T0267250

Praise for Joseph LeValley's other
TONY HARRINGTON NOVELS

"5 out of 5 stars. A compelling and heartbreaking look at the best and the worst in us. A terrific story...A sure-fire winner from a composed and confident storyteller."

— **Great Mysteries And Thrillers.weebly.com**

"LeValley draws on his own experience as a newspaper reporter to give the mystery an authentic feel. Fans of reporter sleuths...will be pleased."

— *Publishers Weekly*

"LeValley skillfully weaves an intricate and involving tale even as he keeps his foot planted firmly on the accelerator. This is fiction based unfortunately on a very real problem. As such, it's both entertaining and important."

— *U.S. Review of Books*

"...a chilling tale as smoothly told as the crimes it recounts are brutal, with a reporter hero doggedly in pursuit of a story...and justice."

— *Max Allan Collins, author of ROAD TO PERDITION*

"A chilling mystery-thriller...which will have the reader captivated. A tale full of suspense and twists that builds towards the nerve-racking climax and comes to an ending with every loose thread tied up. Heartily recommend it to readers who enjoy thrillers/crime dramas."

— *Online Book Club*

"This book is filled with suspense that begins in the courtroom, and keeps readers on edge through a reporter's emotional investigation of a double-homicide. Overall score: 9 of 10."

— *BookLife Prize*

THE THIRD SIDE
OF
MURDER

THE THIRD SIDE
OF
MURDER

JOSEPH LEVALLEY

BookPress®
publishing

Published in Des Moines, Iowa, by:

Bookpress Publishing
P.O. Box 71532
Des Moines, IA 50325
www.BookpressPublishing.com

Publisher's Cataloging-in-Publication Data

Names: LeValley, Joseph Darl, author.
Title: The Third Side of Murder : a Tony Harrington Novel / by Joseph LeValley.
Description: Des Moines, IA: Bookpress Publishing, 2021.
Identifiers: LCCN: 2020919142 | ISBN: 978-1-947305-22-9
Subjects: LCSH Journalists--Fiction. | Murder--Investigation--Fiction. | Organized crime--Fiction. | Italy--Fiction. | New York (N.Y.)--Fiction. | Mystery and detective stories. | BISAC FICTION / Mystery / General Classification: LCC PS3612.E92311 T45 2021 | DDC 813.6--dc23

First Edition
Printed in the United States of America
10 9 8 7 6 5 4 3 2 1

For Jane

"There are three sides to every story.
Mine, yours, and the truth."

— *Joe Massino, reputed former boss
of the Bonanno Organization*

Chapter 1

Spring, Amalfi Coast, Southwest Italy

She was dancing on the seawall, aware she was being watched, but not aware she was being watched by *him*. A breeze fluttered across her face and the early rays of light welcomed her smile. As the sun rose from behind the mountain peaks, she stood on one foot and stretched the toes of her other foot toward the sky, her torso parallel to the wall. A glance to her right showed the worn stones of a street built centuries before, bordered by the blooms of spring flowers that awed the tourists who fed the cash boxes of many merchants in this seaside village. To her left, she could see the water far below, its waves pounding against the black boulders protruding from the surface. To the right, beauty, safety, happiness. To the left, an angry sea and certain death at the bottom of the abyss.

She thought it the perfect metaphor for life. Every day, a person faces choices. On one side, a clear path to health and happiness. On the other, an easy plummet to despair and death. She pondered these things with no sense of melancholy or fear, but with absolute joy. Her exuberance flowed from her confidence in her abilities as she danced atop the wall, and from her certainty about the rightness of her choices. She always chose life. How could she not? How could anyone even contemplate the alternative? With the warm spring breeze in her face, and the scent of roses calling from the carts on the street, life was the only option.

Her name was Noemi. She was twenty-six years old, raven-haired, tall, and slender, but with a dancer's muscular tone. She was well educated, talented, and single. She preferred the term "carefree." This village was her home, but she had traveled the world as a student, a model, and an interpreter. She enjoyed the love and support of her family, the adoration of handsome young men, and the appreciation of her employers, who were good people doing important work. Why shouldn't she dance? She smiled broadly as she raised her torso, lowered her leg, and lifted it again in front of her, pulling it high until the flesh above the knee touched her nose. She slowly lowered the leg again, lifted her elbows, touched her fingers together, and spun full-circle on one toe.

Noemi had been on the wall many times before. People in the village had grown accustomed to seeing her there but were still enchanted when they happened past and caught the image of her spinning on her narrow stage, the morning sun serving as her spotlight.

And what of the risk of balancing atop the seawall, the very dividing line between life and death? It never occurred to Noemi to be concerned. She had trained as a dancer all her life. She had even travelled to the heart of America and spent a year learning gymnastics from, ironically, an eastern European master, simply to prove to herself that she could. As someone who could do a backflip on a four-inch-wide beam of wood, surely she should not be concerned about a two-foot-wide seawall.

If the breeze stiffened and caused her to sway, or a crack in the wall surprised her toes, it only increased the thrill of the dance. Let the sea beckon. Let death reach out of the depths with waiting arms. She chose life, and the choice was hers to make.

If she had shared this thought aloud, the man lurking in the alleyway across from the seawall might have laughed. He too was enchanted by the young beauty. He had followed her 4,000 miles, from New York City to the Amalfi Coast of Italy, because he wouldn't take "no" for an answer. He was going to have her somehow.

The man in the shadows wouldn't have used words such as "enchanted" or "adoration." Where he came from, it was more likely men would say he was "hot" for her and would label her with crude, unacceptable terms. The man didn't care how anyone else chose to put into words his pursuit of the woman. *Obsessed. Micky said I'm obsessed. Okay, I'm obsessed. That don't mean I'm wrong. She's gonna be mine.*

On the wall, Noemi danced. She smiled, happy and content with her life, her choices.

Believing the choice was hers to make was Noemi's first, and last, mistake.

Chapter 2

Orney, Iowa

The attacker's kick just missed Tony Harrington's left temple. Tony had anticipated the move. He couldn't pause even an instant to congratulate himself. He jerked right and forward, leaning in and throwing a mighty left jab into the attacker's side. Except the attacker wasn't there. He had used the momentum of the kick to spin out of the way. Hitting nothing but air caused Tony to lunge awkwardly, lose his balance, and fall hard on his left side. His attacker was upon him in an instant, twisting his right arm behind his back, slapping the side of his head with the back of a hand, ending the spar, and claiming victory.

"Dammit," Tony said, smiling and rising to his knees. He rubbed his left shoulder. "I'm gonna feel that one tomorrow."

The attacker, Pak Junsuh, was the owner of Jun's Martial Arts and Tony's instructor in tae kwon do. He bowed graciously, also smiling, and said, "Take heart, young friend. You are much less terrible now than three months ago."

"That's great," Tony said, clearly not meaning it. "The next time I'm attacked, it will take the guy ten seconds to kill me instead of five."

The elderly Korean chuckled. "Oh no, I say at least twenty seconds."

"Master, I respectfully suggest you shut up," Tony said, urging his five foot, ten inch frame into a standing position. He grabbed a towel, wiped the sweat from his face, then ran it through his dark, wavy hair.

The banter was interrupted by the sounds of Big Head Todd and the Monsters erupting from Tony's cell phone. Normally phones weren't allowed in the dojang. However, Tony had convinced Junsuh to allow it in his case. As a reporter for the *Orney Town Crier*, the local daily newspaper, Tony received calls at all hours and from all types of people, including law enforcement officers and elected officials. He had explained to Junsuh that he couldn't sign up for martial arts training unless his phone was accessible.

Junsuh had relented, but on one condition. He had required they meet for training three days each week beginning at 6:30 a.m. Junsuh believed the early sessions would at least minimize the interruptions from the accursed electronic device. Tony was half convinced the early hours would kill him before any attacker would. As an employee of a morning paper, his workday usually fell between the hours of noon and midnight.

Tony picked up the phone. He knew from the ring tone the call was from his father, Charles Harrington. It was 7:15 a.m. His father never called at this hour. It couldn't be good. He punched the green "Answer Call" button.

"Hey, Dad. What's happened?"

The line was quiet for an uncomfortable beat. Then his father's rich baritone said, "I'm sorry to tell you this, Tony, but Noemi's dead."

Tony was stunned. It took him several moments to process what he had heard. "Noemi...my cousin Noemi? That's not possible. How could that be? Oh, my God." Tony felt his legs turn to rubber, and he sank to the floor.

"Tony," his father attempted, but he sounded tired and a little hoarse. He swallowed and started again, "Tony, I'm so sorry. I know what she meant to you. She meant the world to all of us."

"But how...?"

"We don't know much yet. Apparently, she fell from the sea wall in Amalfi. Her body was found on the rocks below. Her mother said Noemi liked to dance on the wall." His father started to cry. "I'm sorry..."

Tony wanted to respond but had no idea what to say. In his twenty-nine years, he had never heard his father weep.

Charles continued, saving Tony from forcing a response for which he had no words. "You know, it was just like her to dance on the wall beside the sea, heedless of the risks."

Tony knew it was. He had seen her do it. He moaned, "Noemi...Dear God, not Noemi. She was so alive. How could anything extinguish that flame?"

His father didn't respond, and Tony's mind began to shift to thoughts of Noemi's immediate family. "How is Aunt Martina? Jesus, this is going to kill her."

"It's hard to say. She was able to tell me what she knew. It was a struggle, but she got through it. I have no idea what the coming days will bring. Obviously she'll have plenty to do."

"And Mom?" Noemi was Tony's only female cousin. Noemi's mother, Martina Moretti, was a sister of Tony's mother, Carlotta, known as Carla to her American friends. Tony's mother was a native of Italy. She had met Charles when he was in Europe working as an advisor to the director of a motion picture he had written. Carla had moved to the U.S. with her American husband, but Martina and the rest of the extended family still lived in their hometown of Amalfi on the southwest coast.

Tony's father said, "Well, to be honest, your mom's a wreck. She's strong. You know she'll get through it. But it's going to be tough. She hates being so far away."

"Of course." Tony nodded, staring at the mat on the floor beneath his knees. He felt drained, and longed to just crawl away; to find a dark corner in an alternate reality somewhere…someplace where talented, loving young women didn't suddenly die. Instead, he pushed himself up and twisted around so he could lean back on the cold bricks of the dojo's wall. He swallowed hard and said, "I assume we'll go immediately?"

His father hesitated again, then spoke softly. "Actually, Tony, that's been on my mind since we heard. As you can guess, it's a terrible time for me to get away. I loved that girl like she was one of my own children, but it's the tail end of the school year. Trying to leave now would be an absolute nightmare. Will it be possible for you to take some time off and accompany your mother to Italy? I'll pay for everything, of course."

Tony's father was a successful author and screenwriter. Fourteen years ago, he had accepted a position at the University of Iowa in Iowa City as a professor of English and director of its well-known writers' workshop. Leaving that post in May would, indeed, be a nightmare. Also, it immediately occurred to Tony that his only sibling, Rita, would have an equally tough time getting away at the end of the school year. She was a graduate student in music at the University of Chicago.

"Yes, Dad, I want to go, and it won't be a problem. You know

Ben well enough to know he'll not only agree, he'll insist I go. Have you told Rita?"

"Your mother's talking to her on the other phone right now. I'm sure they're both sobbing, so I'm glad I got the assignment to call you."

Tony smiled grimly as his own tears welled up. He asked, "Any word on arrangements? When do we absolutely have to be there?"

"No word at all," his father responded. "They just found her body this morning. Of course, it's seven hours later there, so it was just before noon their time when Martina called your mom. We waited a couple of hours to call you kids."

"I just can't believe it," Tony said, knowing he was wasting his breath and his father's time. "Sorry, Dad. Should I make the travel arrangements?"

His father said no, to leave that to him, but to assume they would be flying out of Chicago later today or first thing tomorrow.

"In other words, Tony, I need you here in Iowa City as quickly as you can make it."

"Three hours, Dad. I just have to pack and call Ben. Everything else can wait."

"Thank you," his father said, breathing an audible sigh. Then, reasserting his typical father-in-charge voice, "But don't speed to get here. One tragedy is enough."

"I promise, Dad. I love you."

Chapter 3

Amalfi, Italy

Twenty-four hours later, Tony and his mother were checking into the Hotel Santa Catalina, a beautiful old hotel high on a mountainside, overlooking the sea. Tony thought it might be a record for getting to southern Italy from Iowa without advance planning. They had driven to Chicago the same afternoon, and had taken a Delta flight directly from O'Hare to Milan. In Milan, they had boarded an Air Italia regional jet to Naples, where they had boarded a train to Sorrento. From there, it was just nineteen miles to Amalfi by car.

Negotiating all the obstacles, such as airport security and customs, was made easier by the Harringtons' experience, having made the trip to Carlotta's home town many times before. The reduced passenger loads, a holdover from the height of the COVID-19 pandemic, also helped. Tony's dad had booked them into first class, so the flights were as pleasant as could be expected under the circumstances. There had been periods of tears and hand-holding with his mother, but mostly she had slept or thumbed through magazines to pass the hours.

Tony had spent his time—far too much of his time— reminiscing about Noemi. They had known each other since they were very young. Because Tony was older by nearly three years, Noemi had looked up to him. She had been fascinated by this American cousin who came to visit once a year, talking his odd form of English with words like "gonna" or "lit" or "totes" and sharing the latest music or books.

Tony, in turn, had thought his young cousin adorable and had enjoyed playing the role of her big brother for a week or two every summer. Then when Noemi was sixteen, she had come to live with the Harringtons in Iowa for a time. She had wanted a year of training in gymnastics to accompany her lifelong love of dancing, and Iowa City was home to an internationally recognized teacher and training school. Tony had been proud to watch Noemi master the balance beam, parallel bars, and floor routines. It had been a fun and exciting year, having his exotic Italian cousin, now blooming into a beautiful young woman, living in their home in Iowa City and attending the local high school. She had turned the heads of all Rita's friends at school, and truth be told, all of Tony's fraternity brothers at the University of Iowa. Tony and Noemi had grown closer as friends, even as Tony had watched over her to ensure she was "protected" from boys with big ideas.

He had been keenly aware of the double-standard he was applying while he himself had pursued his own interests in female classmates at the university. What he had found acceptable for himself and a female companion was very different from what had been acceptable for a young man dating his cousin or his sister. Tony had known he should be embarrassed by these thoughts, but simply wasn't. He had often smiled as he thought, *It's my job to keep Noemi and Rita out of the clutches of over-zealous young men like...well... like me.*

Noemi hadn't been his responsibility, but she might as well have been. With each of her accomplishments, his pride in her had grown. Nothing seemed out of reach for her. She finished college with a major in marketing, then achieved some modest success as a model. Along the way, she mastered three foreign languages in addition to English. She then spent most of a year working as an interpreter for the International Red Cross and some American companies doing business in Europe.

Tony knew a lot of exceptional and successful people—his father, his sister, his boss—but Noemi was alone on the highest pedestal. Her life was a like a classic car show, in which all the cars in the room are cool, and the guy with the '65 GTO in mint condition thinks he has the title of Grand Champion in the bag, but then the red-and-white '61 Corvette convertible with 26,000 original miles rolls onto the showroom floor and steals the show. Noemi was the 'Vette—a classic beauty, supercharged, and ready to win it all.

Tony was devastated as he contemplated the loss. He had never considered what growing old would be like without occasional texts, social media postings, and telephone calls from Noemi. If he was hurting this much, he couldn't imagine what his mother and his Aunt Martina were feeling.

***

The Hotel Santa Catalina was beautiful, comfortable, and quiet. Built in 1880, the hotel had just sixty-six rooms with a staff of two people per room, all of whom appeared dedicated to ensuring their guests were steeped in luxury and hospitality. Tony appreciated all of it but didn't enjoy it much. It felt wrong to be so comfortable and cared for while Noemi's body lay on a cold slab in a mortuary somewhere.

The hotel's attention to detail was evident when the first words out of each staff member's mouth, from the bell staff to the desk clerk to the restaurant's waiter, were, "We are so sorry for your loss. Please let us know if we can do anything to ease your pain while you are mourning with your family." Tony desperately wanted to respond by telling each one to shut up and leave him alone. He knew he should be ashamed for reacting so negatively to their kindness, but he was making no apologies for how he felt. He had suffered loss before and knew the resulting raw emotions were not always reasonable or predictable. *Just go with the flow and concentrate on helping Mom,* he kept reminding himself.

***

After checking into their respective suites and unpacking their bags, Tony and his mother immediately left the hotel. Tony gave the address of his Aunt Martina's villa to the taxi driver, then added in his half-baked Italian, "If you want a tip, you will drive slowly." Of course, with Tony's lack of proficiency in the language, he could have actually said, "Tip me over and slowly drive on me." He couldn't be sure. But his mother nodded her approval, so he figured he had come reasonably close to saying what he meant.

The driver still drove too fast and honked his way through busy intersections, but the trip was half as crazy as some of the Italian cab rides he had experienced over the years. Because Amalfi was a small village, the journey was also blessedly short. So when Tony paid the driver, he included a good tip and simply said, "Grazie."

It was nearly 4 p.m. as they walked up the path to the dark

hardwood door of Aunt Martina's villa. A stranger answered their knock, an elderly woman who introduced herself in Italian. Tony's mom spoke with her, exchanging comments too rapidly for Tony to follow. The conversation ended with a brief hug. The woman pulled the door open wide. She looked at Tony and said in English, "Welcome. It was good of you to come so far."

As they entered the foyer, Tony looked quizzically at his mother. "A neighbor," was all she said.

Three more steps toward the parlor, and Aunt Martina's wail erupted through the house. "Carlotta! Tony! Oh my God, oh my…" She rushed to them, and the rest was drowned in sobs and embraces.

***

For most of the next two hours, Tony was left to his own thoughts, unable to follow the conversations in Italian and not really wanting to immerse himself in the grief of his aunt's extended family and friends. He spent a portion of the time grazing at the table covered in food. He had expected a feast, but this? He was overwhelmed by the mountain of home-cooked Italian flatbreads and focaccia, Neapolitan-style pizza, osso buco alla milanese (slow-cooked veal and vegetables), carbonara, lasagna, and a dozen other dishes less recognizable. A separate table was covered in bottles of wine. As Tony filled his plate a second time, he looked around for something non-alcoholic to drink. He wasn't a big drinker, and considering his jet lag, exhaustion, and melancholy, it wouldn't take much wine to knock him out or worse, turn him into a sobbing, grief-stricken mess. He finally asked for help.

After some digging in the pantry, another stranger found a bottle of Coca-Cola. While Tony would have preferred diet, he grate-fully accepted it. He carried the Coke and the plate full of food out through a side door and sat down on the flagstone patio to eat.

As Tony finished a piece of pizza and turned to the veal, he realized he wasn't alone. He looked up and saw a young boy, perhaps eleven or twelve years old, staring at him from a perch on top of the stone fence separating Martina's back yard from her neighbor's.

"Hello, there," Tony said. "Do you speak English?"

The boy jumped down and trotted up to Tony, smiling. "English most excellent, yes?"

Tony smiled back. "Well, I hope so because my Italian is terrible. What's your name?"

"I am Amedeo," he said, beaming. "It means God's love."

"That's good. I could use some of that right now. I think I remember you from before. You're a neighbor, right?"

"Yes, umm, three villas, uh, over there, and down the hill." He pointed down, then spun and pointed at Aunt Martina's villa. "I help Signora Moretti."

"Really? That's good," Tony said, and meant it. When Noemi was away at work, Tony worried about his aging aunt living alone and trying to negotiate the steep inclines of her mountainside town.

"I cut." The boy made a cutting motion with his fingers. "No, umm…A better word. I…trim, yes, trim flowers and bushes. I buy food. Well, she pay. I bring food here. Long walk up mountain."

"I'm sure she's glad to have your help. I'm also glad you help her. She is my aunt."

"Yes, I know," the boy said. "She told…No, wait…" The boy paused, clearly struggling to remember a word, "She reminded me she have tall, handsome American nephew. I saw you before. You know, other summers, when I was young."

Tony laughed, both at the comments and at the boy's mastery of English. Also, Tony's most recent trip to Amalfi had been three summers previously. If the boy remembered Tony from that trip, it was further evidence of how remarkable Amedeo was.

"You might have guessed wrong about who Aunt Martina meant, based on that description of 'tall and handsome,' but I have to say you do speak English exceptionally well. Did you learn it in school?"

"Well yes, but Noemi helped me. We practiced together many times."

The comment stopped Tony cold. Both smiles, his and the boy's, were gone. Amedeo stared at the ground as he said, "I will miss her very much. I can't..." He started to cry.

Tony reached up with one hand, gripped the boy's shirttail and gave it a tug. The boy immediately understood and lowered himself to a sitting position on the ground. Tony pulled the boy close and began to cry as well. For a long time they said nothing, leaning on each other in the pale afternoon light, on an ancient Italian mountainside.

***

Eventually Tony stood, pulling Amedeo up with him.

"Are you also an excellent tour guide?" Tony asked him. Because of his past trips to Amalfi, Tony didn't actually need a guide to find his way around, but he had a specific request in mind.

"Yes, yes!" the boy said, wiping his face and sniffling. "The best in Amalfi. I know every house and shop on every street. What you want to see first?"

"Well," Tony said slowly, "to be honest, I want to see the place where she fell."

The boy's face dropped. "Oh, no. Not there. I couldn't. I don't want to see. I can't."

Tony understood and struck a bargain with him. Amedeo would

take him close enough to direct him to the spot, without having to go near enough to see it himself. The boy would wait while Tony finished the last leg of the route and viewed the scene.

Amedeo cautioned Tony that it was a long walk down to the seawall. "And it's an even longer walk back."

Tony chuckled, knowing exactly what he was saying. The trip involved walking a mile or more on winding stone paths. During their return, it would all be at steep inclines. It would be a chore. Fortunately, his months of martial arts training had him in the best shape of his life.

He was quickly reminded that walking down wasn't great fun either, but twenty minutes later, as they made one more turn into a narrow alley, Amedeo abruptly stopped.

"It's there," he said, pointing. "Where this vicolo ends, turn left and follow the street along the seawall. Maybe fifty steps, and you'll be there. You'll see polizia markers, maybe, if they still there."

So he's been there to see it, Tony thought. *He was brave, but he's learned a lesson.*

***

The seawall was exactly as Tony had remembered it: stone, solid, four feet high on the street side, with a narrow pedestrian walkway separating it from the vehicle traffic on the thoroughfare. What he hadn't recalled was its width. As Tony walked along, examining the wall, he noted the narrowest spot was at least two feet across. It made sense, of course. If you're going to build a wall to stand against the sea for a thousand years, you're going to build it thick.

Tony reached what he assumed was the actual place where she'd fallen. It was marked now by a simple pair of orange traffic cones to discourage pedestrians from getting up against the wall at that spot. Tony pushed one cone aside, leaned against the wall and looked down into the dark, pounding waves.

He quickly turned away but forced himself to look again. He wanted to remember this place, this horrible, damnable place that had taken the life of his wonderful cousin. He wanted to hate it, to despise it, to blame it for her demise. He knew it wasn't rational, but he also knew he didn't want to blame her. *Noemi, you…You should have…You shouldn't…Dammit!* Tony gritted his teeth and shouted into the wind, "You stupid girl! Why here? Why take such a chance?"

He quickly looked around to see if anyone had witnessed his outburst, then stepped back from the wall. *Two feet wide.* He thought about watching her do backflips and pirouettes on the balance beam. *That narrow little balance beam. This wall…At least two feet. Could she really have just fallen? It seems narrow to the average person. Hell, you couldn't pay me enough money to climb up there. But to Noemi, the top of that wall was as wide as a basketball court. Is it possible…?*

Tony stopped himself. He had experienced a lot of evil in the past four years. He didn't want his recent experiences with murderers and human traffickers to turn him into some kind of paranoid psycho who saw conspiracies and wrongdoing in every bad thing that happened. *Sometimes an accident is just an accident. But still…Two feet wide?*

Tony turned and headed back toward the alley where Amedeo was waiting.

Chapter 4

Orney, Iowa

Ben Smalley stirred low-fat creamer into his coffee, staring at the eddy of chemicals and caffeine trying to escape from the plain white porcelain cup. Ben was buying time, trying to control his temper. Across the table, in a vinyl booth at Willie's Café, sat his local banker and friend, Bart Mason. Perhaps former friend after today's conversation. Smalley almost didn't notice Mason was talking again.

"Ben, I'm sorry. Really, truly sorry. But you have to understand, we're a small, privately-held bank. We survive by being very careful about how much risk we take. We just can't…"

"Risk?" Smalley interrupted, the hiss through his teeth sounding more ominous than he intended. "Dammit, Bart, eighty percent of your business is farmers. You're telling me they're lower risk than the *Town Crier*? The paper's been published continuously for over a hundred years, for God's sake!" His voice rose. "And it's not going to fail on my watch!"

Ben looked around as numerous eyes from other booths and tables quickly returned to their menus or their food. He held up a palm, stopping Mason from responding. In a more normal tone, he said, "The fact is, Bart, my balance sheet is strong. I still owe you a lot less than I have in available assets. My personal net worth is more than two million. That's not gonna change much. As you know, I don't have kids to send to college or aspirations to own a winter home in Scottsdale, like some bankers I know."

"Okay, let's not make this personal," Mason said, immediately regretting it as he saw Smalley's face.

"Not personal? How can this *not* be personal? I've put my heart and soul into the *Crier*. I would argue it is the best daily newspaper in Iowa by a wide margin. Or maybe our seven major awards, including two Pulitzers for God's sake, don't mean anything to a bank that measures someone's worth by the number of bushels per acre?"

Mason's face turned pink, and his eyes flashed as he said, "Stop it. You know I don't deserve that, and my bank doesn't deserve it, either. We've been a good partner for you and a supporter of everything you've done for the past eleven years. We admire you, Ben. Hell, we care about you and everyone at the *Crier*. We're glad you're here, and we want you to succeed."

"Yeah, I can tell," Ben responded, the sarcasm thick enough to use for roofing tar. "So if you're so supportive…"

Mason interjected, "Putting the brakes on now is simply a response to the numbers. You have to face reality, Ben. Even before COVID-19 hit, the *Crier* was losing money nine out of twelve months a year. Except for Christmas seasons, you haven't actually had a profitable month since the election boon ended. And I don't need to tell you how hard the pandemic hit all of us, which, naturally, hurt the *Crier*, too. Our bank has been honored to provide your line of credit, but…"

"It's the 'but' that gets you every time."

"But," Mason persisted, "we can't just let your debt grow and grow with no clear idea of how you're going to recover. And Ben, we're well aware of your personal financial strength, but you're not going to want to empty your retirement fund or sell your house to keep the *Crier* operating for another year or two. We would not expect you to do that, nor would we want you to."

Ben leaned back in the booth and sighed. "You're right, Bart. Of course, you're right. But jeez…I don't know what else to do."

Mason looked him in the eye and said tightly, "You do what everyone else is having to do. You figure out how to raise some additional revenues, or you cut expenses."

"But we already run so lean." Ben was trying not to whine. "And we've already had to cut back to six days a week."

"Well, maybe shrinking rural towns can only support five days a week, or four. Maybe we don't need a paper that wins prizes. Maybe the smallest daily newspaper in the state should hire less major talent and use a few more stringers."

"Bart, if you think my financial woes are caused by paying too much for writers, you are laughably mistaken. I hang on to talent like Tony Harrington and Evelyn Crowder for very specific reasons unrelated to their meager salaries. As you know, Tony has a rich dad, and Evelyn only works because she gets bored when she doesn't. I'm lucky to have them both considering the crap I'm able to pay."

"Well, Ben, if it's not the pay, then you're just going to have to look at right-sizing."

"God, I hate those politically correct terms. You mean layoffs. Firing people. Abolishing jobs. I don't know if I can do it."

"I hope you can, Ben. I don't want to lose your business. But the message from the owners is clear. Your line of credit expires June

30th. That's about six weeks away. You need to bring us a viable plan for how you're going to get back to black ink, consistently and reliably, or the bank's going to call the loan."

Ben stared and fought the urge to tell Mason exactly what he thought. The urge won. "I hate it," he said slowly. "I mean I really *hate* it, when you talk to me like some small-town storekeeper who has to cower before the almighty source of his financial lifeblood. I may not be the smartest businessman in town—I'm a journalist for God's sake—but I'm smart enough. I'll figure this out, and when I do, don't expect me to come to your pissant little bank for my next loan."

"Now, Ben…" Mason started, but Ben was already out of the booth and headed for the door.

"Everything okay, Mr. Mason?" It was Erma, a creator of amazing desserts and an occasional waitress at Willie's. She was standing at Mason's shoulder, holding the handwritten bill.

"Fine. Just fine," Mason said, snatching the bill from her hand. "I guess coffee's on me today."

***

Ben stared at the income statement for the tenth time in two days, hoping he had missed some magical solution to the newspaper's problems. Of course, he hadn't. None of the businesses in Orney had any magic that would solve the fundamental problem that drove a good portion of their financial woes—the steady decline in rural population over the past fifty years. This simple shift of people, away from the farms that no longer needed them, had taken a toll on local businesses since long before anyone had heard of COVID-19.

It was ironic, Ben thought, that while the Earth was becoming overpopulated almost to the point of being unsavable, the rural parts of America were losing people. It felt like someone had pulled the plug back in the 1960s, and now the water was two-thirds gone from the tub. *When and where will it stop?* Ben wondered. Or even more terrifying, *Will it stop?*

The problem of out-migration was complex, but at its core was one basic, unstoppable trend: the continuous advances in farming chemicals, technologies, and equipment. As these advanced in capabilities and, in the case of equipment, sheer size, the need for people to do the work of farming declined. Compounding the problem was the economic advantage of larger farming operations. As a result, the thousand acres of land that would have supported four or five families back in the '60s was now just a small part of the four thousand- or six thousand-acre farm run by a single family or corporation. Ben knew of one man near Orney who farmed, by himself, an area of land that had supported six families a few decades before. The shocking part was the man did all his farming in his spare time. He held a second full-time job in town. The inexorable march of chemistry and engineering made it possible.

As the need for farmers declined and the number of farm families dwindled, the support for local businesses dissipated like grain chaff blowing away in the wind. As local businesses shrank or closed, the number of jobs in the community withered as well. The cascading effect was devastating and impacted every aspect of rural life: churches, community organizations, hospitals, clinics, and schools. As an example, the consolidated school district based in Orney, Southern Quincy Schools, now included students from Orney and six surrounding towns that used to have their own schools but could no longer support them.

Ben sat back in his desk chair, tossing the income statement onto the desk and rubbing his eyes. He was angry with himself for talking to Mason the way he had. He knew Bart was just doing his job, and he certainly wasn't responsible for the economic challenges of rural communities. Ben had lashed out at a friend and had undoubtedly damaged a relationship he valued. Equally concerning was knowing that the whole town would be talking about Ben's outburst by the end of the day. He had worked hard to build positive relationships between himself and the community since buying the *Crier* eleven years ago. The last thing he needed was a wildfire of gossip sweeping through the town, spreading rumors—or facts— about his financial woes, or more specifically, his fight with the one institution in town that had been here longer than the newspaper.

Sadly, these concerns paled next to the real worry that the *Crier* might need to fundamentally change, or perhaps even close. *No, no, no.* Ben was determined the *Crier* would not become another casualty of the trends that had taken down so many other enterprises, but he had no idea what to do—yet. *Maybe Tony's dad will adopt me,* he mused, then laughed out loud as he turned to his computer to email an apology to Bart Mason.

Chapter 5

Amalfi, Italy

Half of the town's 5,100 residents turned out for the funeral Mass in Amalfi Cathedral. At least that's how it appeared to Tony. He was glad the pews in front were reserved for immediate family because he wasn't sure where he and his mother would have found seats otherwise. People of all ages and stations in life turned out to mourn the passing of Noemi Moretti, the beautiful daughter of Martina and the late Alessio. Before he passed, Alessio was the long-time owner of La Grande Cibo, the city's largest store selling groceries and other household supplies. As a popular and prosperous merchant, he had known every resident of Amalfi, and every person had known him and his family.

It was Monday morning, the fifth day of Tony and Carlotta's stay in Amalfi. It had been a busy four days planning the services, receiving visitors, and working with the local authorities. Tony had found himself most interested in the latter but was relieved when

Noemi's body had been released to the undertaker quickly and the death officially ruled an accident.

Throughout their stay, Amedeo had been Tony's shadow, following, helping, practicing his English, making him laugh. Now Amedeo sat beside Tony in the front row of ancient hardwood pews as they listened to the local Bishop conduct the service. Everything was in Italian, of course, but Tony had no trouble following along. Regardless of its location on the globe, a Roman Catholic Mass was conducted with the same structure and with many of the same prayers. Tony found the familiarity of these rituals comforting, and was grateful he and his European family shared a common religious foundation.

At the conclusion of the Sacrament of the Eucharist, Tony was invited to the choir enclosure to share a song. His Aunt Martina had asked him to do this, so he hadn't been able to refuse. He was practically trembling as he sat at the keyboard of the beautiful old grand piano.

Tony liked to play and was a good, if not great, pianist. But his experience performing was limited to the back room of the Iron Range Tap, a bar in Orney, Iowa, or similar places in Iowa City. Sitting at this polished black instrument, in a Cathedral filled with more than a thousand people, including the town's mayor and the Bishop, he felt completely inadequate. More importantly, he wasn't sure he could get through a song without breaking down. Noemi deserved better than he could give.

Tony knew it didn't matter. He loved his cousin and his aunt, so he would play for them. With determination and a little extra grace from above, he would do his best. He swallowed hard, stretched his fingers and began to play and sing, "Somewhere over the rainbow, skies are blue…"

***

As they walked away from the gravesite, Amedeo was glued to Tony's side. Tony's grieving was interrupted when the boy said matter-of-factly, "You must teach me."

"What?" Tony looked down at his young friend.

"The piano. You must teach me."

"Amedeo, I would do anything for you, you know that. But you have to understand, to learn to play well requires years of instruction and practice. It's not something you and I can do in a few days."

The boy's face fell, and his body sagged. Tony stopped walking and knelt to look him in the eye. "Don't be sad," he said. "I promise, I'll teach you a few basic things before I go, and I'll talk to Aunt Martina about who in town might be able to help you."

The boy nodded but didn't look up. Puzzled, Tony asked, "What?"

"You said a few days. I hadn't thought…I mean, I knew, but I hadn't thought, you'll be leaving soon."

"Yes," Tony nodded. "That's true. I have a job and a family and friends back in America. I'll need to return eventually. But let's not dwell on that today, okay? Today we celebrate Noemi's life, and we don't do that by moping about the future."

"Moping?"

Tony laughed. "Never mind. Let's find some gelato to take our thoughts off our troubles."

***

At 9 p.m., Tony called Ben, his boss at the *Town Crier*. Ben was a Pulitzer Prize-winning journalist who had left his job in Baltimore to buy the small paper in Iowa. He was an extraordinary writer and editor, and an even better boss, which was why Tony was still in Orney after nearly seven years.

It was 2 p.m. in Iowa, and Ben was at his desk. The connection was perfect; he sounded like he was in the next room.

"Hey, Tony! Good to hear from you. How are you and your mom holding up?"

"We're doing okay. There've been some rough spots, for sure, like the burial today, but I'm proud of how mom and Aunt Martina have handled everything."

"That's good."

"And I've made a friend." Tony paused, smiling, allowing Ben's imagination to jump to its inevitable conclusion. He waited to hear Ben's audible intake of air, and then said, "No, it's not a young woman, so stop worrying. His name is Amedeo, and he's twelve. He keeps me busy, and he makes me laugh. Honestly, he's been a godsend."

Ben's sigh of relief was audible. "I'm glad to hear it, both for you and for me. In case I forgot to tell you, Italian women are off limits. That's an official decree from your boss. I expect you to come home single and ready to go to work. If I have to write one more article about a traffic accident or city council meeting, I'm going to stab myself with my editor's pencil."

Tony shook his head, reminded that Ben carried a red pencil with him everywhere, even though no one had written a news story on anything but a computer for more than forty years.

"Seriously, boss, is my time away becoming a problem?"

"No, no!" Ben said quickly. "It was a joke. Things have been quiet so it's not been a problem at all. You stay as long as you need to."

Tony was relieved. "If you mean that, I really would like to stay another week at least, maybe two."

"Have you run into a problem?"

"No, not really. It's just that Aunt Martina is overwhelmed with all the details of Noemi's affairs. Mom doesn't want to leave until things are more settled, and I hate to leave before she does."

"I understand completely," Ben said, not surprising Tony even a little.

"And," Tony added, "my young friend wants some piano lessons. I'm going to spend some time with him, and with luck, find him a permanent teacher before I go."

Ben chuckled. "Of course you are. Knowing you, they'll be naming an orphanage after you before you leave."

Tony could feel his face getting red. "Well, I'll be sure to shoplift some fresh fruit off one of the merchant's carts just to keep any hero worshipping by the masses under control."

Ben laughed again, but then said more quietly, "Seriously, Tony. It's great to hear your voice, and it's great to learn you're faring so well. Go save the world and come back when you're ready. Orney will still be here."

"Thanks, boss, but how about you? Are you doing okay, really?" Tony had detected something in Ben's quiet tone that sounded just a bubble left of center.

"Of course, Tony. Just the usual headaches of trying to run a business when what I really want to do is run a newsroom."

"Yeah, I get that. Maybe you should hire a business manager or chief financial officer or something so you don't have to do that numbers crap."

"Yeah, sure, good," Ben said, his voice fading. Then, with a more upbeat tone, "Don't worry about me, Tony. You've got enough on your plate. Just keep me posted and come back when you can. Give your family my love."

"Will do, Boss. You're the best," Tony said, and ended the call.

***

Having such a perfect boss had just one downside, Tony knew. It created a Gibraltar-sized block of guilt when Tony wasn't completely honest with him. It wasn't that he had lied. He hadn't. In fact, in this case, he hadn't really omitted anything specific. But he also knew there was another reason he wanted to stick around a little longer—one he didn't share with his boss, one he hadn't overtly admitted even to himself. But there, in the back of his brain, he could feel a tingle. It was the tingle he felt when he needed to dig deeper. When he needed to be sure he had the whole story. Maybe he would nose around just a little bit, just to be sure there wasn't something more to Noemi's death.

Two feet wide…? Can it be…? Tony shivered and climbed into bed. It had been a long day.

The next two weeks were going to be a lot longer.

Chapter 6

Tuesday morning, Tony got up early and took the long walk down the mountain to the village's shopping district. He had no specific purpose except to say hello to a few shopkeepers he had grown to like during his annual visits in years past, and perhaps to try to meet a few new people. Most importantly, he wanted to find some diet soda.

In the latter quest, he failed miserably. He found Coca-Cola in numerous shops, and a few other American soft drinks in some, but diet soda was nonexistent. *Some things never change.* The thought caused Tony to pause and take in the extraordinary surroundings— the postcard-perfect flowers, the picturesque hills, and the ancient architecture. Everything here was too old to be called old, and it was perfect. Tony was forced to acknowledge that the unchanging nature of Amalfi was a blessing, not a curse.

This thought was amplified as Tony found that many of the old merchants were still in their stores. Not every shop and restaurant had survived the pandemic, but most of his favorites were open and appeared to be recovering reasonably well. More remarkably, nearly every person seemed to remember who he was. They welcomed him into their shops with smiles, condolences, and often hugs.

In his Uncle Alessio's store, the new proprietor spoke perfect English and offered to fix his diet soda problem. "I can get it for you," he said. "Two days. Three at most."

Tony laughed and waved him off. "No, no. Please. It's not worth the trouble. I'll be leaving soon."

The man persisted, insisting Tony write down his preferred type of drink so he could have it for him the next time he visited Amalfi. Tony finally relented and printed for him on the back of a cash register receipt, "Diet Dr. Pepper."

"A doctor? Medicine?"

Tony smiled. "No, a soda with a funny name. Grazie."

At the far end of the street, just past the last shop, Tony could see the traffic cones marking the spot where Noemi had tumbled off the wall. If anyone had seen anything, it most likely would have been from that shop. It was not a business Tony had frequented in the past. It sold pottery and other works of art—things low on Tony's list to buy while in Italy, or anywhere else for that matter. Tony approached the shop with growing trepidation.

His concerns were alleviated at first when the elderly woman inside the door smiled broadly, said "Welcome" in English, and embraced him. The top of her head was inches below his chin. When the woman released her grasp and stepped back, she looked up at him and said, "I glad you came. My heart is breaking, and I hoped to meet you before return to America."

Tony wasn't sure how to respond. The woman clearly knew who he was. He stammered, "I wanted to see the place, you know, where she…"

"I know, I know," the woman said. "I once love watching her

dance on the wall. It was such joy to see. She was much love to know. Now... Now I no bear to look out my window. The view of the sea is ruin for me."

Tony reached out and held the old woman's shoulders. He looked down into her eyes and said quietly, "No, signora. You must not feel that way. It is not the fault of the sea, and Noemi would not want you to be hurt so deeply by her misfortune."

"You are right, of course," the woman said, backing up a step and dropping into a wicker chair near the shop's sales counter. "But it is hard. Yes? It is hard?"

"Yes, it is very hard," Tony swallowed, contemplating how to ask and finally deciding there was no way to sugarcoat it. "May I please burden you a little further?"

The woman cocked her head and raised one eyebrow.

"Did you see it happen? Do you know for sure, just what... how...she fell?"

"No," the woman replied quickly, turning her head away. Tony knew immediately she was lying. *Why? What doesn't she want me to know?*

"You're certain? It would mean a great deal to me to know for sure, to understand how such a tragedy could happen to someone who had danced on the wall so many times."

The woman turned and glared at him, saying more slowly, "I see nothing. Mister Tony, please. No ask me again. And please, go back to America and grieve this... She is gone. You only make heartache and trouble if you chase her ghost."

"I know you are right," Tony said, turning to stare out the window at the wall, "but I..."

He turned back and realized he was talking to himself. The woman had gone through the curtains in the back and had left Tony alone in the front room. *What the hell just happened?* Tony felt an all-too-familiar sense of dread growing like a lead weight in his chest. One very brief conversation had settled the issue. Now he had no choice; he had to find out what had really happened to Noemi.

***

He left the shop and walked to the town's headquarters for the Polizia di Stato. When he entered the door, a chime announced his arrival. A young woman in uniform behind the desk greeted him in English. "Welcome, Mr. Tony. Forgive me for not trying to pronounce your last name. How may we help you?"

Tony again marveled at the universal knowledge of a small town and the average person's command of English.

"You know me," he said, speaking the obvious.

"I saw you play and sing at the funeral yesterday. It was lovely."

Tony, embarrassed, managed a quiet thank you and asked, "Did you know my cousin?"

"Yes," the young officer said. "We were in the same school. She was a year ahead of me, so we weren't close, but I always liked her, admired her. Everyone liked and admired her. This was a great tragedy."

"Yes, thank you for sharing that," Tony said.

The woman nodded and repeated her inquiry, "So how can we help you today?"

Tony said, "I was wondering if I could speak to your chief, your questore, about Noemi. I assume he was involved in looking into what happened?"

"Of course," she said, stiffening a little. "I'm sure you know a full report has been given to your aunt."

"Yes, of course," Tony said. "I've read it. I'm sorry to be a bother, but Noemi and I were...very close. I'll just feel better if I'm able to speak to someone directly involved in the investigation."

The woman nodded and picked up the phone, saying "Of course" as she dialed. She spoke briskly in Italian, apparently answering a question or two, then hung up. "This way."

She led Tony through a door in the back of the room, turned left, and proceeded down a corridor ending at an open doorway into a modestly-sized office. The woman nodded and left as Tony stepped through the door. The room was filled with furniture—a large desk, chairs, shelves, and file cabinets—but it was reasonably tidy. The short, round man behind the desk, dressed in a light-colored civilian suit with an open-collar shirt and rimless glasses, stood and spread his arms wide.

"Mr. Harrington, welcome. It was good of you to come. My name is Marco Ricci. I am the questore of our beautiful city. It was my great misfortune to oversee the investigation of Miss Moretti's accident. How may I help you? Oh, please, please sit. May I get you something?"

A diet soda, Tony thought, but said aloud, "No, I'm fine, but grazie. You are very kind."

The chief's smile remained pasted to his lips, but he waited while Tony decided how to approach the topic.

"Questore, I..."

"Please, call me Marco," smiling.

"Well, uh, Marco, I want to say first that I have no questions about you and your colleagues, your officers' abilities, or thorough-ness in determining what happened to my cousin."

Marco continued smiling and offered an interested nod.

Tony continued, "It's just that Noemi and I were very close friends. It would give me great comfort to understand better...to know if you...if you found anything that explained what caused the accident. I wondered if you might have omitted something from your report, you know, out of kindness to my aunt."

"No. No, nothing like that," the questore said flatly, still smiling. "Is there anything else?"

Good Lord, is that it?

Tony tried again. "Well, it's just that she was such a talented dancer and gymnast, and we all know she danced on the wall frequently when she was in town. Is there nothing to explain what made this time different from the others?"

"No, nothing. I'm sorry. She was lucky many times, but last week she was not. As far as we can tell, she simply stumbled. A great tragedy for sure, but a simple one." The questore turned down the corners of his mouth as he expressed his great sorrow at Noemi's death and said, "My sincere condolences to your aunt, your mother, and you."

Tony marveled at how the man could force a frown and still appear to be smiling. "Thank you. Grazie," he said, standing and reaching across the desk to shake the chief's hand. "I guess I'll never know what I hoped to know, but it was kind of you to take the time to speak to me."

"Of course. It was no trouble. Please come back anytime. We are here to serve," the questore said, still smiling.

***

Marco Ricci watched through the window of his office as the young American strode across the flagstones and out of the building's courtyard. Ricci turned, sat, and pulled a cell phone from his suit pocket. He pushed one button and waited.

In Italian he said, "Yes, it's me. Sorry to trouble you, capo. Do you have one minute? Yes? Well, I'm calling to make a report. I thought you would like to know about a visitor who just left my office…"

After making his report, Ricci was pleased to get affirmation that he had done well in deciding to call. The call ended and he slipped the cell phone back into his pocket. He turned and stared out the window again, this time past the empty courtyard to the sea that stretched out forever from the bottom of the mountain. He wasn't smiling.

***

At 4 p.m., Tony gave up and trudged back up the mountain to his aunt's villa. It felt like he had spent an entire day poking at wasp's nests but finding them abandoned. Every person he had asked had neither known nor seen anything. Tony thought it odd he had found no one willing to open up, in a town full of gregarious people who loved to talk.

"Why do you ask?" The question had been posed many times. "You know it was an accident, right?" The point had been made equally often.

"Yes, of course," he had said.

"Then let it go, young man. Return to your life in America and let Noemi rest in peace."

In each case, the words had been different, but the message had been similar to an extent that rose to the uncanny. *Why is everyone so anxious for me to go home?*

They had appeared honest, Tony thought. He had believed them at first, sensing their genuine affection for Noemi and their desire to ease his grieving heart. *Yet they're all urging me to stand down. I'm starting to think I should be looking for that third eye hiding under the hair…*

Amedeo was waiting on Aunt Martina's front step. It was time for a trip to the cathedral to borrow the piano for a lesson. Tony was glad to have the diversion. As he approached, Amedeo grinned and ran to him. Tony thought it was the first genuine display of emotion he had encountered all day.

***

Tony reached up and set the sack on the garden wall behind his aunt's villa. He turned, grabbed Amedeo under his arms, and hoisted him onto the stone wall as well. Amedeo stuck out a hand, which Tony grabbed as he climbed up to join him. They had the routine down—Batman and Robin swinging into action, ready to tackle the most sinister, uh…pints of gelato. No matter that their presence likely wouldn't be intimidating any super-villains. Tony was proud of how he and the boy worked together as a team, few words spoken between them.

"Lemon or strawberry today?"

"Strawberry!" Amedeo shouted gleefully, knowing Tony would pretend to be devastated.

In reality, it made no difference. Amedeo never finished his pint, so Tony was able to enjoy plenty of both. *Whoever said, "All things in moderation," was full of crap,* Tony thought as he pried the lids off the containers and dug into the lemon delight with unfettered enthusiasm.

Amedeo had been unusually quiet throughout the piano lesson and seemed to return to an even more somber state as he ate his fill of gelato. He finally broke the silence, asking, "Tony, have you ever been afraid?"

Tony laughed. "Of course I've been afraid! Everyone is afraid sometimes."

"No," the boy said, "I don't mean that everyday kind of afraid. I mean really...uh, big afraid. Afraid like you thought you were to die, or so afraid you wanted to?"

Tony turned and looked at his young companion. "What's this about? Are you okay?"

"Yes, yes," the boy said quickly. "I am fine. I am just asking. My mom said you are a hero. I just wondered..."

Tony's laugh cut him off. "Amedeo, I'm not a hero. Tell your mom thank you for the compliment, but I'm just a guy who keeps bumping into bad people. Other people, the real heroes, always have to come rescue me." As he said it, Tony realized his comment was mostly true.

"So you were afraid? Before the rescues?"

"Of course," Tony said. "I was so scared I wanted to curl up into a ball and hide under a bed."

Amedeo looked skeptical. "What could make you so afraid?"

Of course Tony couldn't share with a young boy the details of his worst experiences—of being shot at, threatened, kidnapped, chained to a wall, and forced to witness a cold-blooded murder. Ironically, it didn't matter that he couldn't tell the boy about his encounters with true evil as an adult. When Amedeo asked about being afraid, Tony's mind wandered back to a camping trip. "Let me tell you a story," he said.

One summer day when Tony was fourteen and living at home in Iowa City, he and his longtime friend, Dean Gebbard, packed knapsacks with all the essential provisions for one night of camping. Tony's dad drove them to the state park that bordered Coralville Lake just a few miles north of Iowa City. After being dropped off in the designated campground, the two boys said their thanks and made their promises about being careful. Then, as soon as Charles drove off, the boys set off hiking.

They had no interest in camping in the commercial areas with the recreational vehicles and decked-out trailers. They were determined to find a remote spot where their two-man pup tent and simple tools would give them a "wilderness" experience. After more than an hour of hiking through the woods, they found a clearing with a view of the lake not far to the west, a pasture to the north, and the woods in a semi-circle on the east and south. They agreed it was perfect, unpacked their gear, and set up for the evening.

As he told the story, Tony found himself having to explain to Amedeo the landscape of Iowa and the simple beauty of rolling hills, lakes, and forests. He knew it sounded lame, and probably was lame compared to the mountains and sea that surrounded Amedeo every day. However, the boy had no trouble understanding the thrill the teenagers felt when allowed to camp overnight, alone, in a place they had carefully chosen and made their own.

Tony then described how he had set about clearing an area in the pasture for a fire. He and Dean gathered sticks and cut some larger wood from fallen trees in the forest, using a hatchet from Dean's pack. Dinner was still two hours away, but having a fire was part of the fun, so Tony crumpled up and lit some newspaper, brought specifically for this purpose, and set the wood ablaze.

As the initial flames settled down to a comfortable level, the boys scavenged in their packs for graham crackers, marshmallows, and Hershey's chocolate bars. It seemed odd to be making s'mores in broad daylight, but awkwardness never stood between Tony and a favorite snack. They whittled some long sticks from the wood they'd gathered and proceeded to roast their first marshmallows.

In an instant, everything changed. A gust of wind from the south caught a piece of burning paper as it floated out of the fire. It landed in the pasture and immediately set fire to the dry grass. Urged on by the wind, the grassfire was soon six feet wide, then ten, then twenty.

Tony and Dean leapt to their feet and ran to the fire line, trying to stomp out the flames with their hiking boots. In only a few seconds, it was clear to both boys their boots were not the solution. The fire was spreading left and right, to the west and the east, as the breeze pushed it toward the north.

Tony pulled his flip phone from his pocket. His dad had insisted the boys carry a phone in case of an emergency. However, no bars appeared in the display at the top. Fifteen years ago, cell towers covered far less territory in Iowa. Obviously this remote spot was devoid of signal.

Tony tossed the phone to Dean and yelled, "Head back toward the campground. As soon as you have a signal, call 9-1-1. If you don't get a signal, tell the ranger at the check-in station!"

Dean didn't argue. He simply yelled, "Be careful," and took off running.

Tony wasted no time. He knew he couldn't extinguish the blaze on his own, but he also knew he couldn't let it reach the forest. Burning off the grass was embarrassing, and probably illegal in a state park, but starting a forest fire was a whole other level of catastrophe. He ran to the pup tent, pulled out the two sleeping bags, and ran toward the lake. Once there, he kept going, dragging the bags into the water with him.

When thoroughly soaked, Tony pulled the bags up onto the shore, scrambled up the embankment, and headed for the pasture. He dragged the bags along the ground and then over grass as he passed through the field. Exhausted but unwilling to give up, Tony turned and dragged the wet bags to a position between the fire and the forest. *Let the fire burn north, toward the open pasture. Let it burn west, toward the water, but do not let it travel any farther east toward the trees.*

Tony's arms ached from the weight of the wet sleeping bags.

He was gasping for air, and his legs felt like concrete bridge pylons. But he kept moving, dragging the bags back and forth over the eastern leading edge of the fire.

He had no idea how much time had passed. Sweat dripped into his eyes, making it hard to see, and his lungs began to burn from the smoke. He felt like he was going to pass out. Through clenched teeth, he kept saying, "Please God. Please God. Please God." Determination and fear, aided by adrenaline, were all that kept him moving.

When firefighters arrived, they found Tony unconscious at the edge of the forest. His fingertips were burned, and he was missing most of his eyebrows, but he was otherwise unhurt. The sleeping bags were burned black but had done their job. The fire was racing north through the pasture, but the forest was undamaged. With the help of two pumper trucks, it took the firefighters less than ten minutes to extinguish the grassfire.

They had been lucky. A farm to the north of the state park had provided easy access to the pasture. The firetrucks had reached the site without disturbing the park or any of its visitors.

Tony still felt a chill every time he thought about how close they had come to causing a major disaster.

"So did you have to go to prison?" Amadeo asked, interrupting Tony's reminiscence.

Tony laughed. "No. Even if I had been charged with a crime, I probably would have just had to pay a fine. But I wasn't." Tony stopped and looked at his young friend. He had thought about this many times and now he decided to share it. "I was very lucky, Amedeo. If the authorities had charged us, it would have changed our lives forever, and not in a good way."

Amedeo was wide-eyed. "How do you mean?"

"Well, think about it. If we had been arrested, it would have gone on our permanent records. We would have been labeled as criminals in some people's minds and, at the very least, as trouble-makers by others. That label would have affected how people treated us, from teachers to parents of friends to, well, just about everyone."

"Wow."

Tony noticed the boy had tears in his eyes. He said, "I'm sorry, Amedeo. I didn't tell this story to upset you. I shared it because you asked what made me afraid, and because it has a happy ending."

The boy looked away, and Tony continued, "The fire chief and the park ranger said they weren't charging us because we acted quickly and honorably. We didn't run away and hide. We reported the fire immediately and tried to stop it. Their kindness and under-standing made this a complete non-issue in my life. I'm still grateful to them. I also learned two other lessons that day."

Amedeo turned back to Tony, his brow furrowed.

Tony said, "I learned that what they say is true. Being brave has nothing to do with being fearless. Being brave means doing the right thing despite your fear. I was terrified of that fire, but I'm proud that I didn't back down. The second thing I learned was how quickly a wonderful, happy day can turn to tragedy if we're not careful. We have to find a delicate balance between living life to the fullest while not taking unnecessary risks. We always have to be alert and ready when that gust of wind comes along and pushes our fire where it doesn't belong."

"Like Noemi?"

Oh crap. Tony sighed, "Yes, I'm sorry. I guess it's true. Just like Noemi. If she..." Tony didn't finish. Amedeo interrupted him by jumping down from the wall and running off.

Tony sighed again, hopped down, and picked up the bag con-taining the trash from their gelato feast. He cast his eyes toward the path Amedeo had taken, now empty. *When will I learn to keep my mouth shut?*

Chapter 7

Orney, Iowa

Ben Smalley pulled the hood up on his sweatshirt, wishing he had brought an insulated coat and a cushion for his butt. He was enjoying the Little League game, but his backside was not enjoying the hard aluminum bleachers at Kiwanis Park.

As the sun sank lower in the sky, the breeze picked up. It wasn't cold, exactly, but the sixty-some-degree air seemed to ignore his layers of clothing and find its way directly to his skin. *Maybe the food will warm me up,* he thought, taking a big bite of a Johnsonville brat that had just come off the grill behind the concessions stand.

Ben loved baseball and was happy to have the newspaper sponsor one of the local teams. However, the *Town Crier Tigers,* named for his beloved Detroit Tigers, were losing 11-3 in the second inning. *A perfect ending to a perfect day,* he thought, taking another bite and turning his attention back to the game.

Ten of the eleven runs had been given up to walks, which was pretty common with teams of nine-year-olds, causing Ben to wonder whether he should have sponsored an older team. Then he thought about how intense the rivalries became in later years and, more to the point, how ridiculous some of the parents acted. Once again he assured himself that putting up with a lot of bad pitches was better than putting up with a lot of bad attitudes.

He glanced to his right as Fritter Jones's big frame settled in beside him. Fritter, who was Francis to his mom but not to anyone else, was a very large man. His down-filled winter coat and stocking cap didn't exactly have a slimming effect. Fortunately, on a Tuesday evening in May, the number of spectators was small, and the people in the rows behind him had no trouble sliding to one side or the other to preserve their views of the field.

Jones was the owner and operator of KKAR, the local AM/FM radio station. He yanked open a bag of peanuts and began cracking shells as he greeted Ben. Their pleasantries concluded, the two men watched the game without much discourse. As the inning ended, Ben turned to him and asked, "So what brings you out to the ballpark on a cool evening in May? Do you sponsor a team?"

"Nope."

More peanuts were shelled and consumed. The breeze was blowing chaff from the peanuts onto Ben, but he didn't mind. It was all part of the baseball experience.

Jones pulled a bottle of cola from his coat pocket and twisted open the lid. He took a large swallow, replaced the cap and said, without turning his eyes from the field, "I heard you and Mason had a row today."

Ah, shit, Ben thought, but said aloud, "Well, no, not a row. I just got a little animated when my banker and I didn't see eye to eye on the details of a business deal. I worried that someone would make more of it than it was, but trust me, Bart and I are still friends." Ben desperately wanted to say, "What business is it of yours?" Or, if he was being honest, "Go piss up a rope," but he knew that was not the path to minimizing any damage done by the talk.

"Sorry, Ben. It probably was rude of me to mention it. I didn't bring it up for any reason except to say misery loves company. I got the same problems."

"I'm sorry to hear it, Fritter, really, but I'm not surprised. Everybody's struggling."

"Well, I wanted you to hear it from me first, but I'm hanging it up."

The two men turned and faced each other. Ben said, "Wow, really? After what, twenty-five years? You're getting out?"

"Twenty-nine years, and yeah, I've had enough. The ad for the station will be in *Broadcasting & Cable* tomorrow, and *RadioInk* the next day."

As the *Crier's* primary competitor for news as well as advertising dollars, changes at the radio station were of great interest to Ben. He realized immediately that Jones had sought him out at the Little League park as a simple act of courtesy.

"Thank you for going to so much trouble to tell me. I hate to see you go," Ben said, meaning it. "You've been an important part of the community for a long time. Have you made plans? Will you still be around?"

"Ah, crap, who knows?" Jones responded, shifting his weight and cracking more peanuts. "It'll take a while to find a buyer, you know, considering I don't have great financials to show anyone who's interested. Once it's settled, I suppose I'll use the cash to buy a place down south. Maybe spend summers up here, but winter somewhere warm."

"Sounds nice," Ben said, less sincerely than before and distracted by worries about what a new owner of the station might mean. If one of the big media companies bought it and infused some cash to improve it, Ben's financial situation could get even worse. He liked the friendly competition he had enjoyed with Jones. He didn't relish the thought of doing battle with a gorilla. He fought a smile as he realized the irony of that thought, when sitting next to Jones's enormous bulk.

The men made some small talk through another long inning of multiple walks and nearly as many errors. When the inning ended, Jones shook Ben's hand, thanked him for their years of friendship, and excused himself.

Ben returned his attention to the game. Ten minutes later, the Tigers had three players on base, thanks to equally poor pitching from the Astros, and Allie Perkins was at bat. Little League was coed, and Allie was one of the better players on the team.

She took the first two pitches, both a mile wide of the plate, but clearly wanted to swing the bat. On the third pitch, she stepped over the plate to reach it and swatted it just past the second baseman's glove. What would have been a single with one RBI for a high school team, emptied the bases and earned Allie her fourth home run of the season. The Astros were still looking for the ball in the corner beside the dugout, where it had gone on their third errant throw, when Allie stomped on home plate and began high-fiving her teammates.

Well, maybe this will turn out okay after all, Ben thought.

Chapter 8

Amalfi, Italy

At 7 a.m. the next morning, Tony marched down the mountain again. Having given up on trying to find diet soda, and to avoid a 4,000-calorie breakfast at Aunt Martina's, Tony decided to have a pastry and coffee at La Trattoria Paesaggio. Tony had been to the small, family-owned café many times over the years. He loved to sit on the terrace, just a street above the main commercial district, and watch the shoppers and tourists below.

At this early hour, the terrace was nearly empty. When Tony ordered his coffee with cream and sugar, the waiter made a visible face but refrained from comment. Tony leaned back, closed his eyes, stretched his legs under the table, and enjoyed the warmth of the sun as it peaked over the mountain ridge to the east, across the Tyrrhenian Sea.

When he heard dishes being placed on the table, he opened his eyes. He didn't see the surly waiter, but was greeted instead by the smiling face of the longtime proprietor, Enzo.

"Mister Tony, welcome home!" Enzo said.

Tony rose to embrace the old man. "It's good to see you, my friend."

"Yes, but such a sad reason," Enzo replied, the smile fading.

Tony nodded gravely, feeling his gaze drift downward.

"Please, sit," Enzo said. "You will love the sfogliatella! The flakes are so light, they may disappear with the breeze."

Tony smiled. He genuinely adored Enzo and knew that anything from the kitchen of the "café with a view" would be a delight.

Enzo said, "When I saw the waiter ruining our wonderful coffee with all that sugar and cream, I knew mister Tony must have finally come to see us."

Tony laughed, holding his hand in front of his face to avoid spitting out any of the precious pastry. "Busted," Tony acknowledged. "You know me too well, Enzo."

"Well, I knew you were in town. You sounded wonderful at the funeral Mass, by the way."

Tony nodded his thanks and gestured for Enzo to join him at the table. "I didn't see you there. Of course, I probably didn't see most of the people who were there."

"I would not have missed it. I knew Noemi her whole life. She and my daughter were dear friends, you know. She was a guest in my house many times. I'm not ashamed to admit I still am crying at night when I think of it."

Tony looked across his coffee cup and noticed tears in Enzo's eyes. He reached across the table and gripped the old man's hand. "Me too, my friend. Me too."

Tony thought that would be the end of it, but Enzo surprised him by saying, "That is why I must tell you something."

Tony set down his coffee and wiped his mouth with the crisp, white linen napkin. "What would you like to tell me, Enzo?"

Enzo's hand started to shake, but Tony gripped it tighter.

Enzo dropped his voice to nearly a whisper. "There was a man…" He faltered, and Tony was afraid he might not go on.

"A man? Please, my friend, tell me. What's on your mind?"

"There was a man here, watching her."

"Watching Noemi? Here? You mean here in the restaurant?"

"No. Well, yes, but…" Enzo's face was flushed. He had every appearance of a trapped animal, desperately wanting to flee.

"Tony, please understand. This is very dangerous…dangerous for me, for you."

Tony tried not to sound stern, but did speak more forcefully. "Enzo, please. You must tell me everything. I swear, no one will know you talked to me."

Enzo shook his head, "I would wish for you to speak more quiet, but it probably matters not. This is a small town, Tony. Someone will know. But I have to tell you. Noemi was such a…a gift to us all. We cannot simply look away."

Tony waited, still gripping the man's hand.

"There was a man here in Amalfi. I first saw him the day after Noemi returned from New York. He was an American."

"Can you…?"

Enzo cut him off. "He was tall, perhaps an inch or two taller than you, and well built. He was young. I would say your age, maybe a little older or younger, but close. He had dark, wavy hair, not too long, and a narrow nose that looked a little off-center. I would have thought him a fighter if he'd had a few scars to go with the nose. He wore expensive clothes and tipped generously. He had one of those new watches with the computer in it. His phone would chime, but then he would view his messages on his watch."

"You are very observant," Tony said.

Enzo offered a little bow. "I must be to properly serve my customers. I regret I don't know his name. He always paid in cash and never shared his name with anyone here." Then Enzo repeated the chilling point of his message. "But he was certainly watching Noemi."

"Watching?" Tony forced out the word.

"Yes, watching. I suspected it the second time I saw him here and she was here also, I mean out on the street below. When it happened a third time, I knew it was true, and I started watching him in return. Oh, Tony, I am so sorry. If only I had done something. I am a foolish, frightened old man. I thought I was so clever to watch him, but I didn't do anything to save her."

Tony could feel his own pulse racing. "You're saying this man is somehow connected to Noemi's death? How do you know that? Have you told the polizia?"

"No," the man said, tears now inching down his cheeks. "I don't know anything for certain. But in my heart…He showed up when she did, and I haven't seen him once since she died. He was following her, watching her, I'm sure of it. I mean, how could I not think? How could I not have done something!"

Enzo was half out of his chair, trembling. Tony looked him in the eye and urged him to sit again.

"Enzo, none of this is your fault. Even if this man did something and, as you say, we can't know that, you are not to blame for the evil in others."

"I know, I know, but…"

"No," Tony said bluntly. "There is nothing more. No 'but.' You are not to blame. And I'm very grateful you have told me. But you have not told the questore?"

"Tony," Enzo practically hissed through his teeth. "They… the people in town…They are saying the man is family."

"Family? My family? Noemi's family?"

"Porca miseria!" Enzo cried. "Have you forgotten where you are? Are you an ignorant tourist? This is Italia, my friend. They are saying the man is *family*."

Tony's face flushed and the dread in his chest was back, multiplied a thousand times.

"You're saying this man is mafia, Cosa Nostra?"

"Well, here in Amalfi, more likely Camorra, but yes. If he is family, then he is protected, at least from the questore, and from you or me."

"But you said he is American," Tony protested.

"Yes, and I don't pretend to understand. But you have Italian crime families in America, too, no? Perhaps he is visiting his homeland, or his actual blood relatives. Perhaps the rumors in town are wrong. I only know this. You must be more careful than you have been. You cannot walk all over town asking about Noemi's death, and you cannot start asking people about this man. The Camorra has people everywhere. Most of the merchants in this town pay them for protection and report to them anything they see or hear that might be of interest. The family's soldiers are no doubt aware of who you are and what you have done so far. You must stand down or expect some great unpleasantness at the hands of the local don."

Tony's frustration had reached ignition temperature. He stared at Enzo a long moment. "So what am I to do? Now that I know about this man, I cannot just go home and forget about him."

"I'm sorry, Tony. I should not have told you. I have been selfish."

"Enzo, please. Do not apologize. I am very grateful you told me." Tony leaned back in his chair. Now it was obvious why the woman in the shop didn't want to tell him what happened, and why everyone else was encouraging him to let it go and return to America. Tony not only understood their fear, he shared it. The thought of getting sideways with the Camorra was terrifying. He forced himself to smile as his thoughts returned to Enzo.

"My friend, I make you three promises. First, I promise no one will find out from me how I learned of this man. Secondly, I promise to be very careful and keep myself out of harm's way. I've had more than my share of bruises in recent years. I'm not ready for another one. Lastly, I promise I will figure out a way to identify this man and determine if he did, indeed, do something to harm Noemi, either accidently or intentionally."

Enzo nodded but looked unconvinced.

"Enzo," Tony said firmly, as he stood to go. "I promise. Go back to your kitchen and fatten the tourists while I figure out what to do next."

Enzo stood, pulling Tony out of his seat to embrace him, then turned away.

***

That evening, after consuming another mountain of pasta at his aunt's table, Tony turned to their hostess and thanked her once again for finding, and paying for, a piano teacher for Amedeo.

"Please, Tony," his aunt said, "do not mention it again. He is a fine boy, and it is my pleasure to help him. I am just repaying him for all the help he has been to me."

"Well, I wouldn't know about that," Tony said, "but I know what the lessons mean to him. You may have changed his life."

"He's just a boy. It is early to be predicting his fate. Life has many surprises in store for him. Some good, some bad, as we have learned." She paused to fight off tears.

"Aunt Martina, I'm sorry."

"No. Do not be," she said. "We all will mourn Noemi for a long time, as we should. God forbid this pain should ease, that we should begin to forget her." Tears rolled down her cheeks.

Tony's mother spoke, softly but firmly. "Dear sister, I promise you, Noemi will never be forgotten. She is a hand missing from my arm, the moon missing from the sky. We will carry her memories with us always."

"Of course you will," Martina said with a nod. "Forgive me for changing the subject. Tony was talking of Amedeo, a much happier subject."

"Yes," Tony acknowledged, pleased to have the conversation turn again. "Speaking of Amedeo's happiness, I'm concerned about how he'll be when I leave."

His mother looked puzzled.

Tony continued, "I suppose I'm being a little egocentric here, but he gets pretty depressed any time the subject of my departure comes up. Is there anything else I can do for him before I go?" Tony was looking at his aunt.

"No," she replied. "The boy's family has little money, but much love. He is well cared for. And I agree with you that the piano lessons will provide a much-needed focus for his energy."

Almost as an afterthought, she said, "You may want to think of buying him something. You know, a small parting gift that you would leave with him. I think that would mean a lot."

"That's an excellent idea." Tony said, smiling at the thought. "Any suggestions?"

"Actually, yes," Martina said. "Amedeo loves to fly kites. Many times, he has hiked to that peak to the north, to the meadow near the base, and spent all day flying his kite."

"But if he has…" Tony was interrupted as she continued.

"I think he must have broken or lost that kite. Otherwise I'm certain he would have shown it to you and begged you to go with him to fly it. He must be missing it terribly."

"That settles it," Tony said, pushing back from the table. Tomorrow after my morning visit to Enzo's, I'll find him the best kite in the village."

In reality, it didn't seem like enough. Considering how important Amedeo's company had been to Tony through this ordeal, he felt he owed him a lot more than a kite. However, he fought back his tendency to think like a wealthy man's son and tried to hear what his aunt had said. If the kite had the best chance of being meaningful to Amedeo, then a kite it would be.

Chapter 9

"Mom, I have a question."

Carlotta Harrington turned to face Tony. They were in the back seat of a taxi, returning to their hotel after the long day. Tony's mother looked tired, he thought, and about ten years older than she had a week ago.

"Yes?"

"Do you know the don here in Amalfi? Do you have any connection to him or know someone who does?"

The sag went out of his mother's shoulders. She was suddenly rigid, as if she was an inflatable figure receiving a new burst of helium. "Why would you ask me such a thing? What would it matter?" It came out as a bark. She sounded sterner than Tony could remember hearing from her in many years—maybe since he had been a child and had smeared chocolate on the new family room carpet.

"Take it easy, Mom," Tony said, smiling. "I just thought it would be interesting to meet him. You know, I've been coming here for years and still have no idea who he is. Now that I'm a reporter, I get curious about these things. Maybe he would consent to an interview."

"Don't be ridiculous," his mother snapped, wiping the smile from Tony's face. "The man is a criminal. Haven't you had more than your share of evil in your life? You have to go searching for it here?"

Tony had expected his mother to be curious about his question, and probably anxious, but he had not expected a venomous reply bordering on anger. "Sorry. I didn't mean to upset you. It was just an idea."

"Well it's a terrible idea, and I want you to forget it."

"Okay, okay," Tony said quickly, before his mother could ask him to promise.

The cab pulled into the courtyard in front of the hotel. Tony's mother let herself out, leaving the door open. Tony called after her. "You go on up, and I'll pay the driver. I'm right behind you."

His mother nodded and strode up the three stairs and through the doors.

The driver turned to collect his fare. He was young and had long, blond hair. His eyebrows were nearly white, making his deep blue eyes appear to jump out of his face. He smiled broadly as Tony handed him a few bills.

"You shouldn't lie to your momma," the cabbie said, suppressing a laugh.

"What do you mean?" Tony was surprised to hear the man speak English and was shocked to hear him speak so boldly.

"That was cazzata," the young man said, counting the bills.

"Cazzata?"

"Bullshit, in English," the man laughed out loud. "No one goes to see the capo to ask for an interview. Cazzata. I doubt your mother is foolish enough to believe it either."

"Well, I'm not sure it's..." Tony started, but the driver interrupted him.

"Your mom is right, though. Going to see him is a bad idea. He's a...a...how do you say it? A prick. Yes, a giant prick!" The cabbie laughed again. "You're asking for trouble if you bother him."

The cabbie's boldness, and excellent English, pushed Tony to respond in kind. "Okay, smart guy, what would you do if you needed to know more about a member of the Camorra, and no one in town was willing to talk to you?"

"Hmm..." The cabbie seemed to consider whether he should answer Tony's question. "I don't suppose I get to ask why you need this information?"

Tony considered explaining but slowly shook his head.

The cabbie continued anyway. "It doesn't matter. I can guess. You're Noemi's cousin, right? You want to know about the American who followed her here from the airport in Naples."

Tony was dumbfounded. "How did you...? How could you...?"

The cabbie laughed again. "Tony... It's Tony, right?"

Tony nodded.

"Tony, this is a small village. There are only few taxis and a handful of drivers. Do you really think an American stranger could come here and follow a local girl around for most of two weeks without us knowing about it?"

The cabbie's point was obvious, but his confidence and flippant manner only made Tony angry. "So did you report this? Did you do anything to help her?"

"No, of course not," the young driver replied, but he didn't seem offended. He didn't even stop smiling. "The man never made a move on her. He just watched. So what was I going to report? Besides, the word went out immediately after he arrived that he's family, so we all knew to leave it alone."

Tony was at a loss for words. He wanted to slap the smile off the young man's face. He finally said, "So now she's dead, and the man is gone. How will I find him without the capo's help?"

The cabbie finally looked serious. "The man is not gone. He's staying at the capo's villa. As far as I know, he hasn't left since Noemi's accident was reported. Perhaps he knew her. Perhaps he's in mourning."

"Bullshit," Tony said, mocking the driver's words. "As we say in America, he's lying low to avoid trouble. He killed her, and now he's staying out of sight."

"Careful, sir," the cabbie said. "Your comments are safe with me, but I wouldn't share them with anyone else. You start accusing a member of the family of killing a girl, you're going to find yourself reunited with her in the afterlife."

Tony knew the cabbie was right. The Camorra was infamous for taking care of its own. No one, including the police, would dare go after the man if he was under the capo's protection. Knowing this only added to Tony's frustration. He leaned back on the seat of the cab, threw his head back, and groaned. A word escaped his lips that he hated and rarely used. "Fuck."

After a few moments, the cabbie cleared his throat. Tony lurched forward, saying, "Sorry. I forgot where I was. You probably don't want me to stay in your cab moaning."

"I don't mind, but I do have a job to do." The cabbie was smiling again.

Tony slid across the seat to the open door. "Before I go, can I ask again what you would do? Is there any path to this guy that won't get me tossed over the seawall?"

"Well," the cabbie said, his smile somehow widening, "I wouldn't do anything. I am one of the world's great cowards. I just want to get along. I would let it go."

Tony was tired of hearing this advice and said so.

"I get it," the young man said. "If you're not going to let it go, then all you can do is go talk to the capo."

The cabbie didn't seem to expect a response, which was good since Tony was speechless.

The young man continued. "I want a clear conscience, so let me make sure you understand. My advice is to drop it and go home. But, if you're determined to do something, then you have no other choice. If you take the issue to anyone else, you make the problem worse. The capo will know what you're doing *and* he'll be angry. If you talk to him directly, he will deny everything, but he might admire you for coming to him. More importantly, he'll probably be reluctant to throw you in the metal crusher in his scrap yard after everyone knows you've been to see him. The local questore wouldn't touch him, but a dead American, with a trail leading back to him, would not be high on the don's list of desired outcomes. Visiting him is not an advisable path, but it is better than the alternative."

Tony asked for the name of the capo and how to contact him. He learned his name was Gabrielle Mancini and he could be reached at work. Apparently, the capo had two primary lines of business: security services, which Tony assumed was code for "protection racket," and the waste disposal service for Amalfi.

Tony was about to thank the cabbie for the last time when he said, "By the way, if this fails, is there a higher authority? You know, someone else I can go to? Everyone has a boss, right?"

"Gesù Cristo, you really are looking for trouble," the cabbie said, shaking his head. "The accepted answer is no. The Camorra claim each branch operates independently."

"But?" Tony prodded, noticing the cabbie's emphasis on the word "claim."

"But the rumor is the don of one of the clans in Napoli, uh, sorry, Naples to you Americans, has succeeded, after decades of failed efforts, in pulling at least some of the groups together into one organizzazione, uh…bigger group. I don't know his name, and I don't want to know it, but you won't have any trouble finding it. Now get out of my cab before any of your craziness rubs off on me."

Tony nodded his appreciation, climbed out of the cab, and headed up the stairs. To his horror, he found his mother waiting for him in the hotel lobby. Her eyes narrowed. "That took a long time. What were you up to?"

"Relax." Tony forced a smile and put his arm around his mother. "I was just picking his brain for information about Naples. I might want to spend a day or two there before I head back to Iowa."

His mother grunted and turned to the elevator, leaving Tony wondering whether she was satisfied with his response or hiding her feelings. No matter. He was too old for her to ground him…he was pretty sure.

Chapter 10

As Tony punched the number to Gabrielle Mancini's office into his cell phone Thursday morning, his hands were steady—but just barely. He could feel his palms sweating as Mancini's receptionist answered the call and cheerfully assisted him in scheduling an appointment. To Tony's surprise, she told him to come that afternoon.

He found Mancini in a large but otherwise unimpressive office in a steel building set at the edge of what Tony would have called a junkyard, had he been brave enough to describe the piles of discarded appliances and rusting car bodies out loud, but which Mancini referred to as a "recycling center." Mancini's desk and chair were impressive, suitable for the CEO of General Motors. The desk was massive and made of a dark, highly polished wood; the chair was leather, well-padded, and fitted with wide arms, allowing Mancini to relax while simultaneously leaning forward, intimidating his guest with an unblinking stare. The other office furniture was surprisingly plain, functional, and vinyl-covered. The cabinets and shelves were steel, and small windows were set high, allowing in very little light and providing no view to the outside. One wall of shelving appeared to host a collection of curios and various treasures recovered from the mountains of trash that passed through the yard each day.

Tony had done his research. He knew the Camorra was infamous for taking over the waste disposal services in many parts of Italy, then drastically cutting costs by ignoring environmental regulations and dumping waste into rivers and the sea. As a result, the clans made huge profits and Italy's environment suffered extensively. Knowing this, and suspecting even more unsavory activities in the protection business and likely other criminal enterprises, Tony had a low opinion of Mancini even before the conversation began. Nothing the man did or said helped to raise it any.

Mancini was wearing what appeared to be the company's standard work attire—dark blue short-sleeved shirt and matching slacks. The difference between him and the employees Tony had seen working outside was that Mancini's clothes were clean and neatly pressed, and he had no name tag sewn above the shirt pocket.

Tony's first indication that the meeting would be short and unproductive came when he entered the room and Mancini remained in his chair. He did not invite Tony to sit.

At first, the reputed crime boss was polite, but in a terse and uncooperative way. Speaking in English, he said he had agreed to see Tony out of respect and affection for Tony's aunt, and his fond memories of her late husband, "who had been a client of my firm for many years."

Said by someone else, with a different tone of voice, this might have sounded gracious, even endearing. Coming from Mancini, the clear message was, "If not for your family, I wouldn't give you ten seconds of my time even if I was on fire and you held the only bucket of water."

As the cabbie had predicted, Mancini denied any knowledge

of anything that would help Tony understand Noemi's "accident."

Tony tried to be careful in approaching the subject, saying, "Thank you, Mr. Mancini, for your long friendship with my uncle and his family, and for agreeing to see me so quickly. I apologize for taking your time, but you're a well-established businessman in the community, and I'm sure you know nearly everyone."

Mancini's reply was curt, his gaze never leaving Tony's eyes. "Yeah, that's true; but what business is it of yours?"

"Well, I, uh…I wonder if you've seen any strangers around who might have taken an unwarranted or overly aggressive interest in my niece, prior to her untimely accident?"

"You came out here, to my place of business, to ask me about that lovely young woman's death? Just who in the hell do you think you are? You have some nerve."

Tony swallowed hard, feeling his face burn as he said, "Please forgive any unintended implication. I certainly am not here to suggest anything about you or your colleagues or your…"

"Of course you're not, because you're not that stupid!"

Suddenly, the room felt smaller and twenty degrees hotter. Tony fought the urge to turn and run, forcing his feet to stay planted on the floor's stone tiles.

"Mr. Mancini… Sir, I didn't…"

"Shut the fuck up, mister *'I'm an American so I can bother anyone I want to bother.'*"

"Please, sir, I'm just…"

Mancini suddenly stood, interrupting Tony's plea. The capo pointed a finger at Tony's chest. "Do you know what 'shut up' means young man? Stop talking. Now."

Tony clamped his mouth shut.

"The answer to your fuckin' question is 'no.' I didn't see nobody, I didn't hear about nobody, and I don't know how or why your cousin fell or took a leap off that wall. Any other questions?"

Tony fought down a spasm in his leg as his shook his head no.

"Good," Mancini said. "Now get outta my office before I lose my temper."

"Thank you, sir," Tony said, spinning on his heels and heading for the door.

"Harrington!"

Tony stopped abruptly in the doorway.

"I suggest you also leave my town and leave my country. I'm not going to order you to never come back because I know you have family here, and family matters. But I do suggest you disappear for a while. Return to America, and let Noemi rest in peace."

Tony nodded, but didn't speak, and resumed his flight from the building.

The taxi Tony had used to get to the recycling yard was waiting outside the gate for him when he walked out. As Tony climbed in, a familiar blond-haired, smiling cab driver asked, "Well?"

"Eat cazzata," Tony said, slamming the door in frustration, then flopping back against the seat and exhaling his relief at departing with all of his fingers and toes intact.

***

Gabrielle Mancini didn't wait long. Moments after Tony was out of his office, Mancini picked up the land line connected directly to his villa.

A man picked up the phone on the other end and asked in Italian, "Yes, boss?"

"Get that son of a bitch out of my house and on the way home, now!"

"You mean Costello?"

"Yes! Of course, I mean Costello! Tell him I want him on the bus tomorrow. He has one more night in my house, but that's it. I don't care where he goes, but tomorrow morning he's gone!"

"Right boss. Got it."

Mancini slammed the phone down. *I don't care who his great uncle is. No asshole is coming to my town and killing one of my people, then hiding out at my house. I should kill the fucker myself.*

Mancini knew he was just venting. He had a sweet deal in Amalfi, raking in huge dollars with minimal risk and almost no interference from the bosses in Napoli. The last thing he needed was a fight with them, or worse, the family in New York. That would get everyone pissed at him. Especially since the American denied he had killed her. Of course, that was laughable. Costello clearly had followed Noemi here. His only business in Amalfi, based on everything Mancini knew, was to find a way to get to the girl. Well, he had done that alright. His bonehead play had turned Amalfi on its head and had left the capo to clean up the mess. The more he thought about it, the more he wanted to beat the SOB to a bloody mess with his bare hands and throw him in the shredder.

But no. Mancini hadn't risen to the level of capo by acting on impulses and making enemies of powerful people. No, he would just get this dickhead out of his house and back to New York, and then try his best to forget about it.

Chapter 11

The next morning, a Friday, when Tony stepped out of the hotel's front doors, a familiar taxi was in the courtyard waiting for him. The smiling young man whom Tony now knew was called Montay was outside, leaning on the side of the car, smoking an American cigarette. Tony smiled back and said, "I was planning to walk."

"Ah, but do you know where?"

"I thought I did," Tony replied, ambling toward the cab as Montay opened the door and beckoned to him. Once they were both seated, Tony said, "I need my morning pastry. Enzo will think I've abandoned him if I go anywhere else."

Montay put the car in gear. "Enzo will get over it. This morning you are having coffee at the Amalfi Bus Station."

"Really? What's the occasion?" Tony couldn't imagine passing up Enzo's baked delights for bus station fare.

"Last night I had a thought. And since you're the one chasing Camorra thugs and murderers, I thought you should know my thought and act on it. As you may recall, I am a coward and have no desire to do so."

Tony laughed. "Okay, I give. What's this wonderful thought of yours?"

"Well, I thought your visit with the capo may spark a reaction. In fact, knowing him as I do, I'm certain it did."

Tony didn't get it, and started to say so, but Montay continued.

"So think like Mr. Spock, with logic. If your visit frightened—probably not the right word—uh, created concern for the capo, or angered him, or maybe both, what would he do?"

"I don't..."

"No, we don't know. But it is possible the capo has a murderer staying at his villa. Possible, yes?"

Tony nodded, "Not just possible; very likely."

"Yes, likely. So, what if a worried and angry capo tells the murdering guest he must leave his home to keep the nosy American from finding out he is there? Also possible, yes?"

"Yes, possible."

"Then where would the murdering guest show up next?"

"Ahh!" Tony smiled. "The bus station."

"Possible, yes?"

"Yes," Tony acknowledged. "Of course, he also could have left last night. Or he could be in a private car, driving him to Naples, or on a yacht, leaving by the sea, or at the bottom of the sea with a bullet in his head."

Montay frowned—the first Tony had seen on him.

"Yes, Tony. There are many possibles." The smile came back. "But I choose to believe he will be at the bus station this morning. It seems the most... what was your word? Yes, the most likely."

Montay dropped Tony at the station, reminding him that cowardice didn't allow Montay to join Tony inside. "However, if my rich American friend would like to hire me for the morning, I can stay with the car outside and watch for him. If I see him entering the station, I can buzz your phone so you know it's him."

Though he was just a poorly-paid Iowa newspaper reporter and not the rich American Montay chose to imagine, Tony agreed it was a good plan. Before Tony exited the cab, Montay described the perfect spot to wait where Tony could enjoy the coffee and rolls of the station's ristorante and still have a view of the ticket counter and the boarding area. The station was small. Everyone coming and going would have to pass by the tables outside the ristorante.

Tony thanked him and handed over a generous tip, though he wondered whether this excursion might be a waste of time, or perhaps even a scam by Montay to earn a fare for the entire morning without having to drive anywhere. It didn't matter now; Tony was committed. He hoped at least the bus station food was edible.

He had spied the ristorante during previous trips to his aunt's, on the rare occasions when his family used the bus to go between Sorrento and Amalfi, but Tony had never eaten there. He was surprised to find this had been a mistake. His breakfast was superb, and he laughed out loud when he spotted another surprise on the menu: Diet Coke.

The next couple of hours passed pleasantly as Tony enjoyed people-watching, nibbling on pastries, sipping his soda, and perusing *Local Italy*, an English language daily newspaper.

Tony's phone buzzed. He glanced at it, expecting to be disappointed. Probably his aunt or his mother wondering where he was. He was surprised to see Montay's number on the screen. Tony didn't answer it, but set the phone to camera mode, picked up the newspaper from the table, and watched over the top of the pages. In less than thirty seconds, a tall, well-dressed man with a crooked nose walked into the station. As the man looked at the electronic information board overhead, Tony picked up the phone with his left hand and snapped a quick series of pictures. He then slipped the phone into his pocket and returned to reading the paper, praying he had been discreet enough. Apparently, he hadn't.

The man exited the terminal and strode toward the busses. Tony folded up his paper, dropped his trash into a bin, and headed for the men's room. As he fished in his pocket for the proper coin to pay the bathroom toll, he felt a presence behind him.

A rough, nasally voice said, "Jesus Christ. Hiding behind a newspaper to watch me? You're not only a nosy turd of a reporter, you're a lame-assed, nosy turd of a reporter."

Tony instantly tensed and felt his face turn hot. He spun around and found himself looking into the face well-described by Enzo as that of the man who had been following Noemi. The man's expensive leather coat was draped over his right arm. He clenched a Louis Vuitton travel bag in the other. His exposed wrist revealed an Apple Watch.

"Excuse me," Tony stammered. "I don't think I know you."

"And you're not going to," the man said flatly, pushing up against him until their noses nearly touched. "You may think you're a tough guy because you've taken on some big shots in the past." Tony shook his head and opened his mouth to counter, but the man continued. "Let me tell you, tough guy, you have no idea what I can do, what I *will* do, if I ever see you again."

Tony kept feigning ignorance. "I don't…"

"Shut the hell up. Your little visit yesterday got me bounced out of a nice place in a nice town. I know your name and you weren't hard to find online. Now I know all about you, where you're from, your family. So I'm warning you. Do *not* fuck with me," he said, spitting out each word individually. "Understand?"

Tony nodded, but the man didn't seem to notice. He took one

step back, then suddenly thrust his knee up and forward. Whether it was instinct or his martial arts training, Tony couldn't say, but he spun to his right just in time to avoid a knee to the groin. The man's knee struck Tony's thigh instead, causing Tony to cry out in pain and collapse onto his left side. Tony raised his arms to defend himself, but the man didn't stay to see it. He whirled around and walked out the door.

Tony pulled himself to his feet and stumbled into a toilet stall. After using the facility, he hobbled back to the station's lobby, where he plopped down onto a bench. By then, his hands had stopped shaking enough for him to operate his phone. He punched in a number. After five or six rings, a very sleepy voice said, "Yeah, this is Doug. Who's this?"

"Oh shit, Doug, I'm sorry. It's Tony. I didn't think about the time difference." A quick calculation told him it wasn't yet 5 a.m. in Iowa.

"Hey, Tony. That's okay," Doug said, not very convincingly. "It's good to hear your voice."

Doug Tenney was Tony's best friend in Orney. A reporter for the local radio station, Doug and Tony technically were rivals, but in reality, they often worked together to cover big stories. As two single guys with similar interests, living in a small town, it was almost inevitable that they had become friendly. Over the years, their friendship had grown to be one of the most treasured Tony had ever experienced.

"Really Doug, I'm sorry. I can call you later."

"No, no. I'm awake now. So how ya doin'? How's your mom?"

"We're okay, really. Thanks."

"God, I hated to hear the news about Noemi," Doug said. "She was truly extraordinary. And ya know, I was sure she would come to her senses and marry me someday."

Tony suppressed a groan. It was just like Doug to say something inappropriate, or to try to make a joke regardless of the circumstances. It also was just like Tony to respond in kind. He did, saying, "Well then, I guess she's lucky she died when she did."

Doug chuckled. "I'm glad to see your inability to be funny has remained intact through this tragedy. So are you just checking in, or is there something I can do for you?"

You have no idea, Tony thought. He took a deep breath and said, "Actually, Doug, I'd like to include you in another little adventure."

"Really? Like what? More child molesters, or murderers, or maybe the Mafia this time?"

"Bingo," Tony said, smiling at Doug's ability to strike gold when swinging his pick at random piles of dirt.

"Bingo what?"

Tony could hear Doug climbing out of bed and coming fully awake.

Doug asked again, "Come on...Bingo which one?"

"Well, actually," Tony struggled to say it out loud, "turns out I need your help bringing down a murderer who appears to be a part of an American-based crime family."

"Wait. You're shittin' me, right? Jeez, Tony. You went to Italy to attend a funeral. How in the hell...? What in the...? I'm gonna shut up now and let you explain."

"Good idea." Tony proceeded to describe the events to his friend, up to and including his encounter with the man in the bus station.

When Tony had finished his spiel, it took Doug more than a few seconds to find his voice again. "Okay, so how does getting a guy pissed off at you in Italy have anything to do with me in Orney, Iowa?"

"Well, that gets me to the adventure part," Tony replied. "I need you to go to New York and try to pick up his trail. I'll be there soon, but obviously the guy knows me. I won't be able to get anywhere near him. Besides, I have something I have to do in Naples first."

Doug laughed. It was the kind of laugh you hear from a person shaking his head and trying to communicate that he thinks you've lost your mind. Then he said it out loud. "Have you lost your mind? Am I supposed to wander the streets of New York City looking for a man with a crooked nose? And how the hell do you know he'll even be in New York?"

Tony smiled and explained. "Hang on, pal. Hear me out. When we hang up, I'm going to text you a picture of the guy so you'll know exactly what he looks like. Also, if we assume he's leaving for the states right away, then we can calculate within a twelve-hour window or so when he'll be arriving. The good news is, LaGuardia doesn't have port-of-entry controls, so if he's flying commercial, he has to fly into JFK. At the airport, you'll only need to watch the International Terminal, and the flights coming in from Europe. I know that's still a lot, but hopefully not impossible."

"And if he's going to Chicago or Boston or Los Angeles?"

"You're right. I can't be sure he's headed for New York," Tony admitted, "but I would bet my house, if I owned a house, that he is."

He explained, "I could be wrong, but he looked and sounded like New York to me. And besides, I don't think an entire Italian town would be covering for the murderer of a beautiful young woman unless they believed he was Camorra—that's their term for the local Mafia. As far as I know, most of the major crime families still are based in the Big Apple."

"Okay, okay. I still think you're crazy, but it's worth a shot. And besides, if he doesn't show, you'll be arriving later with a big wad of cash and the desire to thank me by showing me a great time in Manhattan."

"Exactly," Tony said. "And seriously, all the costs of this trip are on me. Now...Are you ready for the bad news?"

"Wait," Doug said, "There's worse news than telling me I need to find and follow a murdering member of the Mafia?"

"Well, maybe not. But if you're in, you have to leave now."

"You mean *now*, now?"

Doug sounded weary, and Tony felt a pang of embarrassment knowing it wasn't the first time he had asked his friend to drop everything and join him for some crazy excursion. He said, "I'm afraid so. Think about it. It'll take you nearly as long to get to New York as it'll take him. If he's leaving right away, it means you need to be at JFK by late this afternoon or early evening. Can you manage that?"

"Sure, no problem. My boss is trying to cut expenses anyway, to make the station more attractive to potential buyers, so he'll be glad to have an excuse to fire me. And all I have to do then is put on my Superman outfit and take to the skies."

Tony chuckled but said, "Seriously, Doug, I don't want to get you in trouble at work. If this is asking too much..."

"Nah, relax. I'll be fine. There's nothing going on here, and I have plenty of vacation coming. I haven't used any since the last time you pulled me into one of these crazy chases. I'll be at JFK before dinner, or maybe earlier. I promise."

"Doug, you're the best. You can't imagine how much I..."

"Can it, Tone-man. This'll be fun. Text me when you know your travel plans, and I'll keep you posted from my end. Now I gotta go figure out how to take a wardrobe designed for the Iron Range Tap and convert it into Studio 54 swank."

Tony laughed again. "Studio 54? What, are you living in the '70s?"

Chapter 12

Orney, Iowa

Doug Tenney was not as lecherous or insensitive as he sometimes appeared to others. At least he chose to believe he wasn't. He thought of himself as someone who liked to have fun and didn't put on airs or pretend not to be thinking what everyone else was thinking. Mostly, he just liked to make people laugh. If that occasionally resulted in being politically incorrect or creating a little embarrassment, well, so be it.

He came by this attitude honestly. His father was an over-the-road truck driver. He drove a sixteen-wheel Peterbilt rig, hauling everything from boxed goods to live hogs to refined petroleum products. He had spent his thirty years on the road accumulating dirty jokes and crass one-liners from nearly every state on the continent.

Doug's dad, Harold "Hoppy" Tenney, believed everyone was a friend until proven otherwise. Hoppy had spent serious time in truck stop restaurants trading stories with strangers, other truck drivers, families on vacation, and on at least one occasion, a group of nuns on their way to a retreat house. Doug had been with his dad once in a fast food taco joint when a seriously obese woman had delivered their food to the counter. His dad had turned to Doug and said, loud enough for all to hear, "Man, she looks like she eats her mistakes." The remark drew an equal number of angry stares and cringes from others in the restaurant. Only Doug had laughed. He couldn't help it. He adored his father and thought everything he said was funny.

One of Doug's earliest memories was of his father teaching him to say "huge." Doug was about four years old, maybe even younger. Whenever his dad had a new audience, he would call Doug to his side and say, "Dougie, how big is my Peterbilt?" Little Dougie would yell, "Huge!" and everyone would laugh, his father the hardest of all. Doug was intoxicated by the feeling of making his father happy.

Doug had inherited his Dad's sense of humor and willingness to say just about anything to anybody. Conversely, he had not inherited Hoppy's wanderlust. He assumed the years he had spent as a kid, wishing his father was home, had dampened that spirit. In any case, Doug couldn't imagine spending his life in a truck on the road. He was very happy to have a radio job in rural Iowa, enjoying his small-town apartment, his friends, his occasional romantic relationship, and his warm summer afternoons on the banks of the Raccoon River with a fishing pole and a cooler full of beer.

Despite his contentment and interest in just having a good time, his friendship with Tony Harrington had a way of disrupting the routine. For one thing, Tony was an excellent writer and an aggressive investigative reporter. Having a first-rate competitor at the local newspaper forced Doug to work harder. He knew that was a good thing, but it didn't mean he had to like it.

Secondly, Tony trusted Doug and was the type of person who

didn't hesitate to ask a friend for help, as evidenced by his latest request—that Doug drop everything and fly off to New York to look for a mafia guy.

A mafia guy! Jeez Louise, I gotta learn to stop answering my phone, Doug quipped to himself as he got to work brewing a pot of strong coffee.

The truth was, Tony had a way of finding trouble. As much as Doug didn't want trouble in his own life, it would never occur to him to say no when Tony asked for help. Tony was a good man, but even if he wasn't, he was Doug's friend, and friendship mattered. Loyalty mattered. *And, yes, keeping that idiot from getting killed mattered too.*

Doug was no superhero. In fact, he thought of himself as the exact opposite. He was the "before" picture in advertisements for fitness centers. Fishing and drinking beer were not exactly the doctor's prescribed activities for getting buff. But, at five-feet, eight inches and 185 pounds, Doug thought of himself as stocky rather than fat and prided himself on his ability to carry a fully-loaded beer cooler more than 200 yards through the forest to reach his favorite fishing spot.

On a more serious note, Doug truly was proud of the fact that he had, on several occasions, set aside his reservations and fears to be at Tony's side when facing evil. *No greater love, Tone-man. No greater love...*

Doug smiled as he threw one last shirt into his suitcase, snapped it shut, and carried it out the door along with a large thermos of java. "Godfather, I'm coming with an offer you can't refuse," he said aloud as he locked his front door and headed for his car.

***

Tony didn't enjoy feeling guilty. Like it or not, he felt overwhelmed by it as he said his goodbyes in Amalfi. He couldn't tell anyone what he was really doing, so he was forced to lie to his mother, his aunt, and even Amedeo. He told them he was going to make a brief stop in Naples, which was true, though the reason he gave them—sightseeing and shopping—was not. He also told them he needed to get back to work, when in fact he knew he would be spending some amount of time in New York. Compounding the guilt was the fact he was leaving his aunt and mother behind in Amalfi, where they would have to grieve and settle Noemi's affairs without him. This was exactly what he had told Ben he didn't want to do.

He rationalized all of this by convincing himself he couldn't leave Doug in New York to cope with Noemi's killer on his own, and he needed to move quickly to stay on the mysterious man's trail. None of this eased his guilt.

His angst peaked again as his Aunt Martina squeezed him in a bear hug and thanked him for coming. "I'm sorry I have to go," he said. "I promise I'll be back soon."

"I know you will, Tony. Just be careful traveling."

Tony shared a similar embrace and apology with his mother, who also thanked him and told him he was wonderful.

Ouch, Tony thought.

Only Amedeo had no interest in sparing his feelings. The young boy was sad to see Tony leaving and made sure Tony knew it.

"I'll be back very soon. You'll see," Tony said as tears spilled down the boy's cheeks. "In the meantime, promise me you'll go to your piano lessons. My aunt spent a lot of time finding you a good teacher, so make her and me proud."

Amedeo nodded but remained focused on Tony's departure. "If you liked me, you would stay," he said with a pout.

Tony laughed and said, "That's a silly thing to say. I like you plenty, and I'll miss you very much. I'll look forward to improving my Italian again when I come back. And I'll expect to hear you playing Bach, or at least Elton John."

"I will play 'Somewhere Over the Rainbow' for you, just like you did for Noemi."

That brought tears to Tony's eyes. He quickly wiped them away and said, "Before I go, I have something for you."

"You have...?" The boy looked up expectantly.

"Yes, a gift. A small gift to remind you every day that I do care about you."

Tony reached into the armoire in his aunt's foyer and pulled out a kite. This was no drugstore kite made of paper and balsa wood. It was a large kite comprised of fabric and flexible polyamide struts. On the fabric's surface, bright colors provided a backdrop for an image of a soaring spaceship. Tony held the kite out to Amedeo.

The boy's reaction was immediate and the polar opposite of what Tony expected. Amedeo reared back, shrieked as if Tony held a rabid dog, turned, and fled out the door.

"What the...?" Tony stopped himself before cursing in front of his aunt and mother.

"Goodness," Martina said, looking forlorn. "I'm so sorry. I don't understand."

Tony put his arm around her shoulder and reassured her. "It's okay. He's just a boy. You never know what's going to set him off." Handing her the kite, he said, "Would you keep this here for a while? He may change his mind and come back for it."

"Yes. Of course I will," she said.

Tony didn't believe for one minute that Amedeo would change his mind, but he hoped the possibility would make his aunt feel better. If he was honest with himself, perhaps he was trying to make himself feel better too. The boy's reaction had not been normal. Tony wished he had time to chase him down, understand what had happened, and make it up to him. Unfortunately, all that would have to wait. He had a bus to catch.

***

Not having train service in Amalfi was irritating but not the end of the world. The bus ride to Sorrento was an adventure in itself. Others had commented many times that Italy needed no amusement park rides; it had the Amalfi Road. The winding, narrow highway made reading impossible because of its numerous sharp turns, one-lane curves, and frequent near-collisions, all accented by the spectacular views of the mountains and the Tyrrhenian Sea.

Having ridden the bus more than once as a young boy helped Tony overcome the abject terror felt by some tourists, though he had to admit to white knuckles a few times along the way. At other points, he was able to relax, enjoy the views, listen to music on his phone, and contemplate his next steps.

When he arrived in Sorrento, he immediately boarded a train for Naples. He knew the ferry was faster, but only by a few minutes. Also, Tony had always loved trains. Conversely, his feelings about boats ranged from indifference to outright fear, depending on the boat, its crew, and the weather. In this case, Tony had no knowledge of any of the three. Choosing the train was even easier given his perception that Italians had endured more than their fair share of boating tragedies. So he chose to risk the tunnels of the Circumvesuviana rail line rather than the open water of the Bay of Naples.

Chapter 13

Naples, Italy

Tony arrived in Naples in the late afternoon. He grabbed his bag off the luggage rack and began walking. He had not made a reservation for a room, but using his phone, he identified several attractive and surprisingly inexpensive options in the heart of the historic district. Because he needed no particular amenities and would only be staying a night or two, he didn't worry about finding a room. Almost anything would be acceptable.

In the end, he chose the Palazzo della Loggia, a small bed-and-breakfast style hotel. His room was small, but the facilities were modern and clean, and the central location was perfect.

He tossed his bag on a chair and unzipped it, removing the toiletries but not bothering to unpack anything else. He opened a curtain and sat down on the edge of the bed. Pulling out his phone, he ran a Google search for information about the Camorra and Cosa Nostra in the Campania Region which included Naples.

What he learned was similar to the rumors he had heard in Amalfi. The polizia now suspected that one man had succeeded in uniting multiple clans into one massive criminal organization. Historically, the Camorra was an umbrella term for a large number of smaller crime syndicates, or clans. In Italy, these clans were notorious for feuding with each other, with more than 3,000 deaths attributed to gang warfare in recent decades. In the mid-2000s, inter-clan killings averaged ten per month and sometimes ran as high as one a day. But recently there had been a noticeable drop in gangland murders, and authorities suspected at least a portion of the hundred or more Camorra clans finally were coming together, perhaps realizing everyone would profit more if they spent less time and money killing each other.

If that one don really existed—if there was one man overseeing the entire criminal operation—then Tony wanted to find him. The problem was, nothing in the popular media or web postings gave any hint regarding who it might be. Tony didn't know if the name was unknown or was being withheld by the press out of fear of legal or physical retribution. He hoped to find out at breakfast tomorrow.

***

Miles Andreson looked more like an overworked bookkeeper than an award-winning journalist. He was short at just under five feet, five inches, but he looked even shorter because he never quite stood up straight. He had gray hair that appeared to be in retreat from the battle being waged on his face by the scars of long-ago childhood acne, the two-days growth of reddish-gray whiskers, and the lines of present-day worries. His slightly misshapen glasses appeared to have been plucked off a figure in a wax museum, circa 1920.

Tony's immediate impression was of a less attractive and more hyped-up version of the long-ago TV detective Columbo. When Miles spoke, he even had a bit of the raspy Peter Falk timbre to his voice. However, when he grasped Tony's hand and smiled broadly, Andreson was transformed from a scurrying bookworm into a Chamber of Commerce ambassador. The man seemed genuinely happy to welcome a fellow American. Tony felt immediately at ease.

"I'm Miles," Andreson said, pulling out a chair at Tony's table and sitting. "I assume you're Tony Harrington. If not, I'm gonna be damn embarrassed."

Tony smiled back and nodded his assurance that Andreson had found the right table. "Thank you for taking the time to meet with me on such short notice."

"Hey, no problem. I gotta eat anyway. I'm happy to do it on your dime, especially here." He waved his hand to indicate the terrace where they were sitting at the Caruso Roof Garden at the top of the Grand Hotel Vesuvio. "I never get to come here if I'm buying. The Associated Press would reject my expense claim, and I could never pay it myself. We both know what the news pays."

Tony rolled his eyes and nodded. "All too well."

"Which leads me to ask," Andreson continued, "how are you covering this? Surely the daily paper in Orney, Iowa, doesn't pay better than the AP Bureau in Rome."

This time Tony laughed out loud. "No, it sure doesn't. It's pretty simple. I have a rich dad." Tony wasn't surprised by the question. When he had called Andreson to ask for his time, he had shared his name and where he worked. Because the *Orney Town Crier* was an AP-participating newspaper, a certain amount of cooperation could be expected. He also knew that before arriving at breakfast, Andreson would look him up on the internet and quickly learn about his past work, including the more sensational stories and the Pulitzer Prize.

Likewise, when Tony had gone looking for help, he had found the AP had a full-time bureau in Rome and a reporter who lived and spent a lot of time in Naples. Getting the number for Andreson had been easy enough; finding him available for breakfast the next morning had been lucky. Tony hoped it was a good omen.

Hearing the "rich dad" comment, Andreson shrugged his understanding and moved on. "So what brings you to me? How can I help? You onto a story here I should know about?"

Tony had thought a lot about how much to share with Andreson and had decided it shouldn't be much. He didn't know the man, so he couldn't predict his reaction to all the facts. Tony didn't want another reporter looking into Noemi's murder case. One nose in mafia business was dangerous enough, and he didn't want to drag a total stranger into a potentially life-threatening situation.

"No," Tony said. "No story this time. It's a personal matter I'm handling for my aunt who lives here. Well, not here, but down in Amalfi. I hope I can keep it personal. I don't want to ask for your help if it's going to bother you not knowing all the facts or being able to publish anything about it."

"Nah, no worries. I've got enough to do without worrying about a little dust being stirred up by an Iowa boy," he said with a grin. "How can I help?"

At that point, a waiter arrived and took their breakfast orders. Once he had departed, Tony took a deep breath and explained he was looking for the leader of the Camorra.

Andreson looked stunned as he fought and failed to keep a neutral face. "Well," he said, forcing a smile. "That's not what I expected to hear coming from an American. Any idea which of the clans you wanna reach?"

Tony shook his head and explained he had heard the rumors about a don possibly unifying the clans. He hoped the rumors were true and hoped to find the man.

Andreson leaned back in his chair and looked at Tony for a long time before responding. "Let me be perfectly honest. I'm not inclined to help you. You may think you know what you're asking, but you have no idea the level of violence and blatant disregard for human life that exists with these bastards. One clan killed nine innocent bystanders last month in an attack aimed at one man they believed was a police informant. You can't just march into that lion's den and say, 'Excuse me, my aunt respectfully requests that you stop polluting her water,' or whatever the hell this is about. They will have you cut into pieces and served to their dogs for dinner before you can finish your first sentence."

Tony leaned across the table and spoke as forcefully as he could without raising his voice. "Believe me, Miles, I do know. I've spent hours reading these horror stories. I wouldn't dream of talking to this guy if I thought he would have a negative reaction to the message I'm bringing. You have to trust me on this. Besides, I'm not asking you to do anything. Just give me a name, and I'll take it from there. After breakfast, you can go about your business and forget you ever saw me."

"You can bet your ass on that," Andreson said. "If I tell you anything, then we both better forget we ever had this conversation. I'm no coward, but I've lived here long enough to know I can't get sideways with the Camorra and expect to live to see my grandkids."

It took another forty minutes of pleading, plus an outstanding egg casserole and some delicate pastries, before Andreson finally said, "Okay, okay. I give. But dammit Tony, promise me you'll be smart with what you do with this. You're young and have a great life ahead of you. I don't care to have your blood on my hands."

"I promise," Tony said.

So, Andreson told him, quietly and carefully, that the rumors appeared to be true. There was a growing awareness that the clans were being united by a single don based in Naples. Andreson refused to say the name out loud, but told Tony the man owned a legitimate construction business that built commercial buildings—high-rise offices, airport terminals, schools, and other large projects. The man used the legitimate business to hide his criminal activities. Andreson said Tony could learn the name easily enough. He could simply read it off the side of the crane across the street.

Tony looked over and saw the name in big, bold letters—Lastra. He made a mental note but wrote nothing down. He was about to ask if Andreson knew the man's given name, when Andreson spoke first. "I hear this man is a real angel. And that's all you'll get from me. Let's talk about my grandkids."

Tony was puzzled for a moment until the lightbulb popped on. *Ahh, Angelo Lastra. Still a very common name, but probably the only one plastering his name across the city on construction equipment.*

Chapter 14

Two hours later, in the late morning of a sunny, spring day, Tony stood in the lobby of a twenty-two-story steel and glass office building along the Centro Direzionale, the heart of the business district in Naples, or Napoli, as the natives called it. He was staring at the business directory on the wall. His limited ability to read Italian was no hinderance. The name "Lastra" appeared at the top of the list next to the logo matching the one he had seen on the construction crane. *The top of the list—the penthouse—of course*, Tony thought as he tried to work up the courage to take the next step.

Suddenly a voice forced his hand. "Posso aiutarti?"

Tony turned to see what could have been a heavyweight wrestler or the center for an NFL team, if not for the maroon jacket, gray tie and highly polished shoes.

Tony knew the man had asked, "Can I help you?" He replied to the security guard, "Do you speak English?"

"Yes, enough," the man said, speaking clearly but without much warmth.

"I am an American," Tony said, unsure if that was a helpful introduction or not. "Can you tell me what the process is…uh, the protocol…? Sorry. I don't have an appointment, but I'd like to see Mr. Lastra. Do you know how I might do that?"

"Uh, much often I say call his office and ask uh…prenotazione …uh time to see him. But, you here, so I ask."

Tony thanked the guard and followed him back to the large reception desk in front of the elevator lobby. The doorman, or receptionist, or guard, or whatever he was, went behind the desk and used the telephone on the credenza by the wall, so Tony was unable to hear the conversation.

When the guard came back, Tony had one of the biggest shocks of his life. The guard asked, "Are you Mr. Harrington?"

Tony swallowed hard, tried to fight back the flush coming to his face, and nodded.

"Do you have I.D.? Passport?" the guard asked.

Tony pulled out his U.S. passport and handed it over.

After examining it closely, the guard handed it back and said, "Very well, signor. Follow me."

Tony wasn't sure if it was courage or a simple lack of options that allowed him to get his legs moving in the right direction. The guard escorted him into an express elevator, and moments later, they stepped out onto the 22nd Floor. They were in a huge lobby with marble floors and a bank of windows looking over the city and out to the bay.

A female voice said, "Thank you, Vincent. I'll take care of Mr. Harrington from here."

Tony turned and saw a middle-aged woman with dark hair approaching with her hand offered. He shook it and said, "Thank you. I appreciate your help. I didn't expect to get to see Mr. Lastra so quickly. I wasn't even sure he would be here on a Saturday."

The woman smiled and nodded but turned to lead him across the lobby, through a hardwood door, and down a hall to a meeting room. The woman was short, but her slender build and stately manner, combined with her dark plum-colored dress and high heels, made her seem statuesque, even elegant. Tony's assessment was that she could be three feet tall and still command the attention of everyone in the building.

The meeting room appeared to be an executive conference suite or perhaps a boardroom, with a dozen plush leather chairs around a hardwood table with gold inlays. Indirect lighting behind wall soffits created a warm glow on the long fabric-covered wall opposite floor-to-ceiling windows that stretched the length of the room. What appeared to be original paintings hung on the fabric wall. The doors and a wet bar lined a third wall, and the fourth had an A-V center with a giant flat screen TV.

The woman indicated the chair in which Tony should sit. He sat.

"May I get you something?" she asked in perfect English. "Coffee, tea, soft drink?"

Tony's first impulse was to decline, but he realized his mouth was so dry he may need it. "A soft drink or just water would be very nice," he croaked.

The woman smiled and went to the bar. When she opened the refrigerator and removed a can of Diet Dr. Pepper, Tony nearly fainted. The woman poured the soda into a glass with ice and set it in front of Tony. She settled into the chair to his left as he watched the cubes crack in his drink.

"My name is Bridgette. My mother was French," the woman said, as if she automatically explained to everyone why her name didn't sound Italian. "I am Mr. Lastra's assistant. Not his receptionist or his personal secretary. I have been with him for more than twenty years, and now I assist him with matters that require being away from a desk."

Tony nodded as if he, too, had three people helping him throughout the day. He took a large swallow of his drink.

"Mr. Lastra is very busy, as I am sure you guessed. But you were lucky. He instructed me to watch for you, and you picked a good time to come. He rarely books meetings that interfere with his lunch hour."

Tony glanced at his watch involuntarily. It was 11:45.

"Don't worry," Bridgette said. "You won't be here long."

She smiled, stood, and excused herself, saying she would let Mr. Lastra know Tony was waiting.

What the hell? Tony was beyond uneasy. He had been told the dons were well-connected, and certainly if Lastra had achieved what people claimed, and had somehow become the one don over multiple clans, he would have informants everywhere. But it was still remarkable that Lastra had known, or at least guessed, Tony would come here. Obviously, someone in Amalfi, probably Mancini, had alerted him to Tony's inquiries. *But how in God's name could he have known about the soda?* Tony thought back to his inquiries of shopkeepers in Amalfi. *Is it possible...?*

Tony's fear was subdued slightly by his growing fascination. What kind of man could build all of this, lead a huge construction business, and simultaneously command a massive, complex, and unstable criminal enterprise? And in the midst of it all, keep track of what was happening in a village miles away? He didn't have to wait long for the answers.

The door burst open and a burly man bounded across the floor with his hand outstretched. Angelo Lastra's hair was thick and pure white. His face was weathered, square, and flat with a mouth wide and expressive, giving the impression it might leap out to kiss or snap at you at any moment. When Lastra took Tony's hand, Tony could feel his rough skin and joints swollen from apparent arthritis. Despite this, Lastra's grip was strong. He was two inches shorter than Tony, perhaps five feet, eight inches, but outweighed Tony by thirty pounds. Lastra was thick but gave every appearance of being muscular and light on his feet. *If I didn't know he was Italian, I would assume he was one of Hemingway's Greek fisherman,* Tony mused.

Tony stood to meet him, trying to match the man's smile.

"Mr. Harrington! Welcome!" Lastra's voice boomed in perfect English. "Sit, sit. I see Bridgette found you something to drink. Good, good. Just let me grab something for myself."

Tony found his first response was spoken to Lastra's back as his host reached the bar. "Thank you, sir. Uh…thank you for the soda, but thank you even more for seeing me without an appointment."

Lastra turned with a tumbler in his hand and strode back to the table. In seconds he was in his seat and drinking—Tony couldn't tell if it was iced tea or whiskey.

I hope I don't ever have to run away from this guy, Tony thought, half-jokingly. *I'm pretty sure he would beat me in a race.*

"So, you are enjoying Napoli, yes?" Lastra raised his white, bushy eyebrows, emphasizing the question.

"Yes, it's beautiful. Of course, I've been fortunate enough to have visited before."

"Of course." Lastra nodded. "You're practically a native."

"Well, I hadn't seen the plaza before—the uh, Centro Direzionale. It's beautiful."

"Yes. No better place to work in all of Europe!" Lastra boomed. "So what brings you here to my office, Tony? May I call you Tony?"

"Yes, absolutely," Tony said, taken aback by the abrupt change of subject and wondering if it was Lastra's technique for putting unwanted guests on edge. *Man, if I get any closer to the edge, I'll be falling into the abyss,* he thought glumly.

Before Tony could answer, Lastra continued, "It's about your cousin, Miss Moretti, am I right? And I apologize, Tony. I should have begun by telling you how sorry I was to hear of your family's tragedy."

Tony cleared his throat and said, "Thank you, sir. It's kind of you to mention it. Yes, I came to see you because I believe you can help me find a man who can answer my questions."

"But Tony, what questions?" Lastra beamed. "The polizia have investigated and have said the poor girl's death was an accident. There is no man to find."

"I understand," Tony said. "But there was a man in Amalfi watching her. He may have seen what happened to cause her accident, if it was an accident."

Lastra said, "I understand the deep sense of loss you must feel, Tony, but I believe it has clouded your judgment. I have friends in Amalfi, and they have mentioned no such man. Even if there was, I would have no way of knowing who he was. I have many friends, but that does not mean I know every stranger, every tourist, who visits our villages."

Tony realized he had come to the inevitable fork in the road. He now must decide to say thank you and excuse himself or plow ahead and risk everything.

Crap. In for a penny, in for a pound. He forged ahead.

"Sir, by the way the people in the village are acting when I ask about the man, I believe he is family."

"Family? Your family, you mean?"

*Oh please…*Tony fought back a groan and shook his head. "If I may speak more clearly, sir, I believe the man is somehow connected to the Camorra."

"Ahh." Lastra responded with a frown. "Those are powerful

and ruthless people. If the man was Camorra, that would be a good reason to leave him alone."

"I agree," Tony said. "I have no desire to cause trouble for the Camorra. I just want this one man, to talk to him. To ask him what happened. I believe he was American, so I thought perhaps the Camorra would be unhappy if he was involved in Noemi's death and, if so, wouldn't mind if he was made to account for whatever he did."

"I think that may be a naïve assumption. Even if it isn't, why bring this to me?" Lastra asked, the sparkle in his eyes fading to a steely stare.

"Well, you are a well-established and successful businessman. You know many people. I thought perhaps you would know who to ask, or whom to have me ask."

Lastra leaned back in his chair for the first time, as if debating with himself how to respond. His eyes never left Tony's, never blinked, as he said quietly, "Bullshit."

"Sir?"

"Tony, do not speak to me as if I was a fool or an idiot. I am neither." Lastra leaned forward again, glaring. "You are the fool. You are here because you have heard rumors about me being Camorra. If you're wrong, you have offended me and have foregone any chance of soliciting my help. If you're right, then you have asked me to help you at the expense of a man you are saying is one of my 'family.' Either way, your cause is lost. You have wasted your time and mine."

"I apologize for any offense," Tony said quickly. "I only thought…"

He was interrupted by Lastra's bellowing voice, "No! Enough. I have help for you, but only in the way of advice. Leave this alone. Do not pursue your fictional American. Do not cross the Camorra. There are many tragedies worse than losing one cousin. Some people lose whole families when they anger the Camorra. Do not be one of them. And, Mr. Harrington, do not bother me again. I am happy to make time for friends, and I am happy to make time for business associates. You are neither."

Lastra stood, and the door opened. Bridgette appeared at the threshold. Tony wondered if she had been listening, or if Lastra had some way to summon her. In any case, she said, "Mr. Harrington, if you'll follow me, I'll help you find your way out."

"Thank you," he said to her, then turned to Lastra and said, "Thank you, sir, for your time."

Lastra nodded but did not reply.

***

As Tony rode the elevator down to the first-floor lobby, he nearly shook at the thought of Lastra's words, "Some people lose whole families..." It was a poorly disguised threat, as Tony was sure it was meant to be. *Dear God, what have I done now?*

***

Angelo Lastra sat at the boardroom table for several minutes after Bridgette and the young visitor had gone. He spread his fingers out on the table's surface and pressed down—an old habit from trying to reduce the lumps in his joints. He pushed down hard until the pain in his joints cried out for him to stop. He didn't stop. He was angry, but not at the American who had just left. He was angry with a different American, the one sitting in his office just on the other side of the wall.

"Fucking Costello," Lastra said aloud.

The door opened and Bridgette stepped in. Lastra simply nodded at her, and she turned and left, returning shortly with Roberto

"Robbie" Costello in tow. Bridgette nodded at a chair, and Costello sat. She left, closing the door behind her. After a full minute of silence, Costello finally asked, "So what did he want?"

"What do you think he wanted?" Lastra growled, staring at the tall American with a crooked nose. "He wanted me to give you up. He wanted me to use my connections to see that you're brought to justice."

Costello snorted, "That little prick. I'll kill him."

"No!" Lastra shouted. "You stupid bastard. You did this! You brought this trouble to my door. Use your head and think of someone other than yourself for once in your life. Think about the fact this so-called prick is a reporter. And he came to my office. If he turns up dead now, the spotlight of news media from all over hell and gone will be shining right on me." Lastra was practically spitting. "No. Leave the kid alone and stay out of sight for a few weeks. Maybe this will blow over by then. Mr. Harrington will have to go back to work in bum-fuck Iowa or wherever, and all he will have is his suspicions."

"Okay, okay. I get it," Costello said, with a hint of a whine in his voice. "It's hands off for now. But if this 'kid' as you call him keeps pushing, I'm gonna have to do something."

"Jesus. Just get out of here," Lastra said. "But remember, if you make any more trouble for me, you're going to find yourself in a place much worse than prison."

Costello was red-faced with anger and humiliation, but he rose out of his chair and left without another word.

As Lastra watched him go, he hoped he wouldn't regret letting him live.

Chapter 15

New York

It was nearly noon on Sunday when the sound of the Delta Airbus's screeching tires woke Tony from a deep sleep. He realized the jet was on the runway at JFK just as the cabin lights came up and the flight attendant announced it was now okay to use cell phones.

Tony pulled his from his jeans pocket and turned it on. It immediately began vibrating in his hand as he counted more than a dozen text messages and three times as many emails awaiting his responses. Most were from people he needed and wanted to get back to, but he ignored all but the texts from Doug.

I was bored so I came back to the airport to meet you. Still bored. Worried the bar will run out of Jack Daniels before I run out of cash. Let me know when you land.

Tony smiled and typed, *I'm here. With luck I'll be deplaned and thru Customs in less than an hour. Meet you where?*

Doug's immediate response read, *Flannigan's. First set of*

tables on right after exiting past security.

***

Tony had very little luggage and nothing to declare, so he made it through Customs with no glitches and exited into the arrivals lobby of Terminal 4 in half the time he had guessed. Doug spotted him coming out of the glass enclosure, and by the time Tony arrived at his table, an icy glass of diet soda was waiting for him.

Tony embraced his friend before sitting.

"Doug, thank you so much for being here."

"No problem, Tone-man. What'd ya bring me?"

"Uh, sorry pal, I never thought to…"

Doug laughed and gave Tony's shoulder a soft punch. "Relax, man. It was a joke. Unless, of course, you found a hot Italian babe looking for a chance to live in rural Iowa with a really sexy radio reporter."

"Well, of course," Tony smiled. "I kept bumping into women like that everywhere I went. I just couldn't think of any sexy radio reporters to hook them up with."

"Smart ass."

"You were asking for it." He paused, then said, "Seriously, Doug. You look like you haven't slept. How long have you been waiting?"

"Relax, it's only been three or four hours. I've only had to make up excuses five times as to why I'm hangin' around: three times to the waitresses and twice to the security guards."

Tony groaned. "Oh, man. I'm sorry. Really."

"I told you to relax. They're starting to like me here. See the brunette behind the bar? She actually stopped scowling at me a couple of hours ago. I'm thinking of taking her dancing tonight."

Tony shook his head at his friend and asked, "So. Anything to report?"

"Well, maybe...If you're really nice to me." Doug grinned and gestured down the long concourse to the other end of the terminal. "As you can see, there are two exits out of Terminal Four. I had to run back and forth to catch the people deplaning from flights originating in Europe. Did you know international flights arrive here every ten minutes during the busy part of the day? It got to be pretty humorous, before I finally spotted him."

"Okay...So you worked hard. Then...wait, what?" Tony was on the edge of his seat. If Doug had spotted "Dracula," why was he sitting here drinking beer?

Doug surprised Tony when he sat up straight, raised his glass of beer, and said, "Tone-man, here's to you, my genius friend. Dracula arrived last night on a United flight from Rome. His name is Costello and he lives at the Ostrich, a luxury apartment building in Manhattan."

Tony's glass hit the table hard, spilling soda, and causing people at neighboring tables to look up. "Jesus, Tenney," he hissed. "How the hell do you know all that?"

Doug smirked and waited, letting the suspense build. "Well, I'd love to tell you about my incredible sleuthing abilities, but the fact is, it was pretty simple. I followed your man out of the terminal building. One of the limos waiting in line had a driver standing in front of it, holding a sign with 'Costello' written on it. Dracula headed right for him, shook his hand, and chatted for a couple of seconds before climbing in. I made up a question to ask the driver at the limo next to his so I could get close enough to read the name Costello. I noticed the 'Ostrich' logo in the corner of the driver's sign. It matched the logo on his coat, so I assume he came from there."

Tony was wide-eyed in amazement as Doug continued, "Later, after checking into the hotel, I spent some time looking up the Ostrich. It looks spectacular. If your guy lives there, and isn't just visiting, he has some serious dough. The apartments in that joint rent for something like $12,000 a month."

"You're amazing," Tony said. "Just awesome."

"Well, yes, thanks, but now what? I s'pose you're gonna ask me to go visit him and slap him around a little?"

Tony laughed again but quickly sobered. "No, obviously not. The truth is, I didn't get the help I had hoped for in Naples. In fact, I got just the opposite. So I need to think about what's next. The good news is we know where to start. That means we can take a night off and have some fun."

"Two nights, I hope," Doug said. "After being up most of the night, I'm not gonna make it past dinner. So you have to take me out on the town tomorrow night."

"Okay, deal," Tony said. "Let's get into the city, get me checked into your hotel, and find some chow. Then I'll let you sleep while I go find the girl of my dreams."

"If you do, I'm gonna punch you in the face," Doug said, sounding like he might actually do it.

***

At 7 p.m., Tony was standing in line at the half-price booth for Broadway tickets. True to his word, Doug had called it a night after finishing two-thirds of the extra-large pizza they had ordered at Lombardi's in Little Italy. Doug had wanted pizza, and Tony hadn't quibbled despite his having eaten Italian food three meals a day for more than a week.

They were staying at one of the major chain hotels near 46th and Broadway, so it had been a quick walk to Times Square once Doug had settled in and Tony had cleaned up for an evening out. Tony loved New York and had enjoyed every Broadway show he had ever seen, so he had decided half-price tickets were fine. He would grab whatever was available. The line was long, and Tony had been waiting twenty minutes or so by the time he was close enough to the ticket window to read the electronic sign. He didn't mind. He was actually glad the crowds had finally returned to the city after the devastating impact of the pandemic.

As he scanned the sign for a musical that sounded good, he sensed someone at his right shoulder. He turned and found himself face-to-face with a young woman. No, not just a woman—a goddess. She was nearly as tall as Tony in her leather ankle boots. She was looking up at the show postings, so her face was just below his when he turned to her. She had raven-black hair, parted in the middle, that rolled into curls as it passed her shoulders. Her eyes were large and brown, accented by dark eyebrows. Her nose was slightly longer than average, but narrow and finely sculpted. She had a wide mouth with perfect white teeth. Her smile seemed natural and permanently affixed to her face. Tony absorbed it all in an instant, and stopped himself from expressing out loud his reaction of *holy shit*.

Down, boy, he thought instead, and turned back to the postings to avoid staring. The woman, however, spoke to him.

"Any idea what you're going to see? God, I hate deciding," she said. "At these prices, I only allow myself to come every couple of months, so choosing is agony."

Tony turned back and said, "Well, to answer your question, no, I just started looking. And, by the way, I'd like to have your problem. I only get here every couple of years."

"Really? Are you from out of town?"

Tony laughed and turned to face her fully. He held out his hand.

"I'm Tony Harrington, and I'm from about as far out of town as you can get. I live in a place called Orney, Iowa, population 15,000 if you include the dogs and a few cows."

The woman laughed. It was a deep, warm sound. It washed over Tony like a Caribbean wave. He wished it wouldn't stop. A laugh like hers could melt steel. She said, "Wow, I can't imagine. I've lived in New York all my life. I think there might be 15,000 people in my building."

It was Tony's turn to laugh.

The woman continued, "So you're visiting from Iowa? Vacation or business?"

"Actually neither," Tony replied. "I'm just getting back from a couple of weeks in Italy and decided to spend a few days in New York before going back to work." Tony was partly proud and partly ashamed of himself, for working the Italy trip into the conversation so quickly and easily. He knew he had done it in an effort to impress her. He suddenly realized she was still holding his hand. He looked down and she pulled it away, chuckling.

"Sorry. I'm Erica Pappas."

"Don't be sorry. You can hold on to me for as long as you want," Tony said, immediately regretting it and wondering if he had overstepped. But Erica didn't seem to notice and was still smiling.

"Uh…" Tony stammered, his embarrassment showing. "Pappas. Greek heritage?"

"Very good, Mr. Harrington," she said. "My father is first-generation American. He's in real estate. He does well. My mother is a CPA. They're both successful, which is why I can afford to live in Manhattan."

"Nice," Tony said. "My parents are also pretty well-off, so I'm able to do the work I love, though it doesn't pay worth a crap." *Is 'crap' too crass a word? You're blowing it, Tony.* Still, Erica smiled.

Suddenly, a voice growled, "Hey, pal, you buying tickets or are you and your lady friend gonna hold up the line all night?"

Tony swiveled and realized he was first in line. He didn't know what to do. He wanted his conversation with Erica to continue, but he didn't want to be too forward. He didn't even know if she was single. She could be here with a date or, God forbid, a husband. Fortunately, Erica came to rescue.

She said, "Tony, if you're here alone, let's see a show together. You pick."

Confused but excited, and still unable to decide the best course of action, he said, "Are you sure?"

"Welcome to New York," she said with a little shrug and that brilliant smile. "Remember, you'll be doing me a favor. I hate choosing."

Tony quickly decided to duck the responsibility by leaving it to the ticket seller. He said, "What show has the best seats left?"

The man said he had two seats on the center aisle, main floor, for "Beautiful," the musical about Carole King, featuring her compositions.

Tony turned and asked, "Have you seen it?"

"Nope," Erica said, smiling. "But it sounds perfect."

"Two for 'Beautiful'," Tony said, pulling out his Visa card.

***

The show was indeed perfect—great music, a good story, and just the right tone to put two strangers at ease with each other. Erica was beaming as they left the theater and went to search for a drink.

"I've got an idea," Tony said. "Since we both had dinner before the show, let's go to Sardi's for dessert."

"A Broadway show and then Sardi's? This is going to be the

most expensive first date in history," Erica laughed.

Tony's heart leapt, both at the sound of her laugh and at her reference to their evening as a first date. He felt like a middle-schooler getting the attentions of the high school's best-looking cheerleader.

Conversation during dessert covered all the basics. She was single, having split a year ago from a longtime relationship with a college sweetheart. He was a physics major who turned out to be more interested in the attractions of ionized particles than in those of his former girlfriend. She claimed to feel a mix of mourning and relief.

Tony couldn't imagine anyone finding science more alluring than the woman sitting across the table from him. *The ex-boyfriend had to be crazy,* Tony kept the thought to himself as he shared a little of his story in return.

Eventually, he related the story of his late girlfriend who'd been murdered four years ago. He had considered glossing over this, but realized if Erica had any interest in him at all, she would Google him and immediately learn all about the events that had earned him his national recognition as a reporter.

Erica was understandably horrified and appropriately sympathetic. Tony also related that he had enjoyed one brief relationship after Lisa but had discovered it was more of a recovery therapy than a real relationship.

At one point, Tony took the plunge without noticing he was doing so. He said, "In all honesty, Erica, meeting you tonight has been the most significant thing that's happened to me since Lisa's death. In a few hours, I've realized I can move on. I didn't know I could feel such…" He stopped himself.

Erica sat motionless for a moment, then reached up and caressed the side of his face with her hand. Tony's face burned and his heart melted. They changed subjects and continued chatting about everything from favorite bands to favorite books.

At midnight, as they left Sardi's, Erica said she would walk back to his hotel with him and catch a cab from there. As they walked up Broadway, they stopped to window shop and, occasionally, to enjoy the craziness of Midtown at night.

They laughed when Spiderman and a snowman from "Frozen" hit them up for spare change. They laughed even harder when they spotted a homeless man sitting in a doorway and holding a sign that said, "Career Advice – $1."

Tony pulled Erica toward the man and said to him, "I'll pay you two dollars if you'll let us take a selfie with you." The man nodded, and they did. The image on Tony's iPhone screen showed them both laughing. *That is so perfect,* he thought.

He showed it to Erica and said, "I'll send you this, but it means you'll have to give me your phone number."

"I would have been pissed if you hadn't asked," she said. "Give me your phone, and I'll send it to myself. Then you'll have it."

In front of the hotel, under the bright lights of the awning, they kissed. It was warm, long, and perfect.

"Call me," was all she said before stepping into the taxi waiting at the curb.

Tony danced a jig in the elevator as it took him up to his room.

Chapter 16

Tony lay awake in his hotel room, wondering if the previous night had been a dream, when his cell phone blared the obnoxious ring tone assigned to announce unknown callers.

"Tony Harrington." He swung his legs over the side of the bed and sat up.

A man's voice said, "Tony Harrington from the *Town Crier*?"

"Yes…Who's this?"

"Tony, my name is Everett Powell. I'm assistant editor for hard news—well, that's not my actual title, but in effect, that's what I do. Anyway, I'm an assistant editor at *The New York Times*. We heard, I mean I was told this morning, that you're in town, and we'd like to meet you."

Tony's mind was reeling. "Wait, wait, slow down. How did you hear I was in town?"

"Ah, that was just dumb luck. You went to see 'Beautiful' last night, on Broadway, right?"

Tony was nodding as Powell continued, "One of our staff

people was sitting in front of you. She heard enough of your conversation to catch your name and a few comments about stories you've covered. She got curious and looked you up online. What a world, right? Anyway, she stopped at my desk this morning to suggest I look at your stuff, which I've done. The Pulitzer Prize is a nice resume-builder, but I was even more impressed when I read your actual work. I'd like to talk to you. Can you get away?"

"Well, uh, sure," Tony said, still trying to catch up. "I'm on vacation, so my time is pretty flexible. What did you have in mind?"

"How about lunch today with me and a couple of other people from the Times?"

"Well, doing a meal could be tough. I'm traveling with a friend."

"The woman you were with last night? If she's your significant other, she's welcome to come along."

I wish, Tony thought, but said, "No, she's a friend from here in town. I'm traveling with a buddy from Iowa. I just got in yesterday, and he was here for a couple of days on his own. So I hate to leave him alone for another meal."

"Understood. Hang on." Tony could hear the phone being set down and Powell pounding the keys on a computer, presumably looking at people's schedules. "Afternoons are tough for editors because of late-night deadlines for the morning edition, but of course you know all about that. I can't get people free quickly enough this morning. How about 10 a.m. tomorrow?"

"Sure," Tony said. "Tell me where, and I'll be there."

"Can you find the *Times* building?" Powell didn't wait for an answer. "Come there, ask for me at Reception, and I'll come down and get you. And don't dress up. Nowadays everybody in the newsroom dresses like they work in their moms' basements. Wear whatever you'd be wearing for sightseeing."

"Sure..." Tony said, wondering why he would dress up anyway.

"And Tony," Powell said. "Thanks. We're all looking forward to meeting you."

***

"Holy shit, Tone-man, *The New York Times* is going to offer you a job!" Doug was wide-eyed as Tony related the conversation to him while they sat in the hotel lobby enjoying coffee and bagels.

"Well, now, let's not get carried away."

"Carried away, my ass. He's read your stuff. He loves your stuff. Now he wants you to meet with him and other execs. What the hell else could it be? So are you going to take it? Can I come with you? I wonder if they need someone with an extensive and impressive history in broadcast journalism."

"Whoa, whoa, whoa," Tony said. "Just stop. In the first place, I've never met the guy or anyone else from the *Times*, unless you count the woman who came to Iowa to cover the governor's trial. Secondly, despite your brilliant insights into a conversation you didn't even hear, we don't know what he wants. Lastly, even if you're right, I have no idea what I would do with it. If he offers me a million bucks a year, that might settle it, but otherwise I'll be damned if I know whether or not I would even be interested."

Doug nodded and took another bite of bagel, making a face as he caught a chunk of onion. "Fair enough, my friend, but if you decide to say yes, you better start laying the groundwork for your most excellent best friend to get a second spot there. Or even better, on the NBC news team!"

Tony smiled. "Care to explain how me being a peon at the *Times* has anything to do with you getting a job at NBC or anywhere else?"

"Nope," Doug said, and Tony laughed.

***

The two friends spent most of the rest of the day being tourists. They walked through Central Park, enjoyed lunch at an Irish pub, and strolled down Fifth Avenue. They didn't enjoy the prices on the merchandise in the stores. They went to the top of the Empire State Building, and they bought T-shirts in a novelty store near the Ed Sullivan Theater.

As they strolled, Tony told Doug about his "date" with Erica. He winced as his friend made jokes about her and poked fun at him for letting an obvious chance to get lucky slip through his fingers. Tony had debated not telling Doug, but really didn't want to keep secrets from his friend. Besides, Tony knew if he wanted to see Erica again while he was in New York, Doug would have to know about her.

They also discussed next steps regarding the primary purpose of their time in New York but found themselves at a loss.

At one point, Doug said, "The way I see it, Tone, we've got limited options. One, you just get a gun and kill him. Two, we kidnap and torture him into telling the truth about what he did to Noemi. Or three, you spend all your dad's money following the guy around until he jaywalks or something, and you sic the cops on him."

Tony smiled, but felt no glee in it. "Your options suck, Doug."

Both men sighed, knowing it was true.

Tony added, "While you figure out a better solution, let's at least take a look at this guy's digs."

They hailed a cab and asked to be taken to the Ostrich. The driver stared at them blankly, so Doug pulled out his phone and looked it up online. However, before he could share the actual street address, Tony stopped him. He instructed the cabbie to take them to the Intrepid Museum on West 46th. They could walk the few blocks from there.

"This is better," Tony said. "If he dropped us in front of the building, with my luck, Dracula would come out the door just in time to bump into us."

The name Dracula drew a quick glance from the cab driver, and Tony and Doug both smiled. A few minutes later, they stood on the sidewalk a block away from the Ostrich. Tony whistled in admiration. The Ostrich was thirty stories of highly polished steel and mirrored windows, configured in a complex pattern that made it appear the building was twisted in a gradual spiral reaching into the clouds.

Doug nudged him with his elbow and said, "It's even more spectacular than it looked online. I wonder if a *New York Times* reporter could afford to live there?"

Tony "nudged" back with a sharp elbow to the ribs, hard enough to cause his friend to stumble and cry out, "Hey, it was just a joke!"

"The views from the upper-floor apartments must be spectacular," Tony said, glancing away to spare his eyes from the sun's reflection off the building's south face. As he turned his head, his eyes refocused on the building across the street. Half as tall and more traditional in design, it had a third-floor restaurant with a large outdoor dining area built on a portion of the building's second floor roof.

With his eyes trained on the dining area, Tony said, "You know, Doug. If we do decide to keep an eye on Costello, take a look at that. I bet we could sit in the restaurant up there and have a perfect view of the front of his building."

"Yeah, probably," Doug said, nodding, "until they got tired of us and threw us out, or until Costello drove off in his Porsche or whatever and we were stuck on the roof. Then what?"

"I didn't say it was a *good* plan." Tony grimaced. *What are we going to do? Am I going to have to let this one go?* "Come on, let's get outta here. Staring at this jerk's pleasure palace is too depressing for words."

They set off toward Broadway, and Tony's thoughts returned to Erica. He pulled his phone from his pocket and said, "Doug, would you mind too much if..."

Doug cut him off with a snort. "Of course not, Tone-man. Have I ever gotten between you and a chance to get laid?"

Tony shot him a look.

"Okay, sorry, sorry. Seriously, if she's half the woman you described, you'd be crazy not to call her. Go ahead. Make a date for tonight if you want."

"Doug, you're the best, really. But what will you do?"

"Are you kidding? I'm gettin' in line at the half-price ticket booth so I can hook up with the girl of *my* dreams. I assume they also have gorgeous blondes with lots of money waiting to serve the needs of slightly overweight guys?"

Tony laughed, shook his head, and dialed.

Chapter 17

Erica peered over the top of her margarita as she sipped, apparently engrossed in Tony's story of being kidnapped and held prisoner by human traffickers. Relating his experiences from two years previously was a shameless ploy to impress her, but he couldn't help himself.

She wore jeans and a lightweight suede vest over a white cotton V-neck sweater. Had she worn an evening gown, she would have been no more stunning. Just enough cleavage showed to be alluring without the appearance of an overt attempt to be sexy. Except for a touch of lipstick and eyeliner, she didn't appear to be wearing makeup. Tony was fine with that, thinking no beauty product could improve on perfection.

Tony was in khakis and a navy button-down dress shirt. He had realized he was under-dressed as soon as they had entered the restaurant. All the male patrons were in suits or sports coats, and most wore ties. Tony and Erica sat at a table on the far side of the rooftop restaurant. Sitting outdoors, Tony felt a little better about his attire, though there were no differences he could discern between the restaurant's indoor and outdoor décor, appointments, or service. The linens on their table were just as crisp and white, the silver was just as polished, and the hand-painted china was just as elegant.

Tony hated himself for doing it, but he had brought Erica here thinking he might as well kill two birds with one stone—enjoy a meal with her while keeping an eye on the front of the Ostrich.

The conversation flowed easily, with her claiming to be embarrassed by her "ordinary" life compared to his. As she talked about summers on Long Island and sailing in the Caribbean, Tony thought her life sounded anything but ordinary.

Throughout the meal and conversation, Tony worked hard to stay focused and not be distracted by the chrome-and-glass tower across the street, even as he stole the occasional glance at it over her shoulder. As dessert was being served—ice cream for him and something called "Death by Chocolate" for her—he realized he had failed.

Erica was smiling, but something in her eyes turned serious when she asked, "Tony, why are we here?"

"What? What's wrong? Haven't you enjoyed your meal?"

"Don't be silly. The food was wonderful. But why *here*? You're clearly distracted, and this restaurant isn't exactly a destination for most out-of-towners. I've lived in New York my whole life, and I didn't even know this was here." She paused, reached across the table, laid her hand on his forearm, and asked, "Are you working?"

"No, no, of course not."

She pulled her hand back and looked down at the chocolate sculpture on her plate.

"Erica, please. What's wrong?"

"It's okay, Tony, really. We've only just met. I can't expect to know everything. I had no right to ask. I'm sorry."

Tony set down his spoon and leaned back in his chair. He

looked up at the black sky—no stars visible from the heart of Manhattan—and said, "Shit. Uh, excuse my French."

Erica looked up at him, waiting.

Tony made up his mind. He took a deep breath and told her everything.

***

"So, you're saying across the street is a cold-blooded killer with ties to the mob, who knows what you look like?"

"Yep."

"And you brought me here, to…to what? Offer me up as a human sacrifice?"

It hadn't occurred to Tony that bringing her to a restaurant across from the Ostrich would put her in danger too. "Oh, man. Well, I mean, I'm sorry…I never thought."

"Relax, it was a joke," she said, the warmth in her smile back. "I'm glad you told me, and I only resent you a little for not giving me your full attention. But I have to admit, I agree with your friend Doug. I'm not sure what you can do if you spot him. Especially from up here."

Tony acknowledged the point with a nod and said, "I hate to admit it, but you're absolutely right. Choosing this restaurant served no purpose." He paused as it occurred to him, "…except perhaps to make me feel better. Watching the building makes me feel like I'm doing *something* for Noemi. It may not amount to anything important, but at least I'm not ignoring what happened."

"I admire you for recognizing the motivations behind what you're doing," Erica said, "but now it's time to pay the bill and take me out of here. My self-esteem will suffer if I start feeling like you're ignoring me. Let's go find some music."

Tony agreed. Thirty minutes later, they were in an off-Broadway bar with a great quartet—guitar, piano, bass, and drums—playing a wide range of pop and hard rock music. The place was packed, and the dance floor was about the size of the Harrington family's dining room table. When they got up to dance, they were forced to hold each other close, regardless of the tempo of the music. Tony wasn't complaining. She smelled fantastic, and the warmth of her body pressed against his sent his heart soaring.

When the band took a break, Erica excused herself to the women's room. Tony immediately got up and approached the piano player, first to compliment him, then to ask a favor.

When Erica returned to their table, Tony wasn't there. She heard his voice amplified and looked up at the tiny stage. Seated at the baby grand was Tony. He began singing the only song that made any sense to sing to Erica Pappas on a warm spring night, in Midtown New York.

"Uptown girl, she's been living in her uptown world. I bet she's never had a backstreet guy…"

Erica was appropriately wowed, both by his talent and his willingness to risk climbing on stage to perform for her in front of strangers. It helped that the crowd also appreciated the performance and applauded enthusiastically when he finished.

The only disappointment of the night came at the end, when he asked Erica back to his hotel room and she declined. Tony said he understood, and he did, but that didn't make it any easier to walk away.

"Believe me, Tony, I would love it," she said. "But if I go up to that room with you, we'll be up all night, and I have to work tomorrow. Can I take a rain check?"

Tony smiled and said of course, while secretly wanting to fall to his knees and beg.

Once again, they shared a passionate curbside kiss, and Erica climbed into a cab. As he watched the cab disappear around a corner, it occurred to Tony that Erica had never told him where she lived. A dreadful thought rose up and flew from his brain like an arrow into his heart. *She has a boyfriend, or a husband. She's purposely keeping me away from her home.* The thought made him weak in the knees, and he forced himself to dismiss it. He would see her again, and soon enough it would be clear she was available and genuinely interested in him.

***

At 1 a.m., Erica Pappas sat on her bed, staring at her smart phone. Could she do it? Did she have a choice? *No, dammit,* she thought. *I don't have a choice. Get it over with.* She dialed.

"It's about time," said the voice at the other end of the line.

"Sorry. He took me dancing."

"You're not falling for this farm boy, are you?"

"No, no. Of course not," she forced a chuckle.

"So what do you have for me?"

"Well…" She took a deep breath. "It's not good. He knows your name. He knows where you live. He called you a cold-blooded killer. He said you have ties to the family."

Costello growled. "What the *fuck?*"

"Hey, don't blame me. I'm just telling it like it is. That's what you wanted, right?"

There was silence at the other end while he composed himself. "Yeah, you did good, but how the hell did he…?" Another silence and a long sigh. "Now I'm gonna have to deal with this prick."

Erica felt her spine stiffen. Perhaps a beat too quickly, she said, "He'll be headed home soon. He said he doesn't have any evidence against you. Maybe it's safer to let it go."

"Shut your damn mouth. Never tell me my business. I can't have a damn reporter running around who knows what I do, what I look like, and who I am."

"Okay, okay," Erica said quickly. "Anything else you need from me?"

"Nah, thanks. I'll call if I need you," he said, hanging up immediately.

Erica turned off her phone, lay back on her bed, and began to weep.

Chapter 18

At 10 a.m. Tuesday, Tony was seated at a modern vinyl conference table in a modest-sized room on an upper floor of the *New York Times* headquarters. Also at the table were Everett Powell and five other people whose names he couldn't remember—two senior reporters, two editors, and the vice president of human resources.

Tony should have been excited to realize Doug was right, the eff-ing *New York Times* wanted *him*, Tony Harrington. Surprisingly, Tony found himself anything but enthused. Confused? Yes. Conflicted? Yes. Distracted? Certainly, by thoughts of Costello and even more so, by thoughts of Erica. But as Powell explained their interest in him, Tony was not experiencing any of the excitement or gratification a moment like this might have generated under other circumstances.

The people from the *Times* must have sensed it because as the conversation progressed, they slowly moved into an all-out sales pitch.

They said the paper had an opening for a local reporter to cover crime and the courts. Tony's background was perfect for it. More importantly, the *Times* needed people who could write clear, compelling news copy. Tony had proven his ability to do so. New York is an exciting place. Tony would find many opportunities to write important news and make a difference in people's lives. It's also a great place for a young, single guy to live. The one-sided conversation went on like that for the better part of an hour. Then the HR guy explained the salary and benefits they were offering. Tony tried to ignore the fact it was five times what he was making currently. The last impression he wanted to give was that the money alone had turned his head.

He was polite. He answered their questions. He asked a few questions.

As the discussion was winding down, a staffer stuck his head in the door to call one of the editors away. "The White House is on the phone," he said. "They're fuming. I think you'd better take it."

Tony found himself wondering if they had staged the interruption to impress him, but decided it was unlikely. All in a day's work at *The New York Times*, he was sure.

Tony concluded his part of the discussion, saying, "I want to thank you all, sincerely. Your interest in me is extraordinarily flattering, and your offer is very generous. If I seem less than gung-ho about this unbelievable turn of events, please remember I'm just coming home from a funeral, I'm still suffering from jet lag, and I was up late last night dancing."

The five remaining faces all smiled and nodded. Powell said, "Of course, Tony. We understand completely."

"I promise you, I will consider it carefully. I need to talk to my current boss and to my father, both of whom I rely on for advice. And I need some time to consider it. Obviously, a move to New York is a very different future for me than continuing to work in Orney, Iowa. I may very well say yes, but I owe it to my family and myself to consider all the pros and cons."

Smiles and nods all around. As everyone stood to leave, shook hands, and headed out the door, Tony said, "Mr. Powell, can you spare another minute?"

"Of course, Tony. You have another question?"

"Well, yes. Could we sit down again? It shouldn't take long."

Powell settled back into his seat, and Tony removed his cell phone from his pocket. He pulled up the photo of Costello and slid it across the table. Powell picked it up and looked at it.

"Okay…Who's this?"

"I was hoping you'd know," Tony said. "His name is Costello. I'm pretty sure he's mafia and may have ties to a clan in Amalfi. I was hoping you would know more."

Powell raised an eyebrow, started to speak and then stopped. He stood, went to the door and shouted across the newsroom, "Chopper! Can you join us for a minute?"

A man who appeared to be a middle-aged hippie—longish hair parted in the middle, John Lennon glasses, short and pudgy—strode into the room. Seeing Tony, he approached with a hand out and said, "Thomas Chopin…like the composer. You can call me Chopper. Around here, everybody does." He turned to Powell and said, "What's up, boss?"

"Mr. Harrington here wants you to look at a picture." Powell handed the phone over to Chopper.

"Ah. Bad dude."

Powell looked at Tony and said, "Chopper's our resident expert on syndicated crime. It looks like you've got a hit." He turned to Chopper. "Tell Tony whatever you know about this guy."

"Well, I'm pretty sure this is Roberto Costello. He goes by

Robbie. He's a nephew, or maybe great-nephew, of one of the biggest crime bosses in New York. He likes to lie low. We don't know a lot about him...Not officially, anyway."

Tony said, "I'm not a cop. I'm a reporter like you. But I'm not on a story, either. This is personal. I'd appreciate anything you can tell me, official or not."

Chopper sat down and looked closely at Tony. "I'm sorry to hear it's personal. This is not a guy you want to get personal with. Word is he's not interested in a high position in the family because he likes to hurt people. He likes working in the trenches and getting his hands dirty, if you follow my drift. Everyone's assumption is that he does wet work for his uncle, but of course nothing like that has ever been proven. By all appearances, he's paid very well, and he enjoys his money."

"Yeah," Tony agreed. "I've seen where he lives."

"The Ostrich? That's just one of his places. They say he has a condo on Sanibel Island in Florida and a time share at one of the ski resorts in Aspen. Anyway, he likes staying out of the operations of the syndicate. He wants everyone to know he's content to stay where he is, doing what he's doing. It makes him less of a threat to those who do want to be boss someday, and it keeps him off the NYPD's radar and out of the clutches of the DEA, FBI, and a host of other three-letter agencies. What's your interest?"

Tony swallowed, knowing he'd have to reciprocate with Chopper. He said, "I'm pretty sure he murdered my cousin in Italy. She was tossed off a seawall in Amalfi. He was seen there following her around for several days."

"Ah," Chopper said again. "That would fit the M.O. It's pretty common knowledge Costello has a thing for women. He's not gentle. Some have been hurt pretty badly. Of course, no one ever presses charges against him."

Tony nodded glumly. "Do the authorities ever go after someone like this? Would it help them to know about my suspicions in Noemi's case?"

"I doubt it," Chopper said. "NYPD has disbanded the OCB—sorry, the Organized Crime Bureau. Individual crimes are now addressed by the relevant divisions of the force. Of course, the feds still work pretty hard to stop, or at least slow down, the syndicates. But unless your evidence is pretty powerful, your suspicions aren't going to send them after a guy who hasn't left a trace in maybe a dozen hits or more. You know, a guy like Costello is the toughest to catch. He works alone, so there's no communication trail and no accomplice to pressure or offer a deal. When he commits a murder, he probably doesn't know the person, so he can't be discovered through a motive. As long as he has a secure way to receive his orders and collect his money, he's a ghost."

"That's really helpful, but damn discouraging," Tony said. "By the way, he threatened me to my face, so if I turn up in a dumpster while I'm here in New York, you might want to take a look at him for it."

Chopper looked at Powell and cocked his head toward Tony, asking, "Who is this guy?"

Powell smiled and said, "Oh, you know, just a typical guy from Iowa in town for a Broadway show."

Chopper laughed, reached into his pocket, and handed Tony his business card. If I can be helpful to you in any way, give me a call. But please, try to not have that card in your wallet when Costello offs you. I'd rather not have him coming after me."

Tony didn't laugh, but he did thank Chopper and slid the card into his slacks pocket.

Chopper left and Powell said, "Tony, I'm glad you asked us for help. Is there anything else we can do?"

He had a fleeting thought that he should ask them to check their resources for information about Erica, but immediately dismissed it. That would be going too far. He had no right to send The *New York Times* after anyone, especially someone he cared about. And if she ever found out…Tony was horrified to think what that might mean. "No," he said. "Thank you. I won't be shy if I think of something."

"One more thing," Powell said. Tony looked up.

"If something happens here that leads to a story, I'll give you a month of your regular salary for exclusive rights, after the *Town Crier* of course."

Tony told Powell he wasn't sure the *Crier's* contract with the Associated Press would allow him to agree to that, but he added it didn't matter. He would help Powell if he could—not for money but in appreciation for the information he had received.

"Besides," he said. "Nothing's gonna happen. I've got nothing on Costello. I'm gonna finish chasing a pretty girl, then I'm going to try to forget what happened in Italy."

"You're probably right," Powell said. "It's hard to let go, but the best reporters know when a story has dried up and it's time to move on."

Both men couldn't have been more wrong.

Chapter 19

"You look like someone who just got fired, not a guy being courted by the world's most important news organization." Doug said between bites of roast beef. At the Carnegie Deli, it was called a sandwich. Anywhere else, it would have been called a side of beef, or a cow. The sandwich was as big as Doug's head. But he didn't seem to mind.

Tony poked at his chicken salad. "Sorry, Doug. Everywhere I turn, I hit a brick wall about Costello."

"Yeah, so what? That hasn't changed for days. What's really bothering you?"

Sometimes Doug was too perceptive.

"It's Erica," he said. "I've called her three times since getting up this morning, and she's not answering. I've got a terrible feeling I've seen the last of her."

"That's a bit of an overreaction, don't you think? She probably just has her phone on silent at work. Maybe she's in a meeting or something." Doug returned to his efforts to devour the cow.

"Yeah, maybe," Tony said, completely unconvinced. "God, why did she have to be so… so great?"

"Hey, nffts, neftfghs adgettfivver." Doug attempted, his mouth stuffed.

Tony found a smile and waited for him to swallow.

Doug held up a finger while he chewed. After about ten seconds, he said, "Sorry. I was just going to give you shit about finding such a superb adjective to describe the girl of your dreams. You're sure 'great' isn't overdoing it?"

"Shut up, Doug."

"That's better," Doug smiled. "You're gonna be fine."

Tony was pretty sure he wasn't.

***

More calls and texts to Erica in the afternoon also yielded no responses, so Tony gave up. She certainly had his number if she wanted to respond.

At 7 p.m., Tony and Doug were back in Times Square. Doug wanted to try the burgers at the Hard Rock Café. Tony couldn't imagine eating again. He was pretty sure his lunch would carry him until Labor Day, but he tagged along, knowing it would be interesting to see all the autographed memorabilia in the restaurant.

When Doug had finished another side of beef, this one ground up and served on half a loaf of bread, he asked, "So what's next?"

Tony surprised him by saying, "It's time to go to work. We're gonna stop playing around and make a run at this jerk."

"I assume you don't mean Bob Dylan," Doug smiled, motioning toward the autographed guitar in the case behind his head.

Tony didn't smile. "Sure don't. Get your garlic and your Crucifix. Let's go find Dracula." As they went looking for a cab, the two friends created the basics of a plan, or at least the beginnings of a glimmer of the basics of a plan.

***

Doug walked the final block to the Ostrich. Tony was nowhere in sight. Five limousines were lined up in the circle drive. It was after seven in the evening, and residents would be coming out soon to claim their rides for their respective nights on the town.

Doug approached the first driver, a young man who was using a soft cloth to wipe non-existent smudges from the fender of the gleaming black car.

"Wow, beautiful car," Doug said.

"Fuck off," the man said, straightening up and trying to look intimidating.

Doug thought, *Thank you, Tony, for sending me on this assignment.* Of course, Doug knew Tony was right. Costello would recognize Tony's face, so he couldn't be here in front of the Ostrich. "Sorry, man. I was just paying you a compliment."

"Well, it's not my car, so no, you didn't. Go bother someone else."

Doug didn't give up so easily. "Really, I'm sorry. I didn't mean to put you off. It's just that I'm from out of town, and I've never seen a car like this before."

"You've never seen a limo? Bullshit. There ain't places that far out of town."

Doug chuckled, scrambling to stay ahead of the kid who was smarter than he looked. "Oh, I've seen limos. Just not new ones in this condition. Where I come from, the limos are used by high schoolers going to prom. The cars are older than the kids, and look it."

"I'd guess Alabama, but you don't have the accent. So where's this place that's so remote they don't have new cars?"

Doug didn't want to say Iowa and risk any chance it would come back on Tony or anyone in Orney, so he said, "New Mexico. My mom's an artist. We live up in Taos."

"Yeah? Sounds horrible. I've never been there, but then I've never been anywhere. If you live in New York, what's the point of going anywhere else?"

"Hard to argue that," Doug said, thinking it might be the biggest lie he had ever told.

In another ten minutes, Doug and the limo driver—"Just call me Butch"—were chatting away like old friends. Doug asked Butch for advice on where to find good music, good food, and hot women. Butch clearly loved showing off his knowledge of the city. Every once in a while, Doug slipped in a question about the Ostrich, then the cars, and eventually the people who used them. He learned the cars were part of a motor pool. Residents of the Ostrich could sign up to use one for an evening. Almost always, on weekend nights, every car was booked. Sometimes they served more than one resident if the schedules worked out, but some residents were particular and wanted the car ready and waiting if they decided to leave a party early, seek out a different bar, or otherwise change plans on a whim.

"The beautiful cars and occasional beautiful women can make this job look glamorous, but it's mostly boring. A lot of sitting around, waiting for rich people to tell you what to do. If the money wasn't so good, I'd be outta here like a home run off a leaded bat."

Doug chuckled and pretended to know what Butch was talking about. He was pretty sure there was no such thing as a leaded bat in the high school baseball games he covered for the radio station. "These must be old people," Doug prodded. "I mean, who else can afford to live in a place like this, right?"

"Yeah, mostly. But there are exceptions. This is New York, you know. There's a couple of daytime TV stars up there, and a couple of younger guys who made it big in the markets. And there's one IT geek. He weighs about 300 pounds, but he's always got a babe on his arm. Funny how money makes a man more attractive."

Laughing, Doug said, "Sadly, I wouldn't know."

Butch laughed with him.

"So you have a favorite?" Doug asked.

"Yeah, sorta. I'm not sure 'favorite' is the right word, but driving for this one guy is rarely boring. He's real mysterious. Filthy rich, but never talks about it. Nobody seems to know where he gets his dough. The others like to whisper that he's mafia, you know, but I think it's BS. Most the mafia guys live in more established neighborhoods, and in less flashy places than this."

"Really? He sounds cool."

"Cool's not the right word. He's dark and tough. Men shy away from him, and women are attracted to him like flies to horseshit, you know? Driving him makes me feel like a badass. And you know the best part? He really likes…Oh, shit. I can't tell you that. I gotta be more careful. I'm not supposed to talk about our residents. I could lose my job."

"Hey, relax. I'm from New Mexico. I'll be outta here in a couple of days. Who am I gonna tell?"

"Yeah, well, this is private. I mean it. But this guy likes to do it in the limo. He gets a woman in the back, there's no telling him to stop. She gives it up easy, or she gives it up hard, but she always gives it up. He knows I watch a little—I mean, why wouldn't I? I'm right in the front seat...—but he doesn't even care. I think he likes an audience."

"Wow, that's crazy," Doug said, not having to fake his reaction. "How hard is hard? I mean, does he *hurt* them?"

"Well, sometimes, but I don't watch that part. If she's really putting up a fight, and it starts to get ugly, I close the view to the back. I'm not stupid. I don't want to be a witness to a crime. Being on this guy's shit list would not be good for my health. Know what I mean?"

"Sure, sure. But wow, you've seen some amazing action back there."

"Yeah, it's always fun to see a naked woman, but of course it's frustrating as hell to watch another guy getting it on when all you can do is sit there."

"Good point. I don't think I'd like it. Are you always the one who drives him?"

"Well, he always asks for me cause he knows I'll keep my trap shut. I still don't see him much though. He has a couple of cars of his own including a Maserati he likes to take out at night. He only uses the limo when he's going somewhere with valet parking. He hates giving his keys to some punk who's never driven a stick shift."

"I get that," Doug said. "So is that why you're out here tonight? You taking Mr. Mysterious somewhere?"

Butch looked at his watch. "Yeah, at 7:45. He's coming down with a date, and I'm dropping them at a show. It's less than ten blocks, and for that I get to wait here for an hour, there for three hours, and then who knows where? It's getting close to that time now. You'd better take a hike. Mr. C...Mr. Mysterious won't like it if he sees me talking to a stranger. He's very private."

"Yep, you mentioned that," Doug said. "Well, it's been fun to meet you. Thanks for the look inside the lives of the rich and famous. I'll go back to the Super 8 now and cry myself to sleep."

Butch laughed heartily and slapped Doug on the shoulder. "Chin up. Maybe you'll win the lottery, and someday I'll be waiting here for you to come down from your glass palace."

"Don't hold your breath," Doug said as he turned and walked down the block.

Tony was waiting around the corner, in a late-model Chevy Impala rented that afternoon from Enterprise. As Doug climbed in, he said, "Did you get anything?"

"Boy, did I," Doug croaked, and flopped into the passenger seat.

***

It was midnight. Tony and Doug sat quietly in the Chevy. They were in a parking lot in Little Italy across the street and half a block down from a nightclub called The Romper Room. Live music from inside the club could be felt, as much as heard, from their car. They watched a steady stream of patrons enter and leave. Tony wished he could go in and check out the band. They obviously attracted a strong following.

Earlier in the evening, they had followed the limo to Broadway and had seen Costello exit the back with a girl on his arm who couldn't possibly have been old enough to be with a grown man. She was blonde and shapely, but wide-eyed and unsteady on her high heels. She could have been inebriated, but at that early hour, Tony thought it more likely she was an adolescent not yet comfortable in evening wear and heels.

In any case, the pair had gone to the show at the Shubert. Nearly three hours later when they left the theater, they walked down the street to a steakhouse, then back to the limo after their meal for the short trip to Little Italy.

It was after 1 a.m. when Costello and the girl exited the nightclub. The limo was waiting at the curb. Thinking about what Doug had told him, Tony had to fight the urge to jump out of the car and yell a warning to the girl not to get into the car. He held back, however, and watched Costello play the part of a perfect gentleman as he helped her into the back.

The limo pulled away from the curb, and Tony reached for the ignition button, hesitating long enough to ensure it wouldn't be too obvious they were following. But before he even touched the button, the limo pulled over about two blocks down the street and stopped. It sat running but unmoving. Tony and Doug looked at each other, both realizing what was probably happening in the back of the limo at that moment.

After ten minutes of agony, Tony could stand it no more. "Dammit!" he said, opening the car door.

Doug grabbed at him but missed. "Tony! What are you doing? You can't go up there. That's a killer in that car, and he knows who you are!"

But Tony was already out of the car. He stooped to look at Doug and said, "I'm sorry. I can't just sit here and let him rape that poor girl."

"You don't know it's rape. Maybe she initiated it."

"I know this, Doug. She's too young, he's filled her full of alcohol, and now he's taking advantage of her. Regardless of what she has said, or not said, he's assaulting her. I can't just sit here and do nothing."

Tony slammed the car door and started jogging up the street toward the limo.

"Shit, shit, shit," Doug said as he opened his door and climbed out. He grumbled under his breath. "Tone-man, if you get me killed, I'm gonna haunt your ass forever."

Tony had a head start and was faster than Doug, so a lot of distance separated them when Tony neared the limo. In the end, it didn't matter. When Tony was less than ten paces away, the limo's brake lights came on, then off, and the car roared away from the curb, turning at the first corner and disappearing from view.

"Son of a bitch!" Tony said, taking off at a run in pursuit of the car, then stopping. It was too late. The limo was gone.

The two friends stood with hands on their knees, gasping for air, then headed back for the car. After two hours of driving around hoping to catch sight of the limo, Tony and Doug gave up.

Tony's frustration had reached the point of a thermonuclear meltdown.

Doug kept saying, "She's fine, Tony. I'm sure she's fine."

Tony was silent until they reached the hotel hallway outside their respective rooms. "Doug?"

"Yeah?"

"Have I mentioned how much I hate this guy?"

"Maybe once or twice. Get some sleep. Tomorrow's another day."

Tony opened his door, entered the room, and pushed the door closed behind him. "That's great," he muttered. "Another day of no progress, frustration, abandonment, and failure. I can't wait."

Chapter 20

"Hey, Tony! Great to hear from you." Ben sounded good—his voice clear, reassuring. It was 9 a.m. Wednesday back in Iowa. Tony knew Ben would be up and hoped his boss wasn't in the middle of something important on a busy weekday morning.

"Hey, Ben. Sorry it's been a few days."

"No problem. I hear you're back in the states. I assume you're in New York?"

"Yes, but how…?"

"No mystery. Your mom called here for you a couple of days ago. She said you'd left Italy but hadn't returned her calls, so she tried the office. She was surprised you weren't here."

Tony groaned. He had failed to call his mother back after receiving more than one message from her.

"Sorry you had to deal with that. I'll get back to her right away. And yes, I'm in New York, living it up with Doug Tenney."

"I've noticed Doug isn't doing the news this week. I actually wondered if he had flown out to meet you"

"Yeah, we've been running around town together the past few days. He's a great friend. The best."

"Anything exciting in the Big Apple?"

"Oh, not much," Tony replied, deciding to unload it all. "I just got threatened by a killer, met a girl, lost a girl, and, oh yeah, *The New York Times* offered me a job."

Whatever Tony had expected, all he got from the other end of the line was Ben's silence.

"Did I lose you?"

Ben sighed. "You sure as hell did. Maybe you should start at the beginning."

Tony did, sharing with his boss his suspicions about Noemi's death and his efforts to follow the man responsible back to New York. Tony stopped short of sharing Costello's name or suspected mob connections but opened up completely about Erica and the offer from *The Times*.

Ben, true to form, didn't interrupt except to ask an occasional question for clarification. When Tony finished, Ben said, "Wow. You packed a decade of experiences into your two weeks away. I'm sorry about the girl, by the way. She sounds lovely. Maybe you'll hear from her yet."

"Maybe. I'm not counting on it."

"So what's next?" Tony could tell Ben was trying to keep his tone light. He also knew that both the major issues—the supposed murderer and the job offer—had to be deeply disturbing to him.

"I honestly don't know, Ben, on any of these fronts. I'm being pulled in a dozen different directions. I want to chase the bad guy, but I also want to run away and leave him alone. I want to take the exciting new job, but I also want to come home to Iowa and settle back into my Orney routine. Mostly, I want to go find Erica, but really don't want to get hurt again, any more than I already have been. I've never felt so adrift."

"Well, you're not asking for my advice, but I'll give you some anyway. If I were you, I would leave the potential killer alone and go after the girl. Once you know for sure where that stands, it may help answer the question about where you want to live."

Tony knew that made perfect sense and said so. He added, "The problem is, Ben, I've now learned this guy I'm following may not be just a one-time killer…Sorry, more on that another time. That makes a huge difference if it's true. You know, I think I could walk away if he'd killed Noemi by accident, or even out of anger, and he was remorseful and unlikely to kill again. But sadly, all the signs say this guy is a complete sociopath. Sources have told me he has a reputation for hurting people, and that he enjoys killing. How in the hell can I walk away from that?"

"It's hard for you, I know. But I have to repeat what I've told you before. You're a writer—a journalist—not a cop or a vigilante. It's not your job to avenge evil and bring bad guys to justice. Your job is to find the truth and write about it."

"I know you're right. But, dammit…" Suddenly, all the frustration, anger, and grief that had been building in Tony for over two weeks came exploding out of him. He pulled the phone away from his mouth as he burst into tears and wailed like a baby. It took a long time to stop convulsing and settle down to a point where he could talk. This, Tony realized, was why he hadn't called his mother. He had feared a scene like this.

He picked up the phone. "Ben, are you still there? I'm so sorry you had to hear that."

"It's okay, Tony. I get it. I really do. How can I help?"

"Well, there is one thing," Tony said.

"Anything," Ben said, without hesitation.

Tony knew Ben would regret those words. He said, "I need you to ship my handgun to me. Here at the hotel."

"Tony, I'm not sure…"

"Please, Ben. You know me. I hate that thing and will never use it except in self-defense. But I feel like an idiot, having a possible killer, a man who knows my name, pissed at me, and me not having any protection at all."

"Your best protection is to get the hell outta Dodge," Ben said. "Are you sure I can't talk you into coming home?"

"Soon, I promise. But not yet. Will you send it? For Friday morning delivery?"

"Yes, of course, but Tony…"

"Yes?"

"Please, I beg you, don't make me regret it."

"You know me, boss. Mister calm, cool, and collected." Tony punctuated the irony of his comment by sniffing back his runny nose.

Ben swallowed a chuckle, and Tony hung up. He took a deep breath and dialed his mother's cell phone.

***

"You look like shit," Doug said, lifting a forkful of lo mein to his mouth.

Tony shrugged. "That's okay because I feel like shit." He tried lifting a piece of broccoli with his chopsticks but dropped it. He tried again, and failed again.

"As if I don't have enough frustration in my life," he said, tossing the chopsticks on the table and picking up his fork.

Doug asked, "So what happened to you while I was out visiting the Lady of the Lake?"

Tony knew Doug had spent the morning on a boat trip around the Statue of Liberty while Tony had stayed in his hotel room, making phone calls and pondering his future. "Oh, not much. I just cried like John Boehner as I talked to my boss, then spent an hour trying to convince my mother to let me back into the family. Then I completely abandoned my manhood and my pride and tried to call Erica again. Don't ask. She didn't answer. I tried not to cry as I left a message, but I'm not sure I quite succeeded."

"Hmm. Pretty pathetic, Tone-man. You should have come with me. Lady Liberty still looks majestic, and the concessions girl on the boat was really hot. Ya know, the cold breeze off the water…Well, you shoulda seen the size of the bumps in her blouse…"

"Shut up, Doug."

"Yeah…" Doug smiled. "You're gonna be fine."

They were sitting in a wonderful old restaurant in Chinatown. This was not a place for tourists. This was a family-owned restaurant in which no one spoke English. It was on the second floor of a retail building, and no one but longtime New Yorkers knew it existed. Tony had been guided here by Jeremy, a friend who worked in the mayor's office at New York City Hall. Jeremy was a former high school classmate who had gone to college at NYU and had stayed in New York to build a life and career. His recommendation for a restaurant was spot-on. Sitting in plush furnishings, surrounded by amazing aromas, and tasting platters of mysterious entrees, it was almost possible to forget one's troubles.

Almost.

Tony set down his fork and stared at his friend.

"What?" Doug asked. "Do I have piece of spinach, or seaweed, or whatever this stuff is on my chin?"

Tony shook his head. "Doug, you need to go home now."

Doug stared at him. "What do you mean go home? Are we done here? Are you throwing in the towel?"

"Not me. You. I've decided to stay and try to do something

about Dracula. It's only going to get more dangerous. You've done what I asked. You've done it brilliantly. Remember how we thought we'd never know anything about this guy? Look what you've accomplished for me. It's all I can ask. I want you to go home. I can't allow you to be in harm's way any longer."

"My friend, the correct response to your command is very simple: up your nose with a garden hose." Doug smiled and took another bite of a pasta-covered clam bit, or lobster bit, or maybe a piece of pork. Who could tell?

Tony shook his head again and said, "What, are you twelve?"

"I didn't think saying fuck you, which is what I wanted to say, would be appropriate in a nice family restaurant like this. In any case, I'm not done here until you are."

"Doug, please. I want you to go."

"I believe you, Tony. You're an honorable guy, and you want to keep your best friend safe. Good for you. Unfortunately, the best friend has a say in this, too, and he says he's not going. So forget it."

"Doug…"

Doug slammed his hand on the table, causing the dishes to jump and Tony to jump even higher.

Doug's face was red. "Listen to me, Tony. I value our friendship. It's the most important relationship I have in my life. How could I go home and let you deal with all this on your own and still call myself your friend?"

"You could. You absolutely could! You don't owe…"

"No! It's settled. If you need to understand why, let me explain it this way. I know I don't have a lot going for me…No, shut up and let me finish. I do an okay job, and I make an okay living, and I have an okay girlfriend from time to time. Occasionally I do okay with a fishing rod or a deck of cards. But the one thing I know I'm really good at—better at than anyone else in the world—is standing by your side when you need help. That sounds melodramatic, I know. So sue me. But the fact is, I would rather die helping you than live knowing I wasn't there when you needed me. I'm staying. Now shut the fuck up and finish your octopus, or tofu, or veal, or whatever the hell is hiding in that pile of noodles."

Tony ate. He didn't try to talk. He had cried enough for one day.

Chapter 21

Tony genuflected and stepped sideways into a pew. Doug looked confused, did a sort of half-bow toward the altar at the front of the cathedral, and slid in beside him.

"I forgot about all the weird shi…uh, stuff you Catholics have to do in church," Doug whispered.

"Relax," Tony replied in a soft voice just above a whisper. "Two-thirds of the people in here are tourists looking at the architecture. No one's going to notice if you're not well-schooled in Catholic formalities."

Doug looked around and realized Tony was right. He'd never seen a church so full of people walking around, talking, and taking pictures, rather than participating in the service underway.

"You gotta admit, it's pretty photo-worthy," Doug said as he settled back in the pew.

Tony nodded as he knelt to pray. It was Thursday morning. They were in St. Patrick's Cathedral, a Manhattan landmark built more than a hundred fifty years previously. The church filled an entire city block at Fifth Avenue and 51st. It could seat 3,000 people.

The neo-Gothic structure was more than imposing; it was magnificent. Doug peered around in awe at the marble finishes and exquisite sculptures. As he gazed up into the rafters, he wondered whether he'd spy Batman and The Joker fighting high above in one of the spires.

Tony was on his knees a long time. When he'd finished praying, he stood to leave.

"Not staying for Mass?" Doug asked, surprised.

"Nah. It doesn't feel right being surrounded by so many gawkers. I'll trust that God appreciates us stopping in. Let's go find some breakfast."

Doug had no inclination to argue.

They walked out the doors and stood at the top of the wide steps facing the street.

"Only in New York."

As Tony's eyes adjusted to the sunlight, he looked around to see what Doug was referencing. Across the street, in the window of a Victoria's Secret store, was a nine-foot tall photograph of a voluptuous woman in a pink bra and thong. "Only in New York," Doug said again, "can you pray and get a boner, all in the same place."

Tony punched him in the arm. "Don't talk like that here."

"Hey, I'm just sayin'! Go ahead, tell me I'm wrong."

Tony was determined not to have that conversation on the steps of the cathedral, so he headed down and turned south.

They found a diner a few blocks south and west, not far from Broadway. As Doug put their name down for a table, Tony went out to the sidewalk to buy *The New York Times* from a vendor there.

As they waited, Tony offered Doug a section and began reading the front page in earnest.

"Like what you see, Tone-man?" Doug's voice was chiding

him.

Tony didn't look up but said, with an edge to his voice, "Doug..." He drew it out so the one word contained a whole paragraph of warnings not to go there.

As usual, Doug was either oblivious or willfully ignoring him. "Hey, your name'd look good there on the front page. I can see it now, 'Orney School Board Cuts Chalk Budget,' by Tony Harrington. That would..."

"Douuug..." Tony now stared at his friend's smiling face.

"I'm just sayin'!" Doug repeated. He stood, rescued by the young woman with an astonishing amount of metal protruding from her lip and her eyebrow, who had arrived to show them to their table.

After consuming platters of eggs and pancakes, Tony and Doug returned to *The Times*. The diner's crowd had thinned, so they didn't feel too badly about keeping the table for a while. When Tony reached one of the inside pages, his hands suddenly clenched tighter. "Dear God," he said quietly.

"What?"

"Dear God," Tony repeated. "Hang on."

Doug got out of his chair and walked around the table to look over Tony's shoulder. On the lower side of the right-hand page was a photograph of a young blonde girl. He joined Tony in reading the article:

New York Times

Body of Brooklyn Teen Found in Central Park

NEW YORK, NY – The body of a 17-year-old girl, the victim of an apparent homicide, was found early Wednesday in a secluded part of northeast Central Park. Police identified the victim as Ashley Boisington, a Brooklyn high school student.

The body was discovered by a couple returning to their apartment on the upper east side after a concert in another part of the park.

Police confirmed Boisington had been sexually assaulted and severely beaten. They declined to give a cause of death, saying it will not be known until an autopsy is completed, but said there was no immediate evidence of a gunshot or knife wound.

One officer, speaking on the condition of anonymity, said it was obvious to him the girl's neck had been broken. "This was a vicious attack and a terrible way for a young girl to die," the officer said.

The officer also said there were no signs of a struggle at the scene where the body was found, and very little blood, indicating the attack happened elsewhere and the body was transported to the remote spot in the park.

Police were asked if the girl's death was related to two other teen deaths in recent months in which girls' bodies were found similarly beaten and discarded in out-of-the-way places. Police refused to speculate.

Family members and school officials were not available for comment on Wednesday, but a classmate of Boisington said she was an excellent student and well-liked. "She was so pretty, and so nice. I just can't believe someone would do this to her," said…

Doug made a face. "Dear God is right." He returned to his chair. "It's horrible, Tony, but don't let it get to you. This is New York City, after all."

Tony was studying the picture. He lowered the paper to the table and looked at his friend. "It's her," he said.

"What's who?"

"It's the girl Costello had in the car." Tony said it with absolute conviction.

"Whoa, Tone-man. And lower your voice. He's Dracula when we're out in public, remember?"

Tony stared, gritting his teeth and clenching the flatware in his fist to try to calm himself. Doug implored his buddy to calm down. "You can't possibly know for certain that it's the same girl. We barely saw her! It was dark, and they were never closer to us than the opposite side of the street. She was blonde and she was young, yes, but do you know how many young blonde girls there must be in New York? About one-point-two gazillion."

"Doug, it was her." Tony was unblinking. "You're right, I can't know it. But I do." He tapped his chest. "In here. I know it. That son of a bitch raped her and killed her. Damn him!"

"Okay, enough," Doug said, noticing a waitress bending the ear of a co-worker and casting sidelong glances toward their table. "We need to get out of here and continue this conversation outside."

***

Two hours later, after much debate and a little outright yelling, Tony finally won the argument. Shortly before noon, the two men took a cab to One Police Plaza near City Hall in southern Manhattan —the home office of the Major Cases Squad. When they identified themselves at the reception desk as reporters from Iowa, the uniformed officer first asked if they were requesting a tour. When they said no, the woman then tried to refer them to the media relations officer.

Frustrated, Tony ignored those efforts and pushed hard, urging her to contact someone assigned to the Boisington killing. The officer then tried to refer them to the homicide squad in another part of the city.

"Look," Tony said, "I can read between the lines. The local media believe, and therefore it's damn likely, that Boisington is another victim of the same man who assaulted and killed at least two other girls. That means the murder is assigned here to Major Cases. You can't ignore the possibility she's a victim of your serial killer. Please, ask if we can talk to someone. We may have information that'll help."

The officer finally relented and made the call. After a few minutes, she led Tony and Doug to a pair of vinyl-covered metal chairs in the lobby.

Forty minutes later, after Doug had begun to nod off, a bleary-eyed, bald Black man in shirtsleeves appeared. "Harrington, Tenney?" he yelled, jolting Doug from his half-nap. "This way."

The man was Lt. Keith Coppestad. He wasn't especially pleasant, but he offered them water, and led them up an elevator and through a maze of corridors to a mostly empty squad room. At a desk on the far side of the room, next to a window fogged over with twenty years of grime, smoke residue, and bird droppings, Coppestad settled into an ancient office chair and leaned back. Tony was sure the chair would collapse under the man's weight at any moment. The detective gestured toward two straight-backed metal office chairs on the opposite side of his desk, and Tony and Doug sat.

Coppestad listened attentively as Tony told his story, starting with his cousin's death in Amalfi and ending with Costello roaring away in his limo Tuesday night with a young blonde girl in the back. "So when I saw the paper this morning, I knew it must be her. It was Costello who…"

"Nonsense," Coppestad barked, interrupting him.

"Excuse me?"

"Mr. Harrington, your tale of woe is touching, and your willingness to walk into the offices of not one, but two, alleged Camorra bosses, tells me you're either brave or completely out of your mind. And, by the way, if your intel on Costello is correct, which I doubt, then you're twice as crazy to be following him around town. If he's mafioso, wouldn't he have friends looking out for him? Wouldn't he know that you're tailing him?"

"But…"

"But nothing," Coppestad interjected. "Let me finish. Even if you're not crazy and all this stuff that led you to believe Costello is guilty of killing your niece is true, there's absolutely no connection to Miss Boisington's murder. Seeing him with a blonde girl means nothing. Absolutely nothing."

Tony wanted to protest, but he held his tongue.

Coppestad said, "Young man, think about it. Even if I was willing to make the leap in logic you've made, and I'm not, but if I was, there's not a thing I could do about it. No judge I've ever met is going to give me a warrant based on what you saw or, I should say, didn't see. This Costello character is just a guy out on a date with a blonde. She could have been forty years old with a good plastic surgeon, for all you really know."

Tony knew Coppestad was right, especially about the practical barriers, but he still believed Boisington was the girl he'd seen. "So you can't even take a look at him? Bring him in for questioning or something?"

"Not a chance," Coppestad said. "And let me be clear: you need to steer clear of him too. I don't want you nosing around in my town, making trouble for people for no credible reason. Understood?"

Tony nodded.

Doug fought to not roll his eyes, knowing Tony too well to believe he'd be put off Costello by the lieutenant's warning.

"I appreciate you guys coming in. I really do. We'll check your description of her clothes against those owned by the dead girl, and we'll look at her phone records to see if there was contact between them. But I don't expect to find a connection. You've got nothing, and you need to admit to yourselves you've got nothing. Go out and enjoy the city while you can."

Tony and Doug thanked him for his time, picked up their jackets, and headed out.

In the elevator down to the lobby, Doug said, "You're not going to let this go, are you?"

"Of course I am," Tony said, smiling grimly.

"Really? I'm surprised."

"The lieutenant's right. I've been chasing ghosts. It's time to relax and have some fun."

Doug was more than surprised; he was astonished.

Once they were outside, they decided to walk down to the World Trade Center Memorial. On the way, Doug began to make suggestions about entertainment for the evening.

Tony stopped and looked at him and said, "You didn't believe that crap I said in the elevator, did you?"

"Huh? Well, sure, I did. Wait, what?"

"I just said we were dropping it in case they have a bug in the elevator. A lot of places that deal with criminals and even civil lawsuits keep microphones and cameras in the elevators. They catch a lot of candid admissions that way."

Doug shook his head, marveling at the trivia repository his

friend called a brain.

Tony continued. "I get it why Coppestad can't go after Costello. Everything he said was true. But that isn't going to stop me from getting this bastard myself. Young women are dying, and I'm going to put an end to it."

"Jeez, Tony. I may have to take back what I said about sticking with you."

"Doug, I was hoping…"

"Shut up. I'm kidding. I'm with you all the way. You're not the only knight in shining armor in the world. I want these killings to stop too."

"Of course you do," Tony said, embarrassed that he might have implied otherwise. "I just wish Coppestad was as easy to convince as you."

***

Keith Coppestad looked through the notes he had taken during his visit with the two men from Iowa. Their story had been incredible —ridiculous even. But something about the name Costello rang a bell. Even if it was BS, and Coppestad was sure these men were full of it, it gave him something to check into. Any kind of lead was welcome after months of chasing the ghost who liked to batter, rape, and murder young girls with his bare hands.

He picked up the phone. "Murray, get the core team assembled this afternoon, and call over to the organized crime guys. See if someone there can join us." He paused to listen and then responded, "Probably nothin', but we're gonna take a look at a guy just in case. I only want the core team, not everybody. This is so tenuous, a feather could snap it. I don't want a bunch of cowboys stompin' around. Thanks."

And when it turned out to be nothing, which Coppestad fully expected, he especially didn't want those same cowboys giving him shit for the next five years.

***

Tony and Doug spent the rest of the afternoon at *The New York Times*, reading articles about the deaths of four teenage girls—not two as acknowledged publicly by the police—who had died and had been found in similar circumstances. *The Times* was reporting the NYPD's line about two other cases because the editors didn't want other media organizations to know yet what they had found by digging through mountains of police records and newspaper clippings in multiple jurisdictions. In short, *The Times* now knew what the police knew: a serial killer was at work.

Tony had shamelessly used Powell's interest in him to get access to *The Times's* archives. They could have gone to the public library but had assumed *The Times* would have everything of importance more readily available. They knew how newsrooms worked. The articles about previous potentially-related murders would have been collected in an electronic file, ready for immediate access when the next victim was discovered.

Powell had confirmed it would be fast and easy for Tony and Doug to access the file, and had agreed to provide them with a desk and a terminal at which to work. He, of course, had asked why they were interested. Tony had said only that his recent work on human trafficking cases in the Midwest had increased his interest in cases involving assaults and murders of young women. Powell may or may not have bought the story.

In any case, it didn't matter. They were here, and they were getting everything.

As Tony finished reading, he found himself impressed that the police had put together the possibility they were dealing with a serial killer, and even more so that *The Times* reporter had picked up on it as well. While it was true the four girls were teenagers and were beaten to death, the similarities ended there. The girls were not similar in appearance, they lived in different boroughs, and in one case, across the Hudson and fifty miles away in New Jersey. One was an athlete; the others were not. One was active in music and drama at school; the other two had no remarkable interests, or at least none that had been reported. Two were white, one was a first-generation Asian immigrant, and one had Hispanic heritage. Two came from single-parent homes and two from nuclear families. On top of all this, the crimes were separated by months and did not appear to be increasing in frequency as was often the case with serial killers. In fact, Ashley Boisington was the first victim discovered in more than four months, the biggest gap of time between the known crimes.

Tony knew, and of course the police knew, that the number of victims could be greater. There was no guarantee all the victims had been found. The killer's MO appeared to involve dumping the bodies in remote places where they wouldn't be found right away. There may be other Ashleys lying in the woods or in a far corner of a junkyard or at the bottom of the river. Tony prayed there weren't.

When they had finished, Doug asked if they were going to stake out Costello's place again.

"Not tonight," Tony said. "I'm expecting a package tomorrow. I'm not going back to Costello's until I have it."

Doug didn't argue or even question him. He could easily guess what Tony wanted before he confronted Dracula again.

Chapter 22

Erica's cell phone rang. A glance told her it was Robbie. She didn't want to answer it but knew she had no choice. She clicked off the large flat screen TV in her apartment and answered the phone.

Typical of Robbie, the conversation did not begin with pleasantries. "Have you heard from him?"

"Well, he's tried about a dozen times, but I haven't responded. I haven't talked to him since Monday."

"I want you to call him."

"What? But you said…"

"Shut the hell up. I know what I said. Now I'm telling you to call him. Apologize. Talk sweet. Get him in the sack. I want you to own that prick. You get me?"

Damn, damn, damn. How can I do this? God, forgive me. Aloud, Erica said, "Yeah, I get you. I'll call him. Can you tell me what happened?"

"What the hell do you care?" Costello shouted at her, causing her to recoil from the phone. She knew how bad it could get when he was angry.

"I'm sorry," she said softly.

He didn't seem to have heard her. "I'll tell you what happened. That little prick followed me. He *followed me... Me!* And today he paid a visit to the Major Cases Squad at the NYPD. Who the hell knows what he told them! I've had it. This fucker has to go. Now do what I told you...or else."

The call ended. Erica's hand was shaking as she set her phone down on the coffee table in front of the couch. She fought back tears, knowing she had to compose herself. She had no doubt Robbie would call back in ten minutes to see if she had completed her assignment. She needed to call Tony right now.

***

Tony and Doug were chewing on sandwiches and watching the Cubs and Mets on TV in Doug's hotel room when Tony's cell phone began playing "All My Loving" by the Beatles.

"Well, I'll be damned," Tony said, a smile spreading across his face.

"Itfff Erifffa?" Doug asked, swallowing a big wad of corned beef.

"Pipe down and inhale your Reuben," Tony said. "I need to take this." He composed himself, lifted the phone to his ear, and answered, "Hey, there. I thought maybe you'd died or left town."

"Hi, Tony." She sounded meek. Or maybe melancholy? "I'm really sorry. I should've called you back a lot sooner."

"No, it's okay, really. Doug and I have been crazy busy. I'm just glad to know you're okay."

"Yes, I'm fine." She managed a kind of half-laugh. "You must be wondering if I'm married or crazy. Maybe a CIA agent or something…" Her voice trailed off.

Tony laughed. "Well, actually, I did wonder about another man in your life. The signs sorta pointed that way."

"No, Tony, there isn't," she said flatly. "I'm single and live alone."

Tony's heart soared. It felt as if a lead blanket had been lifted off his soul. He marveled at how a few words could turn his world right side up. "I'm glad to hear it," he said lightly. "I hate it when husbands come after me with baseball bats."

Erica laughed. "Does that happen a lot? No, don't tell me. In any event, there's no chance of it in my case. I just wasn't sure I wanted to like someone so much right now. I have a demanding job, and I have a great life in the city. I found myself falling for a guy from Iowa. That's not exactly in my life plan."

She found herself falling for a guy from Iowa. Tony wanted to dance. Instead, he said, "Hey, you don't have to move to Orney just yet. Let's at least have a third date before we worry about that."

"That's why I called," she said. "I was hoping you would want to see me again."

"Of course I do! Are you available tomorrow night? Any idea what you want to do?"

There was no response for a long time. Erica finally said, "Tony, I have a very good idea what I want to do. And I… Ah, shit. How do I say this without sounding like a slut?"

Just say it. Just say it. Just say it.

"Tony, how about tonight? Are you busy? If you haven't made plans with Doug, maybe you could come over tonight. I have wine, and a good stereo system, and we could talk and maybe…"

"Erica, you know a category five hurricane couldn't keep me away. Tell me where and when, and I'll be there."

She gave him the address and said, "Come now."

***

Tony was at her door in twenty-two minutes flat. After ending the call, he flew to his room, calling apologies to Doug over his shoulder. A few frantic swipes with a toothbrush and a comb, a clean pair of Dockers, and a maroon crew-neck sweater were all it took to declare himself ready. He debated running down the hotel's stairs, but figured he would be just unlucky enough to trip and break something, so he tolerated, just barely, the wait for the elevator and the ride down to the lobby. As usual, a Yellow Cab was ready and waiting at the curb when Tony pushed through the revolving doors and out into the street.

When the taxi dropped him off, he almost slowed his pace to gaze in awe at the surroundings. The building was a beautiful mix of granite, limestone, and dark tinted glass. It sat back from the street, with a walled courtyard and garden in front. As Tony navigated a winding garden path on his way to the front door, he tried to remember Erica's exact words about her parents. "They've done well," she'd said. *So have you,* he thought. The open courtyard was large, and the garden was immaculately tended and beautiful. At the end of the path, a uniformed man was waiting. He asked to see Tony's identification, then admitted him into the building with instructions to take the elevator to the twenty-ninth floor. The lobby also sported high ceilings and was decorated in marble and a dark wood Tony guessed was walnut. If so, it added to his conviction that he was way out of his league.

When he reached her door, he finally stopped to take a deep breath. *Should I have brought something? A bottle of wine? No, she said she had wine. Flowers? No, it's late. She wouldn't expect that. What else...?* The door opened.

Tony opened his mouth to speak, but Erica was on him, pulling him inside, pushing the door shut, and then pushing him up against it. She gripped him hard, as though she was worried one of them would fall away and be lost in the ocean of uncertainty that awaited most new couples. Tony held her tight in return and looked down into her dark, perfect eyes just as she looked up to kiss him—an expression of raw passion, her mouth open and hungry.

Tony was instantly aroused and only nodded when she asked, "Can the wine wait?"

***

It was as close to perfect as a first time could be, beginning with ferocity and then slowing to savor every sensation. When they finished, Erica was on top and didn't seem inclined to disengage. That was just fine with Tony.

"Thank you for coming," she said, then giggled as Tony smiled at the double meaning of her words. "Stop it," she said, poking him in the ribs. "You know what I meant."

Tony laughed. "Oh yeah, do I ever."

"You want the wine now?"

"To be honest, I don't ever want you to get up. You can stay right where you are for the next twenty years."

"Nice thought, but we would die of thirst, which would cut short our opportunities to do this again, so I say we carve out a little time for hydration and nourishment."

"Hydration and nourishment? Those are big words. I'm not sure I follow you. In Iowa we call it a beer and a burger."

Erica laughed again. "I've heard of those. You'll have to introduce me to them some time."

Tony's smile quickly turned to a groan as Erica slid off of him and rolled over to the edge of the bed.

"I'll be right back," she said.

Tony used his elbows to push himself up, propping his back against the bed's soft fabric headboard. He wondered if the material was satin. This thought caused him to focus on his surroundings.

Jeez...look at this place. Ten-foot high ceilings, hardwood floors, a king-sized bed, floor-to-ceiling windows on two sides, a view of the river. Holy...

Tony was no expert on New York's cost of living, but he knew enough to know a luxury apartment on East 52nd Street, near the river, had to cost a damn fortune. The inside of her apartment certainly confirmed it. The oriental rug covering the bulk of the bedroom floor probably cost more than Tony made in a year. *Who IS this person?*

"Pretty great, huh?"

Tony's thoughts were interrupted by Erica's appearance in the door. She was wearing a pink, fluffy, ankle-length robe, and was carrying a tray with a wine bottle, two glasses, a block of cheese, and an assortment of crackers.

As she approached, Tony asked, "Crackers in bed? That's a little cliché, don't you think?"

She smiled, climbed onto the bed, and said, "Don't change the subject. You were admiring the apartment and wondering how in the hell a twenty-something woman can live like this. You probably even wondered if I'm one of those thousands-of-dollars-a-night call girls."

"I swear that thought hadn't occurred to me," Tony said, a knot growing in his stomach as it now *did* occur to him. "But I must admit I was ogling this place and wondering how you can afford it."

The cork popped, and Tony realized he hadn't offered to help. Erica waved him away and poured. When both glasses were filled, she raised hers and said, "To new relationships."

Tony glanced over at the damp sheets on the other side of the bed and said, "Hear, hear." They both laughed and drank.

Erica spoke first, as Tony grabbed a cracker and what appeared to be a slice of smoked gouda "It's simple, really. My dad owns a real estate company. He has several buildings like this in Manhattan and in a couple of the other boroughs. When I got out of grad school, he made me vice-president of marketing for his company. The apartment comes with the job."

"Wow. Nice work if you can get it. You said he was successful, but I didn't imagine anything like this. I don't suppose he needs an assistant manager of trash collection or anything, does he?"

She laughed. "You wouldn't want it. My life's pretty great, but working for dad isn't all perks and petunias. He makes me earn what I get, and I have to live with all the father-daughter baggage that accumulated during what we lovingly call 'the teenage years.'"

Tony smiled and nodded. "I get it. I love my parents, but there's no way I could work for one of them. I'm lucky, too, by the way. My dad has money and has been generous. Of course, his generosity bought me a Ford and an electric piano. He balked when I asked for a ten-million-dollar apartment."

She laughed and punched his ribs again. "Don't be silly. It wasn't *ten* million."

Tony didn't ask. He rubbed the spot on his ribs where she had poked him. Then he reached over and rubbed a spot on her ribs, sliding his hand inside her robe. He pushed the tray down to the end of the bed with his foot as he leaned into her and whispered, "Let me give you something money can't buy…"

She didn't speak but responded by reaching down and pulling on the tie holding her robe closed. It fell away and she rolled onto her back, pulling Tony on top of her.

"Don't be gentle," she said, hoarsely.

***

Later, as they lay quietly on top the sheets, Erica's head on his chest, Tony found himself marveling at the turn his life had taken. He had a job offer in New York, and now he had a woman in his arms he might very well be able to love. It was too good to be true. That thought, of course, pried open the hole in his mind that allowed his doubts to creep in. *What could this goddess see in me? She's smart, educated, beautiful, and rich. She could have any man she wanted. What chance do I have of hanging onto her for the long term? I'm just a guy from Iowa who likes to write. Some stud from her health club or some rich boy with a yacht is bound to come along and woo her away someday. Why do I do this to myself?*

Tony felt on the verge of tears when he suddenly realized Erica was crying. "Hey, what's wrong?"

She shook her head and sat up, wiping her cheeks with the back of her hand. "You need to go now," she said, choking back a sob. "I wish you could stay, but I have to work in the morning, and I need to get some sleep."

Tony hated the thought of leaving, but he understood and said so. As he pulled on his pants and sweater, he asked again, "Are you sure you're okay?"

"I'll be fine. It's nothing. Just a silly post-sex thing. You'll have to get used to it."

Tony smiled and pulled her up to her feet. He whispered in her ear, "I like the idea of getting used to you." He kissed her once more, then turned and left, unaware that once he was out the door, Erica exploded into uncontrolled bawling.

Chapter 23

Friday morning, Tony was on his laptop, looking for more information about a Pappas family real estate empire, references to Erica Pappas, or even a Facebook page, and was coming up empty. He was surprised, confused, and a little concerned. He hadn't begun the task with any sense of suspicion. It was just his habit—Wasn't it everyone's habit these days?—to look up the person you've begun to date to learn more about her.

At 10 a.m., the front desk called to say UPS had delivered a package for him. Tony closed down the computer and went to retrieve it.

Back in his room, he tore open the seal, pulled out the wads of newspaper, and allowed a hard vinyl case to fall onto the bed. He opened the cover and found what he expected: a Walther PK380 and a box of ammunition. He checked the chamber to confirm there was no round loaded in it, even though he knew Ben would never be dumb enough to send a loaded gun to him, then reached into the case for the magazine and ammo. Satisfied that all was in order, he filled the clip with eight rounds and slid it into place. He made sure the safety was on and pushed the gun into his belt at his back. It was uncomfortable, both physically and mentally, but he didn't revisit his decision. Tony knew Costello was a murderer, and probably a professional hit man. The gun would remain in Tony's belt until this situation was resolved one way or another.

Tony had a permit to carry the gun, though he had no idea if a permit issued in Iowa carried any weight in the State of New York. He had purchased the gun previously, when pursuing a series of articles for the *Town Crier* about human trafficking. He had found himself getting close to some extremely evil people in that situation as well, and had decided he needed protection. He'd only fired the gun once in anger, and even then, only at an inanimate object. Tony couldn't fathom pointing a gun at a human being or ever intentionally harming another person, except in self-defense.

Despite his strong aversion to violence, Tony had seen enough of it during his years as a reporter to know his decision to protect himself with a weapon was rational. This despite knowing the statistics were clear—the average person is more at risk with a gun than without one. Tony also knew he wasn't average. The average person didn't seek out murderers, rapists, or the buyers and sellers of slaves, or for that matter a mafia assassin.

Tony donned his lightweight navy-blue windbreaker and headed for Central Park. He and Doug had agreed to meet at The Boathouse for lunch.

***

"So the sex was great, right?" Doug was grinning as he buttered a piece of warm French bread.

"Shut up, Doug," Tony growled. "You know I don't kiss and

tell."

"Aw, come on. You can't run out and leave me alone with Thursday night television, and then not even share a few tidbits. Be a pal. Tell me about her tidbits."

"Shut up, Doug."

Doug laughed heartily and took a bite of bread. "Ummff," he said, "thiff if goo…" He swallowed. "Sorry, you're right, this bread is fantastic."

The Boathouse was one of Tony's favorite places in New York. As its name indicated, it was situated next to a small lake in the park with one entire wall of glass overlooking the water. Ducks and other wildlife enjoyed the water, as parents strolled around the lake with children in a variety of wheeled conveyances and couples young and old walked past holding hands. The skyline of the city could be seen just above the treetops.

Tony dipped a spoonful of lobster bisque and asked his friend, "Do you think I should be concerned that I can't find Erica online?"

Doug smirked. "Tone-man, you're the worst boyfriend a woman can have. You're either pouting because she doesn't call or trying to find out what's wrong with her if she does."

Tony saw a glimmer of truth in Doug's remark but refused to acknowledge it to him. "Listen, I'm serious. I spent two hours on the internet this morning and could find no references to her. She's a vice president of a big company, but in all that searching I couldn't find a single mention of her or it. Does that strike you as normal, or even possible?"

Doug paused a fork full of salad in mid-air. "Okay, you're right. It's weird. So what?"

Tony started to respond, but Doug cut him off.

"I can think of plenty of explanations, none of which require her to be a criminal, or a witch, or an alien from Planet X."

Tony reached for the basket of bread and said, "I'm all ears."

"What, now I have to make the excuses for her; or I should say, for you? Okay, how about this—she gave you a fake name at the start because she didn't want you creeping on her. In other words, she didn't want you doing exactly what you're doing. Now she likes you, and she hasn't figured out how to tell you that she lied at the start."

Tony nodded. He could envision that easily enough.

Doug continued. "Or even simpler, maybe her real name is Gertrude or Verlene or some family name she doesn't like, so she goes by her middle name when speaking casually or with friends. You want me to keep going?"

"No. I get it. I'm worried, and you're not. I'm paranoid, and you're not. But give me a break. The fact is, I'm falling for her, and you're not."

"I'm happy to take my turn…"

"Shut up, Doug."

They both laughed and dug into platters of roasted chicken with red potatoes and mixed vegetables. They enjoyed the next hour of eating, chatting, and watching the scenery. In the end, the only thing exceeding the meal's calorie count was its cost. Tony knew he couldn't keep relying on his father's generosity. This one would go on his own Visa card, and it was gonna hurt.

***

The two friends decided to walk all the way to Rockefeller Center to work off some of the calories and pass the afternoon. As they reached the third block of Fifth Avenue, Doug said, without turning his head, "You probably realize we're being followed."

"Yep."

"Any guesses?"

"Such as…?"

"Good guys or bad guys?"

"I'm guessing good guys," Tony said as he turned to his right to examine a beautiful pinstripe suit in a shop window.

"Because?" Doug let the question hang, trying his best to follow Tony's feigned ignorance of their pursuers.

"Because they're not trying very hard to hide themselves. I'm guessing Lieutenant Coppestad wasn't convinced we were going to give up on Costello, and he put a couple of goons on our tail to make sure we behave. The fact we've spotted them just makes their job easier."

"Unless we can shake them."

Tony nodded. "Unless we can shake them."

"Do we *want* to shake them?"

Tony nodded again. "Not now. Later."

"Because?"

"Because tonight we have work to do."

"Oh yeah, I forgot. Tonight is the night we grab a mafia hit man, pin him to the ground, and tickle him until he promises to be a good boy."

"Shut up, Doug." No laughter this time.

The men resumed their walk, and after another several minutes Tony said, "I know you're right. We don't have a plan, and I can't figure out what to do short of cold-blooded murder. No, relax. That's not gonna happen on my watch. But the fact is, solution or not, I've decided to stay on him. Maybe I'll learn enough to convince the cops to go after him, or maybe we'll witness something that can be used against him in court, or maybe…Crap, I don't know. Maybe we'll scare him so badly he'll jump off the roof of his high-rise."

"That one," Doug said. "I like that one. Let's work on it."

Tony was tempted to tell him to shut up again, but he decided the joke had grown old. Instead, he steered his friend to the doors of Rockefeller Center and inside to the NBC Studios Gift Shop. His sister Rita was a big fan of the TV show *Friends*, and Tony hoped the shop still carried "Central Perk" coffee mugs.

***

Orney, Iowa

Ben Smalley was cursing his investigative instincts. Maybe not instincts—compulsions, if he was being honest. In any case, Ben had seen the selfie of Tony, Erica, and the homeless man posted on Tony's Facebook page and had immediately agreed with Tony regarding Erica's beauty. In addition to her alluring facial features and shape, she had a natural smile and warmth that shone through the photograph. Ben felt a pang of jealousy. She was the kind of woman he was unlikely to meet in his fifties, especially while living in rural Iowa. There were plenty of attractive women here, but few who were also single, of an appropriate age, well-educated, interesting, fun, mentally stable, and all the other things he wanted in a soul mate. Women with the combination of perfect traits, which Tony had a knack for finding, had eluded Ben for most of his life.

There had been one, though. The thought of her distracted Ben for a moment. He sighed. Her name was Kanna James. Her looks were even more exotic than her name. Her mother was Japanese and her father was Black. The result of their union was a stunning woman with a bushel of curly black hair, dark green eyes, and flawless skin the color of caramel candy. She was medium height, with the body of a long-distance runner and a smile that could illuminate a subway tunnel.

Ben had met Kanna in Baltimore fifteen years previously, while working on an article about criminal sociopaths. Kanna was a psychologist at Johns Hopkins University who had agreed to an interview. At the time, she was involved in a research project regarding the environmental factors that may, or may not, contribute to a child's development of sociopathic traits.

After five minutes in Kanna's office, Ben was smitten. In addition to Kanna's beauty, she was quick-witted and well-read. Combined with her intelligence and education, she spoke with authority on pretty much any topic Ben threw at her.

Two weeks after the interview, and as a result of a persistent series of invitations, Kanna finally agreed to a dinner date. A month later, they were living together. The fact it hadn't lasted was the biggest regret in Ben's past. A short time after it ended, Ben decided to leave Baltimore and buy the *Town Crier* in Orney, Iowa. He made one last play for Kanna, asking her to come with him. She declined, but claimed she was doing so reluctantly. Ben knew in his heart she had simply never loved him enough to spend the rest of her life with him. The opportunity to move from Maryland to Iowa wasn't exactly the enticement needed to tip the scales in his favor.

A year after his move, Ben heard Kanna had married an executive at a large aerospace company based near Baltimore and had opened a private counseling practice in one of the small towns north of the metropolis. He was genuinely happy for her, but that didn't make it any easier to go home alone every night.

As he thought about these things, he closed out of Tony's Facebook page and began an online search for Erica Pappas of New York City. He told himself it was an expression of interest in Tony's future, rather than just being nosy. The first hint of trouble emerged quickly. He found a few women with the name Erica Pappas, but none that matched the age and background of Tony's Erica. This sparked his curiosity, and he dug even deeper.

Hours later, he was still empty-handed, and his curiosity had morphed into genuine concern. He muttered, "Tony, my friend. What have you gotten yourself into this time?" He turned and picked up the telephone.

The voice on the other end said, "Rich Davis."

Ben was glad he'd reached the Division of Criminal Investigation's special agent on the first try. Davis was assigned to Quincy County and was a friend to both Ben and Tony.

"Rich, it's Ben at the *Crier*."

"Hey, Ben. What's up? Everything okay?"

"I'm not sure. It's probably nothing, but Tony's in New York City and…"

"Stop right there. Tony's in New York City, and you think he might be in trouble. I'm shocked. I'm stunned."

"Okay, Rich, I get it. Neither of us is surprised Tony found trouble in New York. If he can find it in Iowa, he sure as hell can find it in the Big Apple."

"Sad but true. What is it this time?"

"Like I said, it's probably nothing, but I'll feel better if you have a way to check it out."

Rich agreed to try, and Ben explained to him about the new girlfriend who appeared to be a ghost. "She says her name is Erica Pappas, but I can't find anyone in New York by that name who looks like her. The photo is on Tony's Facebook page. Could you pull it off of there and see if you can place her? You know, use your magical gizmocallits to vet her without tipping her off?"

Rich sounded unsure. "Jeez, it's tough enough to get our people excited about that level of work when we're chasing terrorists or kidnappers. I may run into resistance if they find out I'm trying to check out a friend's latest romantic interest."

"I understand," Ben said. "I probably shouldn't have asked."

"No, don't say that," Davis said. "I'll do what I can. As you say, it may be nothing, but if she's hiding something, we'd both rather know it sooner than later. I'll get back to you."

Ben expressed his thanks and ended the call. The conversation had not eased his mind; in fact, it had caused his concern to grow. Something wasn't right. He could feel it. *Why is it always Tony? Hasn't he been through enough? And why now? Don't I have enough crap to deal with already?* Ben pounded his fist on his desk in a sudden fit of frustration and yelled, "Dammit!" causing heads in the newsroom to turn toward his office. Ben just glowered at them, and just as quickly, they turned back to their respective tasks.

Chapter 24

New York

Tony and Doug were bored. They were texting each other bad jokes and links to YouTube videos as they waited for something to happen. Waiting was never easy, but it was nearly impossible when you didn't know whether anything would come of it.

Tony was sitting in the restaurant bar across the street from Costello's apartment building. Doug was slouched down in a rented gray Toyota a couple of blocks to the east, out of sight of the building. The plan was for Tony to spot Costello leaving, then call Doug so Doug could follow him. Doug drew the latter duty because Costello wouldn't recognize him if he smelled a tail—or at least the two friends hoped he wouldn't.

It now was nearly 11 p.m., and they had been waiting for more than two hours. Tony knew the club scene in New York didn't get started until very late, but it was Friday night. Tony was sure that if Costello was going out, it would be before midnight.

Almost as soon as the thought crossed his mind, he spotted a Maserati leaping out of the parking garage and turning left on 10th Avenue, heading north toward the Upper West Side. Tony made the call to Doug, who said simply, "On it," and hung up.

Tony left a hundred-dollar bill on the table to cover his meal and five subsequent diet sodas, and scrambled down the stairs to get to his rented Chevy.

He drove north on 10th, praying he was on the right track and cursing Doug for each passing minute that didn't include a call or text with instructions. He had gone more than thirty blocks, or about two miles, and was just passing the signs for the Children's Museum of Manhattan when his phone finally chirped. The text read: *He's in a tavern on 110th near 10th Avenue. Place called Tillie's. Looks like a college bar. Some kids going in and leaving have Columbia U sweats, so it must be close by. I'm parked a block to the south. Two empty spaces. You live a charmed life. I'll wait for you.*

"Good boy, Doug," Tony said through clenched teeth. He was only minutes away.

Tony's phone chirped again, and he glanced down. Erica. His heart leapt, but as he read her text, it sank just as quickly.

I'm home and missing you. Come see me tonight?

Tony spotted Doug's car and eased the Chevy into a spot on the street a couple of spaces behind him. Once he'd turned off the engine, he texted back. *I wish I could, more than you can imagine, but I'm out with Doug tonight. Tomorrow?*

Her response surprised and puzzled him. *It's okay. Be careful!*

It seemed odd to urge two grown men to be careful, especially when she knew he wasn't much of a drinker. It seemed doubly odd that she hadn't responded to his inquiry about tomorrow. Tony was forced to set aside his questions as he heard a tap on the passenger-side widow and turned to see Doug. He unlocked the Chevy's door, and Doug climbed in.

"Up at the corner. Based on the short time I've been watching, I'd say he has to be the oldest person in the bar."

"Well, that fits his MO. He likes his women young."

"So what's next?"

"I hate to ask, but…"

"Yeah, I know," Doug said, trying to sound put out but failing. "I have to go in there because you can't be seen."

"I'm sorry the tough jobs keep falling to you."

"Relax, Tone-man. I like being James Bond while you're stuck in the MI-5 van listening to women fawn over me."

Tony looked up and smiled.

Doug said, "Hey, that was a joke."

"I know, but it's still a good idea."

"Huh?"

"You still have plenty of charge on your phone?"

Doug looked. "About half. I'm fine."

"So call me before you go in there. Then put the phone in your jacket pocket in a way that gives me a chance to hear a little bit of what's going on."

"I'm happy to try, but don't get your hopes up. The music in that place is loud, and a bunch of college kids will be yelling over the top of it. I'll be surprised if you can hear more than the occasional f-bomb, or maybe a girl screaming at some guy—probably me—that he should go to hell."

Tony grinned and pulled a twenty out of his wallet. "You'll need to buy a drink and settle in if you don't want to be too obvious. Try to come back out and give me the lowdown before I go to sleep in my car."

"Ten-four, M." Doug saluted. "God save the queen."

Tony laughed as Doug left the car and headed up the sidewalk.

***

Doug had been right about the phone connection. All Tony could hear was a roar of indistinguishable sounds. He ended the call, turned off his phone, and turned to the radio for entertainment. At least he could preserve one of their phones' batteries. By the time Doug returned nearly an hour later, Tony's frustration was off the charts. He had consumed an entire roll of Certs and could name the type of programming featured on every FM station in New York.

When Doug was back in the passenger seat, Tony was ready with a dozen questions, but Doug held up a hand, saying, "It's pretty simple. Dracula spread around enough money to garner some attention, then settled in with a group of students in the back. He bought about four rounds of drinks in the time I was in there, and now he has a young woman plastered to his side—probably plastered in more ways than one. You should see her, Tony. Blonde, gorgeous, with lots of curves and soft spots. I swear, her breasts are as big as…"

"Okay, Doug, that's enough. I get the picture. But I have to tell you, I can't just sit here any longer. Am I able to get in there without Costello seeing me?"

Doug thought for a moment and said, "Yeah, sure. The whole front part of the club is pretty much invisible from where he's sitting. But there's no guarantee he won't get up and move. I doubt you want to bump into him."

"I'm willing to take that chance. I want to see him in action. I also want to save that girl."

"*Save* her?" Doug shook his head. "You don't know how to save her. You don't know whether you *should* save her. You don't even know she's in trouble."

Tony stared at his friend. "Doug, that may be the most naïve thing you've ever said. Have you not been paying attention? Sure, he may not murder her tonight. I can't imagine he kills every girl he picks up in a bar. But there's no doubt in my mind he'll force himself on her. Even if she's a willing partner, he likes to hurt women. She's almost certainly in over her head. And even if it's okay...I mean, what if it turns out to be a lovely night, and he wants to see her again? Do you really believe a student at Columbia University is hoping to hook up with a mafia hit man?"

"Okay, okay, I get it. But you're assuming a lot. Too much, in fact. But I get your point. She's better off without him. Everyone is. So what do we do about it?"

"I don't know," Tony said, "but I'll think of something." They left the car and headed up the street to Tillie's Tavern.

***

The answer, or at least *an* answer, came very quickly. Tony had just walked up to the bar and ordered a drink when Doug grabbed his arm, leaned in, and said into his ear, "That's her. The girl he was with is headed this way."

Tony glanced over his shoulder and spotted her immediately. She was hard to miss. In a college bar full of nice-looking young people in blue jeans and sweatshirts, she was wearing black yoga pants and a red tube top, partially covered by a black leather jacket. She was tall and fit and moved with self-confidence. If you were the kind of man who wanted to hook up with the most strikingly beautiful woman in the bar, she'd be on your short list. The signs of inebriation were subtle but present if you looked for them: steps a little too deliberate, redness in the eyes, asking to be excused a little too loudly as she pushed through the crowd next to the bar, toward the women's room.

Tony waited for a couple of minutes, then told Doug, "I'm gonna talk to her. If Dracula comes this way, try to slow him down."

"Sure, no problem." Sarcasm swam in Doug's tone.

Tony's timing was good. The blonde was just coming out of the women's room as he reached the hallway leading to the facilities. He spoke quickly, trying to address her before she realized he was blocking her exit back into the bar.

"Excuse me, miss, may I speak to you for a moment?"

"You wish. Sorry, pal, I'm spoken for tonight."

Tony stood his ground. "No, you misunderstand. I need to speak to you about something important. Something important to you."

"Jesus, you sound like an insurance salesman. You're not some religious nut, are you? Never mind. I don't care. Just leave me alone."

Tony was scrambling to come up with something he could say to slow her down.

"Listen, please. I'm working undercover. I'm Special Agent Max Smartly with the FBI. I can't show you my badge because I don't carry it when I'm working an alias." Tony was embarrassed that he pulled a convoluted "Get Smart" reference out of his ear, but he was pretty sure she was too young to catch it.

"Like hell you are. That's the worst line I've ever heard, and I've heard a lot of really terrible lines."

"Listen," Tony pleaded. "It doesn't matter if you believe me about my job. What's important is you're with a very dangerous man."

She finally looked at Tony as if he had her attention. She said, "Dangerous? What do you mean dangerous? He's nice."

"You're with the tall, slender guy, slightly crooked nose, great clothes, lots of money, right?"

"Yeah…" She sounded wary. "So what?"

"Let me say this fast, and simply. The man you are with is a known kidnapper, rapist, and suspected murderer."

"What? Shut the hell up. He's nice. And he drives a Maserati. You ever heard of a murderer who drives a Maserati? Get outta my way."

"I'm warning you, miss. This is no joke. My partner and I have been following this man for weeks. He killed a girl just a few nights ago, and we missed catching him by minutes. We don't want you to be the next victim."

Tony reached into his wallet and took out a hundred dollars in twenties.

"What's that?" she asked, rearing back as if the bills would bite.

"Cab fare. I don't want anything from you in return except to save your life. Does he know your name?"

"My name? Well…Well, he knows my first name."

"Does he know where you live?"

"Nah, he didn't give a shit about that. He said he has a great place in a high-rise. He was gonna show it to me."

I'll bet, Tony thought as he continued. "What about your friends? Will they tell him what he wants to know if you leave?"

"I'm…I'm not sure, but I doubt it. We all just met him tonight. I think they're smart enough to clam up if a stranger starts asking for that kind of stuff."

"Good," Tony said, hoping he had her on the right path. "Anything else? Did you talk about your work or where you hang out?"

"Nah," she said, and laughed. "Now that I think about it, we talked mostly about him. He knows how to be charming. He made himself sound like the best catch in the city."

"He's had lots of practice," Tony said. "Now please, take the money and go. And hurry. He's gonna start wondering what's taking you so long."

"Okay, I'm outta here," she said. "I still think you're full of shit, but I'm not gonna chance it. Thanks for the cab fare."

Tony stepped aside, and she hurried past, turning right to go out the front door rather than left back into the bar. Tony breathed a sigh of relief, then followed. He stopped at the bar long enough to take one drink from his orange juice, grabbed Doug by the arm, and headed out.

As they walked down the sidewalk toward their car, they saw the woman go past in the back seat of a cab. "Mission accomplished," Tony said, a grim smile on his face. "Let's just hope…"

"Harrington!" The scream came from behind, and both men whirled to see Costello bounding toward them. "What did you do? You son of a bitch! You scared her off, didn't you? You bastard! I'm going to kick the living shit out of you."

Costello's yelling ended as he reached Tony, pulled back, and took a swing at him. Tony's reaction was fast. *Thank you, Jun.* Instead of rearing back, away from Costello's fist, and being off balance when a punch found his jaw, Tony leaned into him. The fist swung past the back of his head and Costello's forearm smacked against his ear.

Tony ignored the pain, wrapped his arms around Costello's torso, and drove his right knee up into his crotch. Costello screamed and bent over, clawing at Tony's legs. Tony spun out of his grasp and stomped hard on the back of Costello's leg. He screamed again and fell forward onto the sidewalk. Tony kicked him hard in the kidney, eliciting a third scream. As Costello curled into a defensive fetal position, Tony reached down and pulled Costello's revolver from a holster under his jacket.

Tony put the gun into his own coat pocket. He had no idea what to do or say next, so he simply turned to go, pulling Doug along with him.

Costello yelled from where he lay on the ground, "Taking my gun won't save your life! I have plenty of guns! You. Are. A. Dead. Man. You hear me?" Costello's voice rose to a scream. "I know who you are! I know where you live. You are a dead man!"

Tony wanted to run but refused to give Costello the pleasure. He told Doug to stay close. They'd retrieve the Toyota later. They walked to the Chevy and climbed in. It took Tony longer than usual to find the ignition and put the car in gear, as his hands were shaking violently. Eventually he succeeded, and they drove away.

***

A block to the north, in a white utility van parked at the curb, facing away from the tavern, a man with a camera was staring out of the van's rear window. "Holy shit, chief, you ain't gonna believe this," the man said into a tiny microphone mounted on a wire at the side of his mouth.

A voice from the other end of the connection replied doubtfully. "What? What ain't I gonna believe? And don't call me chief," Lieutenant Coppestad commanded.

The man said, with a distinct note of glee in his voice, "Our young friend just beat the shit out of Costello."

"What! Jesus H. Crowbar, I told Harrington to leave him alone!"

The man in the van replied, "Well, in Mr. Harrington's defense, Costello chased after him down the sidewalk and took the first swing. I got it all recorded."

"I don't give a flying fart if you filmed it in IMAX! I told Harrington to stand down. What's he doing now?"

"Harrington and Tenney drove away in the rented Chevy.

Costello is holding his crotch and trying to stand up. Who would have thought...?"

"Is he going back inside?"

"Nah. He's hurting. He just stumbled over to his Maserati. I'm guessing he's headed home for the night."

"Okay," Coppestad said. "Once he drives off, you can pack up and get back here. I wanna see those recordings."

"Roger, chief."

***

In the hotel, Doug followed Tony to his room. The two men had not spoken a word since getting into the car. Tony could tell Doug was upset. He had decided not to breach the silence until Doug was ready.

Tony hoped Doug was coming to his room because he was ready to talk about what had happened. Once inside, with the door closed, Tony began, "Doug, I'm sorry..."

"Shut up, Tony."

"I..."

"No, I mean it. Shut up. I have something to say."

Tony waited, dreading what was coming.

"As we drove back here, the whole way I'm thinking what an idiot you are. You stirred the hornet's nest with no plan, no thought to the consequences, no damn clue about anything."

"I..."

"Don't make me say it again." Doug stared at him. "Just listen. My second thought was no, he's not clueless. He has a plan. I thought you'd decided to kill him. I feared you'd made up your mind to take this situation into your own hands and end it with a bullet to Costello's head." Doug paused to take a breath. His eyes were stony and unblinking.

"But I've realized I was wrong about that too. I've realized you don't want to kill anyone. I'm not sure you *could* kill anyone, regardless of what they've done. A few minutes ago, it dawned on me. Your plan is worse. You *want* that asshole to come after you."

Tony stood stone-faced.

Doug continued, "You don't have to admit it. I know I'm right. You want Costello to come for you. When this thought first occurred to me, I tried to reject it but, sadly, I couldn't." He turned away and walked over to the window, staring at the lights below. His voice dropped to the point where he could barely be heard. "The truth is… you want him to kill you."

"Doug, wait…"

Doug interrupted, still staring out into the night. "Okay, maybe you think you won't die. Maybe you think somehow you'll pull off another Harrington miracle and escape with your life. But I know it's true. You want this trained killer, this goddam member of the mafia, to come after you so the cops can get him."

Tony couldn't argue. It was the only path he had been able to devise that would put Costello out of commission.

Doug turned back to him, the red rising in his face and the disgust rising in his voice. "You stupid, self-centered prick!"

Tony's eyes grew wide, and Doug strode over and stuck his face into Tony's. "You are so wrapped up in *your* problems, *your* grief, *your* poor cousin, *your* desire for justice, *your, your, your…*" Doug's voice cracked, and tears began inching down his checks. "Did you think for even one *minute* about the rest of us? When this creep kills you, or maims you for life or whatever, what happens to everyone else? What does it do to your mom, your dad, your sister, to Ben…Fuck, man, did you ever think about what it will do to *me*?"

Tony reached out, but Doug backed away. "Don't touch me."

He wheeled around and went out the door, slamming it behind him.

Tony stared at the door for a long time. A part of him was angry. *What in the hell was I supposed to do?* Another part of him was ashamed. *I've put everyone I love through so much hell already. What is wrong with me?* The biggest part of him simply felt lost and alone.

Chapter 25

On Saturday morning, Doug didn't respond to Tony's calls or texts. Tony hoped his friend had simply shut off his phone to avoid being disturbed but feared he was still was angry. Tony knew that somehow, he had to make amends.

At 9 a.m., Tony went down the hall to Doug's room, hoping he would be awake by that hour. When he arrived, he was greeted by an open door and the sound of a vacuum cleaner. "Oh, no," Tony groaned. "Damn it."

He jogged back to his room and called the front desk to confirm his fears. He knew he was right before he heard the receptionist say it. "I'm sorry, sir, but Mr. Tenney checked out early this morning."

Tony thanked the woman and hung up the phone. "Damn, damn, damn. You've done it this time, Harrington."

He hadn't slept much during the night. As he had lain awake, he had replayed Doug's words over and over in his mind. By morning, Tony had decided Doug had been right. Maybe Tony had known it all along. In any case, he now needed a new plan.

***

Tony didn't feel like eating, but he knew he wouldn't do well on too little sleep and too little food, so he found his way to the hotel's restaurant and ordered an omelet and a glass of orange juice. While he waited for it to arrive, he woke his phone and immersed himself in the resources of the internet, researching his next steps for Plan B. He asked the waiter for a piece of paper, and when it arrived, he jotted down a few names and an address. He had just finished when a shadow fell over the table. He looked up and saw Lt. Coppestad gazing down at him.

"Mind if I join you?" Coppestad didn't wait for a response. He pulled out the chair opposite Tony and sat. The waiter arrived quickly with a place setting, but Coppestad put up a hand to stop him. "Just coffee. Thanks."

Tony tucked his notes into his shirt pocket and said, "I was really hoping I wouldn't see you today."

"Likewise. Believe me. But it seems you have a listening problem."

Coppestad tossed a manila envelope onto the table. "Care to explain these?"

Tony opened the envelope and found himself looking at a half-dozen large, full-color photographs. The first showed the blonde woman leaving Tillie's Tavern. The next showed Tony and Doug exiting through the same door. The third showed Costello's back as he ran toward the two friends. The final two showed Tony's knee in Costello's crotch, and Costello writhing on the ground.

Tony shook his head, trying to think of something to say, as he flipped the photos over face-down on the table, out of view of any curious waitstaff.

"Does that appear to you to be a scene in which two tourists from Iowa are staying away from a New York resident? A New York resident whom, I might add, they have been specifically told to leave alone?"

"He came after…"

"Can it, Mr. Harrington. We have a lot more images than these. We know you followed him to that bar. You sparked all this somehow. What in the hell were you thinking?"

Tony found he wasn't intimidated by the lieutenant's words. He was irritated. "Okay, Lieutenant. You want to know what I was thinking? I'll tell you. I was thinking that when I went to the NYPD for help, I was told there was nothing they could do. I was thinking maybe if I followed this asshole, maybe I would see something that would help you. I was thinking that when I saw Costello with that girl—that woman—maybe it would be worth my time to save her life and save you another homicide investigation." Tony leaned back in his chair. "Right or wrong, that's what I was thinking."

Coppestad put his elbows on the table and sipped his coffee. He eyed Tony for a long moment, then said, "What did you do with his gun?"

Tony reached into the pocket of his windbreaker and pulled out the revolver. "I was actually going to bring this to your office today…"

"Jesus, Harrington!" Coppestad hissed. "Give me that thing." He grabbed the gun, checked the safety, and stuffed it in his pocket. "You're gonna scare the shit out of everyone in this place."

"You asked," Tony said, unable to suppress a smile. "Maybe we'll get lucky, and the ballistics will connect it to one of your unsolved crimes."

"You're a bigger fool than I thought you were if you think a professional killer—your words, not mine—is going to hang on to a gun he used in a crime."

"Let's hope he's a dumb professional killer," Tony quipped. His omelet arrived. It was huge, covering an entire dinner plate. "Good grief, I can't eat all this. Get a plate and a fork, and I'll share it with you."

Coppestad eyed the food, clearly tempted. He said, "Okay, but don't think sharing a couple of eggs—well, okay, a dozen eggs— makes us friends."

"I promise," Tony said, waving at the waiter.

While the men ate, Coppestad asked, "So have you had enough? Are you leaving?"

"Not yet. All I've accomplished so far is to make a dangerous man angry enough to vow to kill me. I'm now officially glad you have those two goons following me everywhere."

"You have to understand that can't continue. The NYPD doesn't have the resources to follow every dumbass around the city, waiting for him to get gunned down."

"Yeah, I get that."

"Do you also understand you're in real jeopardy here? If this guy is who you say he is, and I still doubt that, I wouldn't bet a rusty nail on your future. But even if he isn't, even if he's just a typical New York City hothead, you're likely to wake up in a gutter...or a hospital."

"I understand, Lieutenant, I really do. I also understand that the mafia has long arms and enormous resources. I'm no safer in Iowa than I am here. Somehow, I have to end this, or he'll just come looking for me."

Coppestad scoffed. "And just how do you propose to end it? You think you can kick him in the balls again and have him call it quits?"

"I don't know," Tony said. "But like you said, if I hang around, something's bound to happen."

"Jesus, Harrington, now you're talking like you're content to be a target. I may not like you but please don't get killed on my turf. I don't need the extra work."

Tony smiled and looked the lieutenant in the eyes. "I don't intend to die in New York, at least not for a long time. I'll be careful, I promise."

Coppestad shook his head and stood up. "You, young man, are batshit crazy." He pointed his index finger at Tony's face. "So, here's the deal. You don't make another move without calling me first. I want to know what the hell you're doing, before you do it. Unless you promise me that, I'm going to lock you up in protective custody, I swear." He stared at Tony, waiting for an answer.

Tony stared back and said, "I promise."

"Good. Thanks for the omelet." Coppestad picked up the pictures, stuffed them back into the envelope, and left.

As Tony watched him go, he wondered if it should bother him more than it did, that he was getting so good at lying to people.

Chapter 26

Tony returned to his room to trade his windbreaker for a sleeveless vest. He needed something to cover the Walther in his belt, but it was getting too warm outside to walk around with the additional layer of long sleeves. He had time to kill before his next planned task, so he decided to take the subway to the South Ferry Station and walk into Battery Park. He hadn't seen the Statue of Liberty since he was a kid and thought it might be a nice distraction.

As Tony pulled on the vest, he noticed the message light blinking on his hotel room phone. He walked over, pushed the message button, followed the instructions, and heard an automated voice say, "You have one message." Then, "Your friend is waiting for you near the taxi stand."

Tony smiled and yelped, "Yes!" Doug had decided to stay. At that moment, he realized how much he had tried to avoid thinking about Doug's departure. How much more afraid he was to face what was coming without his friend's help.

He hurried to the elevator, and when it opened on the lobby

floor, he nearly ran through the revolving doors to the sidewalk out front. He saw a row of taxis and a couple of limousines lined up, but no sign of Doug. Then he noticed a chauffeur in front of one of the limos holding a sign that said, "Harrington." Tony smiled and walked over. Before he could say anything, the rear door of the car opened, and a voice said, "Get in, Mr. Harrington."

Oh, shit. "No, I'd rather not, thank you," Tony said, quickly glancing around for any signs of Coppestad or his goons or Doug.

The voice said, "I think you will. Come close enough, at least, to have a look at this." Tony took one step toward the door and leaned down. A big, burly hand was holding a large photograph of a young woman Tony recognized all too well—his sister Rita.

The voice said, "We know who she is. We know where she goes to school. We even know the schedule she follows for her cello lessons. Maybe we should send some guys to go check on her? Or you could get in the fucking car."

Tony was terrified, but nodded, stepped over to the door, and climbed in. The man with the sign shut the door and walked around to the driver's door. In the back of the limo with Tony were two men he had not seen before. Both were bald, pale, and enormous.

"What do you want?" Tony squeaked.

"Shut up," the man with the photograph said. "Give me your cell phone. Slowly."

Tony reached into his pocket, pulled out his phone, and handed it over. The man's big fingers did not slow him down as he deftly removed the SIM card from its slot. He handed the phone back to Tony, who hoped it was a good sign. Maybe this wouldn't be his last car ride.

The limo pulled into traffic, and Tony asked, "Where are we going?"

The second man's arm flew out so fast Tony would have missed it if it hadn't delivered a blow to his stomach. Tony doubled over in pain and tried to breathe. *Why is it always the stomach…?*

The first man said, "I told you to shut up. I suggest you learn to follow instructions."

Tony nodded, gasping for air. Eventually he managed to sit up straight again.

The first man held out some black fabric and said, "Put this on."

"You're joking."

Apparently they weren't. The second man reached over and gripped Tony by the throat with his left hand, squeezing tightly. With his right hand, the man grabbed the black hood and pulled it over Tony's head. Once Tony's face was completely covered, the man released his grip, and Tony slid down in the seat, gasping for air again. He nearly spoke, anxious to object, but stopped short. It occurred to him they wouldn't have covered his head if they intended to kill him. *There would be no point in that, right? Right? Jeez, get a grip. I need to do what I'm told, for now. They haven't searched me. My hands are free, and I have a gun. Just stay cool.*

They rode in silence. The car made multiple stops and turns and drove for a long time. Tony had no clue where they were, except he was pretty sure they had driven over a long bridge, so they probably were no longer in Manhattan. The car stopped for a few seconds, and Tony could hear a low rumble under the louder screeches of moving metal. The car pulled ahead, and the darkness under the hood grew even darker. *We've pulled inside a building, or a garage of some kind.*

He heard the sounds again. When they stopped, the hood was pulled from his head. Tony could see they were inside a large, mostly empty building. It had high ceilings with windowed gables and a second-story balcony around the perimeter. The building appeared to have corrugated steel walls, and sunlight bled through a variety of gaps and holes.

"Stay here. We'll get out first."

Tony obeyed. He assumed the men were doing it this way to ensure he couldn't run when he stepped out, for which he was glad. Getting out last meant less chance of the gun tucked in the rear of his jeans being spotted.

When he stepped out of the limo, each of the men took one of his arms and led him past the front of the car to the far end of the old building. Two simple straight-backed chairs were positioned facing each other. In one of them sat Stefano "Stuffy" Montagna, the head of the Montagna Crime Syndicate, one of the most feared mobsters in America. Tony recognized him immediately. He'd come across the face in his research only a few hours previously.

"Sit down, Mr. Harrington," Montagna said, his raspy voice conveying a command rather than an invitation.

Tony sat. Sweat was beading on his forehead, and his hands were shaking. Montagna was reported to be nearly eighty years old, but his grip on his family and his businesses was said to be as strong as ever. Tony had no doubt Montagna could end his life with as little as a nod to one of his "colleagues."

"You're frightened." It was a statement, not a question.

Tony nodded.

"You're right to be frightened, Tony. May I call you Tony?"

He nodded again.

"Thank you. You may call me sir. It wouldn't seem right for you to be too familiar with the man who holds your life in his hands. Wouldn't you agree?"

Tony nodded.

"Good. Do you know who I am?"

"Yes, sir."

"Good! You're good!" The old man chuckled with apparent

genuine glee that Tony had done his homework. But he quickly grew somber again and sighed. "Here's the thing, Tony. You may not know that Robbie Costello is a member of my family."

"Actually, sir..." The old man's hand shot out and slapped Tony across the face. The blow nearly knocked him out of his chair. The side of his face felt like it was on fire. Tony fought back the urge to reach up and rub it.

"I'm sorry, Tony, but you're not to speak until I allow you to. Do you understand?"

Tony sat up straight again and nodded.

"What I was saying is that Robbie is family, not in the slang sense of being in my employ. He's my flesh and blood. He's my sister's grandson. Did you know that? You may speak now."

"No, sir," Tony said softly, his heart sinking as the shaking in his hands increased.

"Ah, well...I guess that explains to some extent why you behaved so foolishly with Robbie. Of course, you're not new to foolishness, are you? I've done my homework too. And I had a call from an associate in Italy who told me about a visit you made to him. That probably doesn't surprise you. My associate said I should keep an eye out for you. That you might try to do something...uh, unwise. I didn't think much of it. What's some farm boy from Ohio going to do to my very tough, very skilled great-nephew?"

Tony didn't correct Montagna's misidentification of the state.

Montagna continued. "You hurt him, you know. I asked to see him this morning. I had a little task I needed done. He actually declined to come, saying he was sick. So I sent a man to check on him. His balls are sore as hell, which is what he's worried about, but I have to say, the gash in his leg is the bigger concern. Just a little harder, and I think you would have broken the bone."

Montagna sat back and took a deep breath. He held up one

hand, and the limo driver appeared in an instant, handing him a bottle of water. He took a long drink, handed the bottle back, and said, "I would like to ask you if you're sorry for what you did, but that would be a waste of time. You would lie to me and say yes, or you would be honest with me and say no. Either answer would piss me off, which is rarely a good idea, so we'll let it go for now."

Tony was struggling to control himself. He had faced evil before, he had been a prisoner before, held by men who intended to kill him, but he had rarely been this terrified.

The old man spoke. "Tony, the only question that has any relevance—in fact, the *only* reason we are having this conversation—is to ask you one question. And that is, is there any reason why I shouldn't kill you now? And don't give me any bullshit about your pals in the Major Crimes Squad. Believe me, your body will never be found, so the police investigation will go nowhere."

Tony was praying hard that someone from the NYPD had followed them, or at least had seen the car that had picked him up. He prayed that if the cavalry didn't arrive in time, he would die quickly. He prayed that if he died, Montagna wouldn't get away with it. He prayed that if he died, the revenge would stop here, and Rita and others he loved would be safe.

"You may speak now."

Tony realized Montagna was waiting for an answer to his one relevant question. He suddenly brightened and said, "Yes I do. I mean, yes, there's a good reason you shouldn't kill me."

"Really?" Montagna smiled broadly. "I wonder how creative you can be. I've heard a lot of reasons over the years, from people in situations similar to yours. I have yet to hear one that carried much weight. Please, tell me."

"I think you would prefer I say it to you privately." Tony nodded at the three men from the limo.

Montagna folded his hands and shook his head. "Tony, Tony, Tony...You must think me a moron. I haven't lived to be seventy-eight by falling for old tricks like that. You're disappointing me." He turned to the limo men. "Gentlemen."

"Wait!" Tony said, his panic rising. "I swear, I know something about Mr. Costello that you don't know. At least I don't think you know it."

"Not good enough," Montagna said.

A thought popped into Tony's head. "I can prove it!"

Montagna crossed his arms and smirked. "How do you propose to do that?"

"In my pocket! There's a piece of paper in my shirt pocket with notes I made to myself. You need to see what it says."

Montagna turned to one of the men from the back of the limo. He asked, "Is that right? Does he have notes in his pocket?"

The man's face turned white, and he stammered, "I'm sorry, Mr. Montagna. I guess I don't know."

Montagna rose from his chair and turned to face the man. He snarled, "You don't know? Are you telling me you brought a man here to meet with me, sat him down in a chair inches away from me, and you never searched him?"

"I'm sorry, Mr. Montagna." The man was on the verge of tears. He rushed over to Tony, but Montagna shouted at him.

"Stop! Don't touch him. You fucking idiots. I would kill the three of you where you stand if I didn't need you today. Go sit in the car, all three of you."

The men slunk away, and Montagna turned back to Tony. "Which pocket?"

Tony glanced down to his shirt pocket. Montagna stuck his hand in and pulled out the piece of paper Tony had used in the restaurant. His notes included a list of tasks for the day. Number three on the list was "Go to Montagna's Restaurant. Try to talk with him."

Montagna's eyebrows went up. He looked at Tony. "Is this for real?"

Tony nodded.

Montagna sat back down. Tony secretly thanked God that the old man hadn't searched him more thoroughly. The Walther was still tucked against his back.

"Okay, you have my attention. What is it you wanted to tell me? Speak. Now."

Tony related the story of Noemi's death but quickly explained that he now knew something more.

Montagna said, "That's good, because Robbie says he didn't kill that girl, and I believe him."

Tony didn't, but he wasn't dumb enough to argue the point. He said, "Please forgive me for saying this, but I believe Mr. Costello is killing people for his own pleasure. People he's not telling you about."

Montagna stiffened in his chair as a variety of emotions flashed across his face. Tony was pretty sure he saw shock, anger, and disbelief. He hoped he also saw a glimmer of concern. If Montagna knew Costello well, and it appeared he did, then he would know the claim wasn't too far-fetched.

Through tight lips, the old man hissed, "That is an astounding accusation, Mr. Harrington. One I find hard to believe. And if you're wrong, you are going to pay for it with a long and horrible death."

"I'm sorry, sir. Truly I am. But I can give you the names and addresses of several young girls, and the circumstances…"

"Young girls? You think Robbie is killing young girls?"

Tony's fear was rising again, but he forged on. "I do, sir. I saw him Tuesday night with the girl who was found dead in Central Park on Wednesday morning. I swear, sir, I didn't come here looking for this kind of trouble, but I believe he's the man responsible for the deaths of those young girls you've read about."

Tony held his breath, terrified of what might follow. When Montagna just stared, not moving, Tony added, "I also know you're the only person on Earth who is capable of confirming it. You can check the dates of the girls' deaths against Robbie's work and travel schedules. If he travels out of town for you, you even could check on cases of murdered and missing girls in places and at times that match his travels."

The old man was still trying to look offended and fierce, but Tony could see the wheels turning. As the realization set in that Tony might actually be right, a deep weariness slowly replaced the anger.

Tony continued presenting his case. "I wanted to seek you out, to tell you this, because I assume you don't want this kind of trouble —for you, for him, for the family. A serial killer will bring a level of attention from authorities and the news media exponentially greater than what you've had to ward off in the past. You…"

"Enough!" Montagna screamed. "Shut your damn mouth." He sat back and stared at Tony. The glare from the old man's eyes made him feel like a flower withering in the blistering sun of an African desert.

Montagna asked, "You have the information about those dead girls? Times, places, names, all of it?"

"Yes, sir," Tony said, reminding himself to breathe.

Montagna pulled a pen from his suit jacket pocket and scribbled on Tony's notes. He handed the paper back to Tony. "You can read that?"

Tony saw it was an email address. He nodded and read it back to Montagna to be certain he had it right.

The old man said, "Send everything you have, everything about those girls, to that email. Then do nothing. I will look into it. I think you're dead wrong, and in this case, dead means dead." He took a deep breath and added, "Dear God, I hope to hell you're wrong."

Montagna stood and walked past Tony toward the limo, saying, almost in a mumble, "I trained that boy. I treated him like one of my own sons. How could he..." The old man stopped and turned to Tony. "Why bring this to me? What do you expect me to do? He's *family*, for Christ's sake."

Tony shakily stood up and turned to face the old man. "If you become convinced I'm right, all I'm asking is that you put out the word he's no longer protected. Let the authorities have him. Get him locked up for a hundred years where he can't hurt anyone else, especially you and your family."

Montagna shook his head and said, "Is everyone in Ohio as fucking naïve as you, Mr. Harrington?"

Tony smiled and said, "Probably."

"You're on your own to get back to your hotel," Montagna added. "I'll toss the card to your phone out the window, so you can call for a taxi or one of those Uber things if you want. Not a word about today, to anyone. Understand?"

"Yes, sir," Tony said, loud and clear.

As the car pulled out of the warehouse, Tony walked shakily over to where his phone's SIM card lay on the floor. He stooped to pick it up, then collapsed to his knees.

Chapter 27

Getting back to the hotel was not simple. The map on his phone told Tony he was in Brooklyn, near the waterfront, in a rundown area filled with old warehouses and assorted other abandoned or poorly-kept buildings. The properties still in use were filled mostly with shipping containers for the commercial wharf or private storage facilities.

Tony had a strong cell signal, but no access to wifi, and he had never downloaded the Uber or Lyft app to his phone—he didn't have much use for either of them in Orney, Iowa—so he called for a taxi. Explaining his location was not easy, and he waited more than an hour before a cab finally showed up. The driver did not look happy and insisted Tony pay him cash up front before he would take him anywhere.

Tony was tired, scared, angry, and sore from his ordeal. He tried to be polite but found it difficult. *Maybe I* could *shoot someone,* he thought, staring at the driver who finally put the cab in gear and headed back toward the Brooklyn Bridge.

***

"Two more nights, then you're done," Costello said.

"I'm not sure I can..." Erica dared to say, wincing ahead of the verbal abuse she knew would come. It came.

"Don't give me that shit!" he barked. "You will do what I tell you to do. Period. Your farm boy is gonna pay for what he did to me. Nothing you say or do can stop it, so get your head outta your ass and call him. What's your problem, anyway? You've done worse for me and the family than seduce some hick."

"I'm sorry, Robbie. It just...I feel like such a whore. I'm not a whore." She held the phone away from her face long enough to wipe away tears. She brought the phone back to her ear in time to hear him say, "You're a whore when I tell you to be a whore, understand? It's too bad if you don't like it. We all gotta do things for the family we don't wanna do."

Bullshit, Erica thought. *You've never had an assignment you didn't like. The more gruesome the task, the more you like it.* "Fine," she said, "I don't want to talk about it anymore. I'll call him."

"Good." And with that, Costello hung up.

To the empty room, Erica said, "You're wrong, Robbie. I've never done anything worse than this." She dialed Tony's number.

***

"All My Loving" erupted from Tony's phone as he was stepping out of the shower. Knowing it was Erica, he answered without taking time to dry off. "Hey, beautiful. What's up?"

"I hope I don't have to remind you that you suggested we get together tonight."

"No, of course not. I just didn't expect to hear from you so soon." He glanced at the clock on the phone. It wasn't yet 4 p.m.

"I knocked off early. I thought maybe we could spend some time at the Met. They're open until eight this evening because they're launching a new exhibit. I thought we could enjoy some art and then walk to a place across from Central Park for Greek food. I'll enjoy treating you to my favorite baklava."

"The art museum?" Tony tried to sound upbeat. He would rather do literally *anything* other than spend hours at the Metropolitan Museum of Art. The entire sum of his art purchases throughout his life was three abstract prints he'd found at the Des Moines Art Festival, and three theater posters of Mel Brooks movies. "Sure. I'd love to."

"Doug won't mind if I take you away again?"

"Uh, actually, Doug had to get back to work. He left for Iowa this morning."

"That's too bad," she said. "I was hoping to meet him before he left."

"Yeah, I was disappointed too." *You have no idea...*

"You sound a little down. Are you okay?"

"You're very perceptive. Actually, I've had a pretty crappy day. Doug's departure took me by surprise, then, well...Let's just say it's gone downhill from there."

"Well, cheer up. I'm a girl with high expectations. I expect you to entertain me, woo me, sweep me off my feet, and then...do other things for me..." she let the thought hang, knowing Tony's imagination would take over.

He swallowed and said with an exaggerated, heavy breath, "Your wish is my command, Ms. Pappas. You rub this genie in the right place, and he'll make your dreams come true."

She giggled and said, "I'll meet you at the front door of the Met in an hour."

Tony scrambled to get dried and dressed quickly. He had to send a very important email before he could go out for the evening. As he brushed his teeth, his cell phone rang again. He glanced down and saw it was his boss. Tony loved Ben, but simply couldn't take the time to talk to him now. He'd return the call tomorrow. He let the phone ring until it went to voice mail, then shut it off. *Just for a little while,* he thought, not wanting his time with Erica to be interrupted by anyone.

When he was finished in the bathroom, he strode to his laptop lying on the desk. He sent everything he had collected regarding the murdered girls to the email address Montagna had provided. He wrote no cover note. He knew it wouldn't matter what he said about the materials or any potential follow-up. Montagna would either take it seriously or he wouldn't. He would do what Tony had asked, or he wouldn't. He would contact Tony, or he wouldn't. All Tony could do was try to relax and hope the return message didn't come in the form of a bullet to his head.

***

Chicago

Making a connecting flight at O'Hare International Airport can be as irritating as it is challenging. Pulling your bag through a mile of corridors when you're angry and despondent turns the task into absolute misery. Doug Tenney could attest to this because on the misery scale of one to ten, he was a sixteen. He was sweating from the combination of too-warm air and the need to hurry. He was worried about getting to the gate on time, and he was cursing the airline executives—*or was it the flight controllers?*—who always seemed to make sure his next flight was in a different terminal from his arriving flight.

But mostly, Doug was angry. He was angry at Tony for being such a self-centered ass, and he had realized on the flight from LaGuardia to O'Hare, he was angry at himself for leaving.

That sure was a lovely speech you made to Tony about always standing by him, he thought, excoriating himself. *"I'd rather die helping you than live with myself if I didn't..."? What a line of crap. If that was true, why am I going home? I must be a bigger ass than Tony.*

His self-flagellation was interrupted by his cell phone vibrating in his pocket. He glanced at the Coke in his hand, the Coke he knew he shouldn't have taken the time to buy, saw there was less than a third remaining, and tossed it into the nearest trash can. Without breaking stride, he reached into his pocket and seized his phone. "Tenney," he answered.

"Doug, this is Ben at the *Crier*."

"Hey, Ben. What's up?"

"I was just wondering if you are there with Tony?"

Doug winced as he admitted, "Sorry, but no. I'm actually at O'Hare in Chicago. I'm on my way home."

"Oh. I didn't realize you were coming back today."

"That's okay," Doug said, considering leaving the conversation with that, but letting his curiosity get the better of him. "Can I ask why you're calling me, if it's Tony you want?"

Ben hesitated a moment, then said, "I didn't mean to cause you any concern. It's just that I tried to call his cell but couldn't get him. I thought maybe he had silenced it and that I might be able to get to him through you."

"Sorry, Mr. S, I'd help you if I could, but I'm pretty sure Tony wouldn't ignore a call from you. You might just try him again in case he was in the shower or something." Even as he said it, Doug felt the dread growing deep in his heart. *Tony wouldn't ignore a call from you. And if he'd missed it, he'd do his best to return it as quickly as possible...*

"I'll do that, Doug. Sorry I bothered you."

"Wait, Mr. S."

"Yes?"

"Is everything okay, really? I mean, if this is important, maybe I can help somehow."

Ben sounded reluctant to reply, even as he said, "Well, I gotta be honest. Something's come up that's nagging at me, and I was hoping to talk with Tony about it. Before you ask, maybe I should ask you something. How's Tony doing? I mean, he's staying in New York a lot longer than expected. He told me you guys have been following a guy he thinks killed Noemi, then he asked for his gun. Do you know anything more about any of that?"

"Boy, Mr. S., you're putting me on the spot. I'm not sure Tony would want me to..." Doug stopped, deciding not to go there. "Nah, I don't know nothing. You first."

Ben managed a chuckle and said, "Okay, look. You know he's met a woman there, right? Erica? Did you meet her?"

"No, I didn't get the chance before I...I had to go. But I sure heard about her. She must be terrific 'cause the Tone-man is dancing on cloud eleven, at least."

Ben's reply came through a heavy sigh. "Jesus, I hope this turns out alright."

The alarm on Doug's internal radar was clanging. "What? You hope *what* turns out alright? What do you have?"

Another sigh, audible over the phone, "Here's the thing. I've been doing internet research on Erica Pappas, and I can't find her anywhere."

Doug breathed an equally big sigh, but his from the sense of relief that spilled out of him. "Oh, that," he said. "Tony noticed that too. He said it's normal to check out somebody on the web when you first meet her. You know, to learn what you can." Almost as an aside, Doug added, "Of course I wouldn't know. When I get a girl to agree to go out with me, I'm so happy she said yes, I don't wanna know any more about her. Anyway, Tony looked for her and couldn't find any information. It concerned him, but not enough to dampen his, uh, enthusiasm. I actually helped convince him it's probably nothing. That's right, isn't it? It's no big deal?"

Ben, too, was relieved to learn that Tony wasn't blind to the issue. He said, "Yes, at least I hope you're right. But I have to confess, it's damn unusual in this day and age not to find any trace of a young woman who's single, lives in Manhattan, and claims to work in real estate. Realtors are notorious for trying to get their photos and information out there. So when Tony didn't answer his phone, my mind started conjuring up all kinds of sinister scenarios."

"Yeah, I get that." Doug nodded to no one. "I'll try him myself. Maybe he's just avoiding his boss."

Silence.

"That was a joke, Mr. S."

"Sorry, Doug. It's been a long couple of days. At this point, I hope that's what it comes down to—being avoided, I mean."

"You're a good man, Mr. S. If you ever need another reporter —you know, at about twice what you pay Tony—you know who to call."

This time, Ben's chuckle echoed back through the connection. Satisfied, Doug said, "I'll let you know if I reach him."

"Hey, Doug, before you go, can I ask you something else?"

"Sure, Mr. S. Ask away."

"You and Tony have an unusual relationship. I mean, considering you're competitors, it's surprising that you seem to share everything."

Doug could feel his face scrunching up in concern. "Well, yeah, I guess so. That's not a problem, is it?"

"No, no. Nothing about it has ever worried me. I'm just curious how you make it work."

"Well, we trust each other. Of course, that didn't happen overnight. We just kinda eased into it as we got to be friends. The rules are unwritten—hell, they're unspoken—but they're clear. We never steal a scoop, we never hesitate to share what's available publicly if we're only saving the other guy some time, and we always credit the other person if we're using his research, or even his prose. You know, that kinda stuff."

"And it's never been a problem?"

"Nope," Doug said quickly, feeling his guilt about leaving New York grow another head.

"Huh. That's great, Doug. Really. Thanks for sharing."

"Sure, Mr. S., but couldn't you ask Tony…"

Doug stopped because Ben had ended the call. He immediately pulled up Tony's number and called him, but after seven rings, it went to voice mail. Doug realized he hadn't thought about what he would say. "Uh, hey, Tone-man. Uh…Look, I'm sorry, okay? Call me." He hung up.

"Oh, hell," he said aloud, stopping in the middle of the stream of rushing bodies. He turned around, bumping into a few irritated soon-to-be passengers, and headed for the ticketing counter. With any luck, he could be back in the Big Apple before 11 p.m.

***

Orney, Iowa

Ben resisted the urge to pound on his disk and scream again. *The staff in the newsroom must be thinking I've lost it.*

He had spoken honestly when he'd said it had been a rough couple of days. His two best reporters were gone—Madeline Mueller had left the previous year after co-writing a series of stories with Tony about human trafficking. So far, Ben had failed to find anyone as good. Her replacement was already gone too. Now Tony was off in New York chasing who-knows-what. That left him one reporter, plus the sports guy, a copy editor who could be pressed into reporting some simple things, and Mrs. Crowder, who now only worked from home. In short, everyone was working long hours, and the job still wasn't getting done very well.

Compounding the problem was the fact Ben was worried, distracted, and unable to sleep at night. The combination made him less productive and extremely irritable. If he wasn't careful, someone else was going to quit. *Even worse, if I don't get my head out of my ass, my readers are going to drop their subscriptions. My paper has been crap lately.*

It was hard enough to keep readers for a newspaper and nearly impossible to make any money. Ben knew the *Crier* had to be exceptional every day to have any chance of surviving.

He stared at his computer screen as he contemplated these troubles. He knew he needed to get to work on his article about the legal challenge being mounted in opposition to the next sea of wind turbines planned to go up on a site east of Orney. Instead, he picked up his phone and dialed Rich Davis at the DCI.

"Sorry, Ben," Davis answered, dispensing with formalities. "Nothing yet."

"Dammit," Ben replied.

"Understand," Davis said, "all I've been able to do so far is check the normal databases. I can tell you she doesn't have a criminal history, if Erica Pappas is her real name, that is. We're hoping to get the FBI's time tomorrow to run her through the facial recognition programs. She can't have lived in Manhattan for twenty-plus years and not have had her picture taken somewhere. Apparently she didn't object to Tony taking it, so I think there's reason to be optimistic we'll find her. By the way, if the FBI asks, we're looking for her as a potential witness to a felony in Iowa."

"Oh?"

"I had to tell them something, or I wouldn't have had a chance of getting their help. If it turns out she's a stripper or a polygamist or some such crap, I won't hear the end of it for…ever."

"Thanks for all your work and for taking the risk. I really appreciate it. And Rich, there are things a lot worse than being a stripper."

"Maybe for you and for Tony, but not for the guy who's begging resources from the feds."

"Ah, of course. You're right."

Rich concluded, "I'll call you as soon as I know anything."

Ben hung up the phone, simultaneously eager to know more and dreading Rich's next call. Would his fear be justified? His gut was shouting, "Yes!"

He didn't know how right his gut was.

Chapter 28

New York

Erica was waiting in a corner of the wide expanse of steps in front of the Met when Tony climbed out of his taxi. She was wearing a simple pale-yellow cotton dress, hemmed to a couple of inches above the knee and gathered at the waist. A white sweater was draped over her shoulders, and a string of pearls hung from her neck.

Against the yellow, her olive skin looked warm and inviting. In her sitting position, Tony could see the underside of her leg right up to the edge of the step. He had to force himself to look up into her eyes.

She stood to greet him. As her thigh disappeared behind the yellow fabric, he wished she hadn't. "You look wonderful," he said, giving her a quick hug and a peck on the lips.

"Thanks," she said. "You, too."

"Nice try, but there's no comparison. I doubt you got that dress off a department store shelf, which is where I got these slacks and sweater."

She smiled. "No, but if you'd shown up in Armani, I would have been irritated. I don't want my date trying to out-glamour me."

"No risk of that when you're hanging with me." He looked up toward the entrance at the top of the steps. "Ready to go?"

She hesitated. "You don't really want to spend time in there, do you?"

Tony wasn't sure how to interpret the question. "Well...sure. I mean, I could use a little culture."

She laughed out loud, and Tony could feel his face begin to burn. She said, "Tony, please. It's okay. I'm not crazy about the idea, either. The more I thought about it, the more I realized we might feel stifled by the atmosphere in the galleries, or worse, get trapped into some conversation about..." she made her voice sound nasal and snooty, "...the infinite dimensions of the universe as depicted in this sculpture of a picket fence and a giant egg."

It was Tony's turn to laugh. "Okay, but if we skip the culture lesson, then what?"

"Let's walk into the park and see what we find. It's a warm evening, so I bet the street performers will be everywhere."

They strolled past the museum and into Central Park. Entertainment wasn't everywhere, but it was easy to find. In less than ten minutes, they had walked into a plaza area near the Great Lawn, where they found a troupe of performers doing acrobatics and comedy. The comedy mostly involved making fun of tourists who were dragged into various roles as props, furniture, and foils for the young men's antics.

When the hat was passed, Tony dropped in some cash, hoping he had been generous enough. He got a big smile and a fist-bump from the tall, muscular Black teenager, so he guessed he had.

They strolled south, following one of the park's major

pedestrian paths as it wound between two lakes. As they walked, they talked about everything and nothing. It was the kind of conversation new lovers have in which they explore each other's interests and ideas. Thoughts of things as minor as favorites—foods, sports teams, vacation spots—and as big as the existence of God or life on other planets. They laughed often, held hands, and fell into a comfortable rhythm, as though they were the hi-hat and snare drum in a jazz drummer's syncopation.

They found themselves at Bethesda Fountain. They bought a couple of soft drinks from a woman selling bottles out of a Styrofoam cooler and sat on one of the marble benches at the edge of the open brick terrace next to the lake.

As the sun fell in the western sky, the skyscrapers of New York enveloped the park in the shadows of a premature dusk. The air grew chilly, and Tony helped Erica into her sweater.

She cuddled up next to him and said, "Don't you wish we could stay like this forever?"

Tony was ashamed of the thought that first entered his head about what he'd rather be doing, so he simply said, "I do." He put his arm around her and pulled her close. After a few minutes, he could feel her trembling. He pulled away a little so he could look down into her face. He realized she was crying.

Before he could ask, she said, "You have to go home."

"Well, sure, eventually. But maybe not for long."

Erica straightened. "What does that mean?"

"I've been wondering if I should tell you. I mean, I don't want to presume too much. You know, we just met, and you have this life…"

"You can tell me, Tony. Please, tell me everything."

Tony took the plunge. He described getting the call out of the blue from *The New York Times* and about the generous job offer. He told her he had been debating what to do, especially since meeting her. He told her he adored her and was excited at the prospect of staying in New York and continuing to explore their growing relationship.

He wasn't sure what he was expecting, but, he realized when he thought about it later, he undoubtedly was hoping for her to squeal with joy, jump to her feet, dance, or something. She did none of these.

Instead, she stabbed him through the heart, saying, "Oh, no, Tony, you can't. You can't stay here. You *have* to go home."

Gaping, he pushed back from her, suddenly feeling faint. Had he misjudged her and their relationship that badly? He tried to form a question, but he couldn't speak.

"Oh, Tony, don't look at me that way," Erica pled. "God, what am I supposed to...? How can I say...?" She drew in a big breath and steadied herself, taking a second to wipe her face. "Tony, please, you have to believe me. I want you to stay, but I'm afraid you can't. You shouldn't! You're...My life is...complicated. I can't do this right now."

Tony stared at her, his eyes growing cold, his anger rising, "Can't do what? What more could we do than what we've been doing? Has this been a casual hookup for you? I'm just some boy-toy entertaining you for a few days until I go running back to Iowa? You're happy to grab a quick fuck from the out-of-towner, but you can't have him stick around? You don't want to make a commitment? Don't want to mess with your perfect little life?" His voice had risen in pitch as well as volume.

His words produced a predictable effect. Anger flashed in Erica's eyes, and she said, "Don't talk to me like that. You have no right. You don't know anything about me."

"Well, you're right about that. I don't know a damn thing about you. But it's not because I haven't tried."

"What does that mean?" she shot back. "I've just been telling you…"

Tony interrupted. "That's not what I…You know what? Forget it. Dammit, you have to explain this. How in the hell can you go from wishing we could last forever to telling me I can't stay any longer in what…? Ten seconds?"

"Tony, I meant what I said. I want you to stay, but you can't. You just can't. I'm sorry…I don't know what else to…"

"Stop it, Erica. I don't want to hear it." He stood. "Thank you for a lovely evening. I'm leaving now. If I want bullshit, I can find plenty of that in Iowa."

***

Through her tears, Erica watched Tony storm away. She pulled a handkerchief from her purse and tried to wipe her eyes, but the tears kept coming.

She had realized almost immediately, as Tony had grown angry, that she could have calmed the storm quickly by telling him everything. He would have apologized, and they would have embraced and cooed and fallen deeper in love. She had also realized that this would have solved nothing.

She already knew Tony well enough to know that if he knew the full story, he would try to "rescue" her. That could only end one way—with Tony being shipped back to Iowa in a box. In fact, even if she didn't tell him everything, but simply allowed him to stay, he'd still be a man marked for death.

Tony's only chance of survival was his immediate departure. And the only way to convince him to leave was to let his anger and disappointment—his rage—control his decision-making. Erica prayed that Tony was headed for his hotel right now to pack his bags and get out of town.

She called for a car as she walked back to Central Park South. It was waiting for her when she reached the street. She paused, opened the passenger door, and handed the driver a twenty-dollar bill. "I've decided to walk."

It wasn't that far, and she dreaded the task that awaited her when she got home. However, even after an extended session of window shopping along Fifth Avenue and a glass of wine in the bar at the Plaza Hotel, she was back at her apartment by 9 p.m.

Reluctantly, she dialed Robbie's number. She knew, somehow, she had to convince him to let Tony return home unharmed. She had to put a stop to this.

She failed. Robbie didn't scream. He didn't even raise his voice. He spoke in a low snarl that sounded more menacing than the rattle of a snake's tail. He reminded her of who she was, the position she was in, and the consequences of refusing him. Then he gave her detailed orders regarding her assignment for the coming day.

For the third night in a row, Erica cried herself to sleep.

***

Tony did not return to his hotel. He couldn't face an empty room and a long, undoubtedly sleepless night. He needed to comprehend what had just happened.

What the hell did just happen?

He needed to think, but he didn't want to. He walked fast, south and west. He stopped at a street vendor's cart and bought a jumbo hot dog, forcing it down as he resumed his walk. He meandered the streets aimlessly for nearly two hours, barely registering his path as he struggled with his anguish.

Finally, he found himself walking into a dance club in the

Chelsea District. The music was deafening, and the main room was packed solid with young people.

The pandemic recovery is complete, or it better be, he thought, as he pushed his way through the crowd. People of all colors, shapes, and sizes comprised the crowd, two-thirds of which was female. Among the women, the most common shape to Tony's eye was "Wow!" He was pretty sure he had never seen so many beautiful women in one room before. Most wore shimmering dresses cut short on the bottom and low on the top.

He continued to wrestle his way through the crowd, not an unpleasant experience, until he reached the bar. He told the bartender to fill his biggest glass with Jack Daniels and ice. Once in hand, Tony turned to the crowd, raised his glass, and said into the roar of hip-hop, "Here's to you, Miss I-can't-do-this-right-now."

Because Tony rarely drank alcohol, the impact of the whiskey was fast and profound. By the end of his second drink, his face felt warm and his brain befuddled. Halfway through the third drink, he was on the dance floor, pressed against a young blonde in a black cocktail dress. She was a head shorter than Tony and wore her hair in a pixie cut. She was stocky, braless, and aggressive. Tony was out of control as a dancer, victim to the whiskey and the fact he couldn't dance even when sober. Periodically the young woman, who said her name was Kerty or Kersy or something like that, would smile, reach out, and pull Tony in close, forcing him to stop waving his arms around.

The feel of her aroused him, but he didn't want to know her. She had shared her name without being asked and repeated it when she wrapped her arms around him for a slow dance. Through the fog of alcohol and noise, Tony realized she was saying "Courtney." He also realized the pace of the music hadn't slowed. Apparently Courtney wanted to get romantic; as she clung tightly to him, she swayed to a beat only she could hear.

Tony had not reciprocated. He just wanted to drink, dance, and drink some more. He wanted to get stupid drunk. He wanted to pass out. He wanted to die. *What the hell had happened back there?*

Courtney put her lips to his ear and said she needed a drink, then pulled him off the dance floor. Tony paid for her drink as well as a fourth whiskey for himself, without hesitation. She smiled and took him by the hand, pulling him toward the rear of the club. There were smaller rooms in the back where the music was less loud and comfortable seats and couches were available. They entered a room where one other couple was entwined on a big chair, apparently trying to swap tongues.

Tony and Courtney sat on a leather couch and took big swallows of their drinks. Courtney set hers down, leaned over, and kissed Tony hard. He kissed her back.

"That's better," she said and kissed him again, this time running her hand up his chest, under his sweater. Soon her tongue was in his ear and she began tugging on his neck, trying to pull him down on top of her as she lay back on the couch. Sensing Tony's resistance, she grinned at him and whispered, "I may not be a genie, but I can make your dreams come true."

Tony looked at her and then shook his head. His voice sounded like he was trying to talk underwater as he said, "You can't shay that. That's myyy line." Then he giggled. Still fighting a thick tongue and a brain on synaptic hold, he slurred, "And no, Coursney, you can't make my dreams come true. Sorrry, but you chan't. My dreams are somewhere… Uh…" He belched and stood. "I'm shorry." He turned and left quickly, weaving just a little as he found the door. He didn't look back.

When Tony stepped out of the club, the cool night air jolted him but didn't seem to clear his head. If anything, the effects of the alcohol seemed to be growing. He didn't see a taxi and was having trouble standing without swaying, so he decided to sit while he waited. He slid his back down the brick surface of the building until his butt was planted on the sidewalk. Then reached into his pocket and pulled out his phone.

He had an urge to talk to his dad but retained enough sense not to make the call. In fact, he couldn't get the phone to work at all. *What the hell?* He pounded it on his leg a couple of times, but it seemed useless. It was dead. Then he remembered. *Oh crap. I turned it off.*

He instinctively looked around, worried about who might have been watching. He chortled under his breath and powered up the phone. He immediately saw a bunch of calls from Doug. Four? No, six? Wait, four? His eyes wouldn't focus. He ignored the voicemail notifications and found the button to return Doug's call.

His friend answered on the first ring. "Tony! God, I was worried about you. Where are you?"

Tony giggled. "Well, Miffter Tenneennee, I'm not in freaking Iowa. I'm…" He looked up at the street sign. It was too blurry to read. "I'm at the corner of whiskey and ice." He giggled again.

"Holy shit! You're drunk."

"Well… Mmaybe just an eensy-weensy."

"Okay, Tone-man. Just take it easy and tell me where you are. I'm here. I mean, I'm back in Manhattan, and I'll come get you if you tell me where."

The whiskey chose that moment to start a rebellion in Tony's brain. The world began to spin and grow dark. Tony slumped over on the sidewalk.

"Tony? Tony!" Doug was yelling his name over and over when the club's bouncer left his post at the door and walked over to where Tony lay motionless on the sidewalk. The bouncer checked to be sure he was breathing, then picked up the phone.

"You can stop yelling," he said quietly, explaining who he was and giving Doug the address where he could find his friend. The bouncer then ended the call, slipped the phone back into Tony's pocket, and made sure Tony was lying on his side so that if he vomited, he wouldn't choke. Apparently the bouncer had dealt with drunks before.

Chapter 29

Tony could feel a hot knife goring out his eyeball. No, not a knife. A laser. Someone was burning his eye out with a laser. No, they were pounding on his head with sledges, or bricks. But the laser…The pain in his eye caused him to twist his head to the side. The burning was replaced with screams from every other part of his head and neck.

"Hey, Tone-man. Welcome back."

He knew that voice…Doug. Doug Tenney. *Why is Doug torturing me?*

"What the heeell?" Tony groaned.

"Easy, my friend." Doug spoke softly. "You have a six-pints-of-Jack-Daniels hangover which, for you, means you had, what? A couple of beers and a strawberry daquiri?"

"Up yours, Tenney," Tony managed to croak. His indignation cleared the fog a little, and Tony opened his eyes. He saw…what? Towels. Shelves. A toilet? He realized he was on the floor of the bathroom of a hotel room, propped up in the corner against some pillows and covered with a bedsheet. He discovered the burning sensation in his eye had come from a single ray of sunshine coming from the other room and reflected off a bathroom fixture into his face.

Kill me now, was his first thought, but he said, "Why am I on the floor?" He wasn't sure Doug understood him. It sounded like he was trying to talk while gargling motor oil and marbles.

Doug said, "I know. It's no way to greet the morning, but I figured you wouldn't wanna puke in your bed."

With his palms against the floor, Tony tried to push himself up a few inches. He said, "But I'm not going to…" Suddenly he grabbed the rim of the stool, pulled his head over, and retched into the bowl.

Doug fought very hard to keep from laughing. After all, he knew his friend had a gun.

***

It was mid-afternoon before Tony had recovered enough to clean up and accompany Doug to the hotel's restaurant for a late lunch. While Doug feasted on a club sandwich, fries, and strawberry pie, Tony had toast and orange juice.

The subjects of Doug's return and Tony's hangover had been awkwardly ignored until Tony finally asked how he'd gotten from the dance club to his hotel bathroom floor. Doug explained how the bouncer had intercepted the call and had given Doug directions. The bouncer had lifted Tony into the back of a cab, and Doug had helped him up to his room.

"Then I slept in your bed and let you have the bathroom floor," Doug said, a grin spreading across his face. "All in all, not a bad deal for me, since I don't have a room of my own anymore."

Tony looked up at his friend for a long beat, swallowed, and said, "Thank you. I'm glad you're back."

"Nah, none of that. I never should've left. If I hadn't, you wouldn't have a marching band drum line performing in your head, and I wouldn't have wasted another plane ticket."

"I'm afraid wasted is the right word," Tony said sullenly.

Doug raised an eyebrow but let Tony continue.

"I've decided to pack it in, for real this time."

"Seriously? Don't sound like you, Tone-man. Have something to do with your three beers and a daquiri?"

"Knock that off," Tony said, trying to sound gruff but smiling for the first time in twenty hours. "It's everything, really. I mean, think about it. We've told the police about Costello. What else can we do with him except stay here and be targets? The cops'll catch him eventually now that they have his name. Or Montagna will discover the truth about him and give him up."

"I happen to agree," Doug said with a nod, "but you didn't get drunk because you decided to let New York's finest deal with Costello. So what happened with Erica?"

Tony gazed down at his half-eaten toast. He rubbed the back of his hand across his moistening eyes. "Yeah, about Erica. We had a...a disagreement?" Tony realized he didn't know what had happened in the park. "We had words. She said she couldn't continue to go out with me, and she walked away. Well, actually, I walked away, but it was only so I wouldn't have to watch her do it."

"Huh. Sorry, man. Truly."

"I gotta admit, Doug, it hurts. A lot. But somehow, I knew it was coming. There was just too much she wouldn't tell me."

"Yeah, about that," Doug said. "Ben tried to call you, and when he couldn't get you, he called me. He was worried because he couldn't find a trace of her anywhere."

Tony wasn't sure whether to be pleased that his boss cared enough to try, or peeved that his boss was prying into his love life.

He decided to assume his boss's best intentions and smiled. "Did you tell him he's in good company?"

"Yeah, I said you're aware she's a ghost. It didn't seem to put his mind at ease much."

"I guess when I tell him it's over and I'm coming home, we all can rest easier."

Doug's stare said he wasn't buying it, but he held his tongue.

In an effort to show he was serious, Tony pulled out his phone and began looking up flights on his travel app.

"When are you thinking of leaving?"

"Soon. Today. Now, if we can. There's no point in hanging around. If Costello recovers enough to get mobile, he's gonna come looking for us. I'd just as soon he not find us."

"Ditto," Doug said with a nod. "Let's go up to your room. I can pack for both of us while you do that on your laptop. It'll be easier on your eyes."

"You mean these two blood-shot, burned-out, unable-to-focus eyes?" Tony deepened his voice, imitating a favorite character from 1950s television reruns— "You make good plan Kemosabe."

Doug chuckled, which made Tony smile. He still felt like someone had started a fire inside his body, then tried to stomp it out with steel-toed boots, but he could tell he was on the road to recovery. As they rode up in the elevator, Tony found he was looking forward to boarding the plane and returning to the routines of Orney, the *Crier*, and the people he loved, including, of course, the man beside him in the elevator. Tony put an elbow on Doug's shoulder and leaned into him. He hoped Doug would assume his hangover had left him needing some support. In fact, he just wanted to be close—to feel the warmth emanating from this best of all possible friends.

***

As he sat and opened his laptop, Tony's phone began playing "All My Lovin'." Erica.

"Jesus Christ," he muttered.

Doug was at his side in an instant. "What?"

"Look." Tony held the screen up for him to see.

"Aw, man…"

"Do I ignore it?"

"I dunno, Tone-man. If you do, it'll drive you crazy. It'll eat at you like battery acid all the way home, then you'll call her anyway."

"Yeah, but…"

"I know. What can she say that will do anything but make it worse, right? If she's sorry and realizes she wants you, it makes leaving harder. If she's decided she was right and just wants to say goodbye on friendlier terms, well, you know, it makes it worse. There's no right answer here, bud."

The phone stopped ringing. Tony wondered if that settled things. It sure made it easier to slip it back into his pocket and pretend she had never called. Then the phone began playing the accursed song again.

"Well, crap." He hit the answer button. "Hey, Erica." He tried hard to sound upbeat.

A man's voice growled, "It's not Erica, you dick. Look at my text, and call me right back. And I mean *right* back." The phone went dead.

"Dear God." Tony was thinking it, but Doug said it aloud. He was still standing at Tony's side and had heard the caller's voice.

A text alert sounded as Tony fumbled with the phone to open his messages. At the top was Erica's number. When he touched it to open the text, a photograph popped up. The sight caused Tony to bolt up out of the chair and scream. Doug pulled the phone out of his hand to look. He looked away and handed the phone back to Tony, who plopped back into the chair, speechless.

Through clenched teeth, Doug said, "That son of a bitch."

The photograph showed Erica, stripped to her underwear and chained to a steel post. It appeared to be a vertical I-beam in a building under construction. She was seated in front of the post, with her arms pulled behind her back, presumably handcuffed, and the chain around her neck.

Tony forced himself to look again, but he wished he hadn't. The right side of Erica's face was purple, darkening to black around her eye socket, and a thin line of blood could be seen oozing from the corner of her mouth. Worst of all, she looked terrified. The unhurt eye was open wide, and beads of sweat stood out on the pale parts of her skin.

"I will kill this bastard," Tony said. "I swear."

"Easy, man. Just…"

Tony had already pushed redial, and Costello answered on the first ring, his voice loud and rough.

"Don't talk! Not one word."

Tony bit back the raging urge to scream at him.

"This ain't a negotiation. You come to me, she goes free. Plain and simple. You die, or she dies. You choose. Now talk."

"Me, you bastard. *Me!* Let her go, and you can have me."

"Spoken like a true-blue farm boy," Costello said. Tony could hear him sneering. "I assume you know the drill, but I'm gonna say it anyway so you don't fuck it up. You don't tell anyone. You don't talk to anyone. You sit on your hands until I call you. I'll call you tonight and tell you where to come. And hear me, smart boy. If I get one whiff of a double-cross, if I or my people see a cop within two miles of this place, if you try anything funny, you'll both be dead. It won't bother me to kill you both. In fact…"

Tony could hear Costello's voice trail away from the phone,

and he could imagine him turning to look at Erica.

"In fact, I'm pretty sure I would enjoy it. So don't give me an excuse. You got it, farm boy?"

"I got it," Tony said, panic rising in his chest and reaching his voice. "Just don't hurt her anymore. Keep her safe, and I'll do exactly what you tell me to do. You have my word."

"Damn right you will." Once again, the phone went silent.

Tony dropped it onto the desk and slumped down on top of it. "What have I done? Doug, my God, what have I..." He buried his face in his arms.

***

Orney, Iowa

Ben Smalley woke to the sound of his phone ringing. He realized he had fallen asleep in his chair. It was 2 p.m. Sunday, and he was sleeping. At this rate, by the end of the week the paper would be as dead as Bill Cosby's comedy career. "Smalley."

"Ben, it's Rich. I've got something. I'm headed your way. I just wanted to be sure you were there."

"Holy crap, Rich. You sound grim."

"Yeah, I do." He hung up.

Ten minutes later, Rich Davis was in the chair in front of Ben's desk, pushing a large envelope across the surface toward him. Ben opened it and saw a grainy photograph of five people on a sidewalk in front of a restaurant. The angle of the photo made it obvious it had been taken from a higher location, probably a rooftop or a second-story window across the street.

Pictured were three men and two women. One of the men appeared to be quite elderly, and one of the women was young, dark, and attractive. Ben looked up at Davis. "That's Erica."

"Well, yes and no," Davis said.

Ben didn't know his anxiety could grow any greater, but somehow it inched up several notches. "And that means what?"

"It means," Davis said stoically, "you're right that the girl, uh, young woman, is the same as the one in Tony's photograph. Her name, however, isn't Erica."

Ben sagged back into his chair. "Aw shit, Rich."

"I'm sorry, but there's something else. I shouldn't tell you, but I know you're going crazy, and besides, you're the one who brought this to us."

"What?" Ben threw his hands into the air. "For God's sake."

"Sorry. The woman is Angelica Montagna."

The name rang a bell from Ben's days working on the east coast. "Montagna? You don't mean the…"

"I'm afraid so. The old man in the photo is Stefano Montagna. You may know him as 'Stuffy.' They say he got the name because he liked to stuff the bodies into oil drums before tossing them into the concrete being poured at one of his construction sites."

"Erica told Tony she's Greek."

"She lied. She's Italian. Stuffy is her grandfather."

"Dear Lord," Ben said, running a hand through his short, wiry hair. "So the FBI found this match?"

"Yeah, they ran the photo we had through the facial recognition software. They found this photo, taken last year, in their organized crime database. It gets better…Or worse, I guess."

"How in the hell could it get any worse?" Ben practically barked.

Davis sighed and said, "Once this popped up, the FBI staffer, as a matter of routine, contacted the NYPD to confirm all the names and check on any recent activity. The special agent running the program wanted to be thorough in case her pals back in Iowa were on to something she should know about. You'll never guess what the woman at the FBI heard."

Ben wasn't in the mood to guess, so he just glared until Davis continued.

"NYPD said one of the people in the photo is Robbie Costello. He's Stuffy Montagna's grand-nephew. They recognized him right away because they've been doing a little research on him recently. Apparently some small-town reporter had come to them and claimed Costello is a serial killer."

Ben sat forward in his chair. "Tony, obviously."

Davis breathed deeply and looked into Ben's eyes. It was up for debate regarding which pair of eyes showed more anguish. "Of course it's Tony. Somehow Tony got on Costello's case, and now it turns out Erica isn't Erica, but is Angelica, and Angelica is a cousin to Costello, and they're both members of one of the major crime families in New York, and who's at the center of it all? Of *course* it's goddamn Tony!" Now Davis was nearly yelling. "How does he *do* this? Every *damn* time!"

Ben's brain was churning. *How indeed?* The common thread among all parties seemed to be the Italian heritage. Tony had just been to Italy. Was there a connection?

"Rich, I have an idea. Can you find out if Costello knew Noemi Moretti? Or, maybe…check to see if he was in Italy recently. Tony was distraught about his cousin's death. He told me he followed a man back to New York, a man he thought was responsible. Could that be Costello?"

"It's a thought. Gimme a sec." Davis pulled out his phone, typed a lengthy text message, and pushed send. "We'll see what's readily available. The travel question should be easy to answer. The other could take a while."

The two men were silent for a while as each pondered what they knew and what it might mean. Rich spoke first.

"Do you think Tony sought out Angelica in an attempt to get close to Costello?"

"Nah, he told Doug Tenney he was frustrated because he didn't know anything about her and wasn't having any luck finding out."

"Then what about the other way around?"

"Yeah, that's the real worry, isn't it?" Ben agreed. "Angelica, using her alias as Erica, sought out Tony. Perhaps Costello knew Tony was looking at him and used his cousin to get close to him. Tony's loneliness made him an easy mark. It was his bad luck that he fell so hard for her."

"God, the poor guy."

"No question." Ben nodded, letting his thoughts settle, then he stirred into action. "If this is ringing as true for you as it is for me, we need to tell him. Angelica and Costello pose a huge threat to him and to Doug. They need to get out of there now."

"So call him," Davis said bluntly.

"Jeez, I've been trying," Ben said. "He hasn't answered his phone for more than twenty-four hours."

Davis stared for a moment, then jumped out of his seat. "Keep trying. I'm gonna get some people in New York working on this." He was out the door before Ben could verbalize his agreement.

Chapter 30

New York

"We have two things in our favor," Tony said, but Doug looked dubious. "Really. Think about it. First, he doesn't know about you. And even if he forced information out of Erica, she thinks you're back in Iowa. I told her you left."

"Great. You have me. I'm secretly 008, every spy's favorite partner. What's number two? Please tell me it's better."

"He doesn't know I have a gun."

"Shit, Tone-man. Everyone in New York has a gun. He's gonna assume you picked one up, or at least have some kind of weapon on you. A professional like him ain't gonna worry about a six-shooter or whatever that thing is."

"It's a Walther PK380, and it's loaded with eight rounds."

"See? It even sounds like a gun 008 would carry. But it doesn't matter. Unless it's invisible, you're not gonna get anywhere near Costello with it."

"Yeah, maybe. So we just gotta figure out a plan. And we'll have to do it fast because I'm sure he isn't going to tell us a location until five minutes before he expects us to be there. He'll do all he can to limit our ability to tell anyone or plan anything."

"You're counting on the fact that he's underestimating his opponent, or opponents? These two highly-trained special forces operatives?"

Tony managed a smile. "No. He's underestimating two Iowa guys who have faced worse than him before, and who are determined to stay alive and rescue the girl."

"And the cops?"

"I say no, but I can't make that call alone. What do you think? We need their help, but my worry is that Costello has connections on the force. That seems likely, so the risk of calling them would be significant."

"Ah, shit," Doug said. "You're right. No cops."

Tony was glad Doug agreed but then heard his friend say, "But Tony, if we're not calling in the cavalry, then you gotta promise me you'll prepare for the worst and be able to handle it."

"Of course," Tony said.

"No. Stop and think about it. You're gonna have to keep your head. When we get there, Erica could be in far worse shape. I wouldn't put it past this bastard to beat on her, even rape her."

"Doug, stop!"

"No, Tony, I won't. You gotta be ready for this. Erica may even be dead. If she is, I have to know you're gonna be able to keep your head. My life, and yours, will depend on it."

Tony stepped back and looked at his friend. He said, "You're right, of course. I promise, I'll be ready. I won't let my anger screw up whatever brilliant plan we devise."

"Good. Now I'm gonna lie down and try to rest until he calls.

Some jerk with a drinking problem kept me up half the night. Feel free to wake me if you come up with that brilliant plan—or any plan at all."

***

While Doug lay on the bed with his eyes closed, Tony sat in a chair and stared out the window. He had faced mortal danger before and survived. However, the first time a paid killer had held him captive, he'd been rescued by Rich Davis; the second time he was nearly killed, his sister had intervened and had prevented his death long enough for Ben to lead the authorities to where he was being held. In short, Tony had always survived because the people around him were smart, brave, and willing to act.

As he thought about a plan to save Erica and stop Costello, he knew the same would be true. Success or failure would fall on the shoulders of his accomplice. He stole a glance at Doug and quickly looked away again.

***

Tony was scared. He stood facing the steel mesh door of a construction elevator. Costello's instructions had been to take the elevator to the eleventh floor. Tony knew it was possible he wouldn't leave the elevator alive. Costello could simply be waiting at the top, ready to shoot him when he arrived. He hoped the man's cruel nature would cause him to act more slowly, to extract a pound of flesh before putting Tony down for good. If so, they at least had a chance.

Tony waited another few minutes. He had to give Doug time to climb eleven flights of stairs. It was dark, as dark as it ever gets on the east side of Manhattan. Tony was wearing blue jeans and a jacket. The warm spring breeze didn't require one, but there was some comfort in being less exposed as he contemplated entering the concrete-and-steel shell of the high-rise construction site.

There was also some comfort in knowing he had been right. As Tony had planned for their encounter with Costello, he assumed it would be inside a building under construction. He didn't believe Costello would risk moving Erica, so he would bring Tony to the site in the photograph, the unfinished building with the exposed I-beams.

His phone buzzed. Tony glanced at it and saw a text message. *Stop dicking around. Get your ass up here.* Tony stepped into the elevator, pulled the cage door shut, and pushed the UP button. The elevator shuddered and began its slow climb.

When he saw the number 11 painted on the steel beam, he pushed STOP. Two men he hadn't seen before were waiting on the other side of the cage. One was dark-skinned and huge, with a fleshy face and a close-cropped beard. He wore a dark suit and held a revolver in his hand. The other was a non-descript white man with neatly trimmed graying hair. He was dressed in slacks and a pale blue button-down Oxford. He could have been an insurance salesman or a store clerk or an Iowa farmer. Tony could see no weapon on him, but the man held a radio—or was it a remote control?—in his right hand. He kept it down at his side so Tony couldn't see it clearly.

The smaller man spoke. "Put your hands on your head."

Tony did.

"Take one step forward and stop."

Tony did.

The insurance salesman quickly stepped up and Tony assumed he would now be searched. Instead, the man's hand came up to Tony's neck, and instantly Tony felt his body convulse and fall to the floor as fifty thousand volts of electricity assaulted his muscles. He was unable to move and completely helpless as the man casually slipped handcuffs around his wrists.

Costello's jeering voice came out of the dark. "Drag him over here. Let him reunite with his girlfriend before he dies."

The larger man grabbed the back of Tony's jacket and dragged him across the floor. Copper pipes and other construction materials were ignored, and Tony heard his pant leg tear as he was pulled over the top of a drainpipe protruding above the surface of the concrete. He couldn't feel any pain and couldn't have cried out if he had.

"Easy, man," Costello said. "We don't want his skin all bruised before I peel it off with my razor." Tony's heart was pounding so hard, he wondered if people on the street below could hear it.

"Put him in the chair."

The man grabbed Tony's arm and lifted him off the floor. That pain, he could feel. He was dropped into a portable cloth-and-wood folding chair like those used on movie sets.

Costello stepped up, swung, and struck an enormous blow to Tony's gut, knocking him and the chair over backwards.

"Just wanted you to know this is not going to be a fun night for you," Costello hissed.

Why is it always my gut? Tony asked himself as he struggled to breathe. The combination of muscles still recovering from the taser and Costello's fist to his gut were making it nearly impossible. He feared he would black out.

"Ethan, I thought I told you to put Mr. Harrington in the chair."

The big man smiled and again grabbed Tony's arm and wrenched him up and into the seat.

"Search him, Mickey."

This time, it was the insurance salesman who stepped up. He was very thorough. Tony was pretty sure he couldn't have gotten past him with a pea shooter, or even just the pea, let alone a gun.

The insurance salesman stood up, looked at Costello, and shook his head.

Costello asked, "Where's your gun, Tony?"

"What gun?"

Costello stepped up and slapped him hard across the face. The blow knocked Tony sideways, and he could taste blood in his mouth, but he managed to stay seated.

"Don't fuck with me, Harrington. Your Walther. Where is it?"

How the hell does he know what kind of gun I carry? "I'm not dumb enough to come here with my gun."

"Well, forgive me if I disagree," Costello said. "But you're pretty damn dumb to come here at all, don't you think? After what you did to me, you're gonna have the pleasure of seeing your balls on a platter before you die. Whaddaya think about that?"

Tony didn't risk an answer. His pain was growing, and the fear had become physical. He couldn't get his legs to stop shaking.

Costello stepped back and said, "Boys, you can go now. This is gonna take a while, and I think I can handle an unarmed and handcuffed farm boy."

The two men nodded, strode to the elevator, and disappeared as the metal cage carried them down.

Tony's heart leapt. With Costello's muscle gone, maybe he and Doug really did have a chance to survive this.

Costello continued, "Besides, I don't want too many people watching when I rape and mutilate Tony's beautiful young girlfriend over there." Costello was nodding to Tony's left.

Tony turned his head and saw Erica about thirty feet away, still sitting in her underwear with her back up against the steel pillar. As soon as their eyes met, Erica dropped her head and stared at the floor. Tony's rage and disgust flared, but he fought them back.

"Don't fret, Tony. I'm gonna start with you. I'm gonna make sure I inflict as much pain as possible before you die."

"No, you're not!" The shout came from the left. Costello whipped his head around and saw a part of man's face from behind the pillar and an arm holding a gun. The gun was pointed at Erica's head.

"What the f...?"

Doug shouted again. "We know who she is! We know you can't hurt her! We know she's been helping you!"

Tony stood up on shaky legs. "Unlock these cuffs and give me your gun, Costello."

Costello spun and struck out. This time, Tony was ready. He ducked down and in. Costello's fist only caught a wisp of hair as it passed his head. Tony simultaneously kicked down on the side of Costello's leg. Costello cried in pain and fell to his right. As he hit the floor, his gun skidded across the concrete.

Tony jumped on top of him, one knee landing on Costello's left forearm. Tony heard a crack, and Costello screamed again. Tony was ready to declare victory, but this wasn't the dojang. Costello was enraged and fighting to get up.

Tony said, "Stop! If you hurt me, my friend over there is gonna blow Erica's—or should I say Angelica's—brains all over the place. We know she's your cousin, and you don't want that." Tony could see Costello's muscles tense, preparing for a strike, so he said, "It's over for you anyway. Don't you wonder how we know about Angelica? My boss told me."

"Your boss? What the hell are you talking about?"

"My boss called and told me all about Angelica. He knows about her because the FBI told him."

Costello's eyes narrowed. "The FBI? You're full of shit."

"I'm not. They showed him a picture of you and Angelica with other members of the family. It's only a matter of time before they come for you."

Costello's face turned beet red, and his fist came up from his position on the floor and caught Tony's temple, sending him over onto his side. Costello was quickly back on his feet and heading for his gun.

"I'm warning you!" Tony screamed.

Costello stooped down, picked up the gun, and stood. In a surprisingly calm voice, he said, "Bullshit. It's all BS. And I dunno who's behind that pillar with a gun, but if he's a pal of yours, he ain't gonna kill nobody. Besides, if he did, his life and yours wouldn't be worth the grease smear on your farm-boy jeans. If you know who she is, you know I'm right. So nice try, but Shut. The fuck. Up."

Costello walked over to Tony, who had managed to get into a sitting position, his hands still cuffed behind his back. Costello clicked off the safety and put his gun against Tony's head. He said, "If you knew Angelica was working with me, why did you come? If the feds were coming for me, why not just leave?"

Trying to maintain his composure with steel pressed against his scalp, Tony said, "I had to be sure your threat was a fake. I had to be sure you wouldn't really hurt her."

"Well, good job, farm boy. You're right. I'm not gonna hurt the little angel." Then he yelled, "Farm boy number two! Come outta there. If I don't have that gun in my pocket in three seconds, I'm gonna end your friend's life right now."

Doug stayed where he was. His voice was unsteady as he yelled back, "You're right. I don't wanna shoot the girl. But if you hurt Tony, I will shoot her and you. After what she's done to Tony, and what you've done to lots of people, I won't even regret it. I know how to use this. One thing we farm boys know how to do is shoot."

Costello laughed out loud. "You're trying to scare me? You little shit. I'm gonna enjoy watching both of you suffer."

"Wait!" The voice was Angelica's.

"I thought I told you to stay quiet," Costello barked.

"Just let me say goodbye. Please."

"Jesus. I knew it. Make it fast." Costello's gun never wavered, and his eyes never left Tony as Angelica stood up and walked over to them.

Tony wondered what Doug was thinking as he let her go, but he wasn't surprised to see that she hadn't actually been secured to the pillar. *She was probably fully dressed and enjoying a cappuccino or some damn thing until she and Costello heard me arrive downstairs.*

She knelt next to Tony. She was crying. "I'm so sorry."

Tony's voice sounded as dead as a corpse speaking from the grave. He said, "Save it. You lied. You set me up. And now you've killed me. I don't want to hear your pathetic attempt to make yourself feel better. Just go away and enjoy your perfect life."

"Good advice," Costello smirked. "Now get outta the way, Angelica. I got work to do."

Angelica's head drooped and Tony's eyes naturally followed the motion down. He was astounded to see his Walther cradled in Angelica's lap. Costello was standing to one side, his view of the gun blocked by her back. Angelica nodded once at Tony, the pleading in her eyes shifting to determination. She stood, moving carefully to ensure she didn't reveal what she held.

Costello shifted on his feet, expecting her to turn and walk away. Instead, she spun a full one-eighty and drew the Walther up. The barrel came to rest on his cheek, pointed up due to their difference in heights.

"Let him go," she said shakily.

"You whore," he growled. "What do you think you're doing?"

"I may be a whore, but I'm not a murderer. At least not yet. But I will kill you if you don't drop that gun and let him go."

Costello didn't reply. He acted. His left hand, now swollen from the damage Tony had done with his knee, shot up and knocked Angelica's hand away, as his right hand moved his revolver from Tony's head to Angelica's face. He screamed, "I'll teach you to point a gun at me."

The sound was thunderous, amplified by the bare concrete surfaces. Tony screamed in horror and shock as he saw Angelica fall back, her torso spattered in blood. Then, to his surprise, her fall was followed by Costello, who pitched forward onto the floor, face first.

Stunned confusion seemed to freeze time as Tony struggled to comprehend what had just happened. Doug ran toward him, then stopped, raising his hands and staring past Tony into the dark. Tony and Angelica both turned their heads and saw the henchman, Micky, as he stepped out of the shadows carrying a large pistol.

He strode up to Costello and kicked his gun across the concrete. As he knelt to check his pulse, he said, "Angelica, are you okay?"

"No." Her voice was soft, almost a whimper. Mickey looked up. She said, "I think your bullet passed through Robbie and lodged in my rib cage. It hurts like hell."

Mickey said, "Just lie back and stay still. I'll check you soon. Costello's still alive, so I need to finish this."

"Wait." Costello spoke, his voice distorted by the concrete pressed against his face and the blood oozing from his mouth. "Mickey, we're friends. What the hell?"

"Sorry, Robbie, but the old man gave the order himself. Seems some guy from Iowa found out you've been killing girls. Not sanctioned hits but some kinda rape and murder thing. You know the family can't let that happen."

"That damn farm boy. Unbelievable," Costello wheezed. His eyes moved to look at Tony. "All because of what happened in Amalfi, right?"

"Yeah, that's right," Tony said. "Once I realized you killed Noemi, I couldn't just let it go. If you'd left her alone, I never would have come."

Costello convulsed, and Tony realized he was laughing. "Fuck me," he said. "No good deed goes unpunished."

Before he could stop himself, Tony asked, "No good deed…?"

"What I did in Italy was the only good thing I've ever done in my life," he said. He convulsed again, this time coughing up blood.

Tony's anger rose. "What are you talking about?"

"I'm telling you, farm boy, I didn't kill her." He paused, gasped for air, and grunted, "If I would've just told everyone what happened, you wouldn't be here, and I wouldn't be…tasting my own…blood now." Costello's voice shifted from rasp to gurgle. "I tried to protect him, and look where it got me."

"Protect who?" Tony sounded incredulous. The idea that the real killer might still be out there was incomprehensible. He didn't believe it. He couldn't believe. It would be more than he could bear. "Dammit, don't lie to me," Tony hissed through clenched teeth.

"It don't matter now," Costello said. "You got your pound of flesh. Now, go fly…" He coughed, then fell silent.

Mickey leaned forward and pressed his fingers to Costello's neck. "He's dead," he said. He moved to Angelica's side. Then, looking at Doug, he said, "There's a black bag sitting on the floor near the wall behind me. Grab it for me."

Doug looked at Tony, who nodded.

"Hurry up!"

Doug trotted to the wall, found the bag in the dark, and carried it back.

"You'll find some forceps and bandages inside. I came prepared."

Doug pulled more from the bag than was probably needed.

Mickey grabbed the forceps from the pile and proceeded to remove the slug from Angelica's flesh, just below her left breast. She gasped, but did not cry out.

"You were lucky," Mickey said. "The bullet may have cracked a rib, but it didn't penetrate beyond the surface of the bone. This will heal quickly."

"Yeah, I feel lucky," Angelica said through gritted teeth.

Mickey quickly applied bandages and instructed her to lie still as he injected her with a painkiller.

"I'm sorry, but it's a small dose," he told her. "I need you functional while we get this mess cleaned up." Angelica nodded and remained on her back.

Mickey turned his attention to Tony, instructing him to turn around so he could remove the handcuffs. Mickey then grabbed a terrycloth towel from the pile of materials Doug had taken from the bag. He reached behind his back and removed his gun from under his sweater. Tony and Doug both stiffened, and Mickey said, "Relax. Do exactly what I tell you, and you'll get back to Iowa in one piece."

He carefully wiped down the pistol and held it out to Tony.

Tony reared back, as if a hot branding iron had been thrust at him.

"Take it," Mickey said. "It's the only way you leave here alive."

Tony took the gun in two fingers.

"Hold it as if you're going to shoot me. But please don't. None of this works if I'm not around to take care of it."

Tony sighed, grasped the gun in a firing position, and asked, "Now what?"

"Slip it back into the holster." Mickey turned his back until he felt Tony slide the gun into place. He turned back.

"Okay, here's what's going to happen. No questions, no deviations, no screw-ups. Okay?"

"Tell us," Tony said tersely.

Mickey laid it out, all neat and tidy. Costello's body would not be found. It would be made to look as if he skipped town after learning the police were on his trail. Only Mickey and Mr. Montagna would know where the body was hidden. The slug would be with the body. Mr. Montagna would keep the gun in a safe place.

Tony would never bother the Montagna family again. If he did, the police would receive an anonymous package, containing the gun, Tony's name, and the location of the body. It would be easy to convict Tony of Costello's murder. The police already knew Tony was obsessed with bringing Costello to justice. They had pictures of the fight between Costello and Tony outside the bar. Ethan and Mickey would both testify they saw Tony here with Costello, and Tony's fingerprints on the gun would seal his fate.

"Very neat," Tony said grimly, hating the thought of living with a sword of Damocles hanging over his head for the rest of his life.

"I know you don't like it, but frankly, tough shit. It's this or you join Costello in the foundation of one of Montagna's buildings. You choose."

"I get it," Tony said. "I'll leave. Tell Mr. Montagna we have a deal."

"And you," Mickey turned and stared at Doug. "You're not supposed to be here. You could really mess up this whole deal."

Doug began to protest, but Mickey cut him off.

"Relax. I've decided I'm going to cut you both a break, and God help me, I'm going to trust you. So the deal is simple—you were never here. As far as I know, no one knows you're even in town. Angelica told us you'd gone home. So I'm not telling anyone you were here. I'm not sure Montagna would do this deal if he knew there was another witness. Angelica, I'm trusting you want these young men to live. I mean want it badly enough to never tell the family I kept this from them."

"Absolutely." She spoke quietly, but with resolve.

"And you?" he looked back to Doug. "You want to stay alive? You're never going to breathe a word of this to anyone?"

"I swear on my father's Peterbilt," Doug said.

"What? Never mind." Mickey turned back to Tony. "Looks like we have a deal, Mr. Harrington. Now go away and let me deal with my dead friend."

Tony nodded, walked over, retrieved his gun off of the floor next to Angelica, and slipped it into his pocket. He turned, took Doug by the arm, and briskly headed for the staircase.

"Tony!" Angelica called after him.

Tony froze, then turned. She had hoisted herself up onto her elbows. She was still spattered with blood. Her hair was matted from sweat, and the dark makeup simulating the bruises still covered half her face. *How can anyone look like that and still be so beautiful?* he wondered.

She said just loud enough for him to hear, "I really am sorry. You're such a great...I really...oh you know." She began to sob. "I know you'll never believe me, but I really do care for you. I didn't want to help Robbie. He forced me to do it."

Her words did little to ease the anger or the hurt.

"It was all a charade, right from the start, wasn't it?" he called back across the expanse of concrete. "Meeting me at the ticket booth was no accident, right? You slept with me because they told you to, right?" Tony didn't wait for answers. He knew the truth now, and the pain of it was more than any punch to the stomach or slap in the face. He also knew it was still true that if she managed to say something to make him feel better, it would only make it harder to walk away. He turned and headed down the stairs.

Chapter 31

Orney, Iowa

"Bart? It's Ben. I have a plan. You still interested?"

Bart Mason at the bank said he was.

"I think you'll like it. I've negotiated a deal that's going to make a real difference in my bottom line. I'm gonna need some capital, but…Hang on, hear me out. This is a solid business deal. I promise you're going to agree with me that it's a game-changer for the *Crier*. I haven't had a chance to write a fancy business plan, but I have all the facts and numbers in front of me. Can I come see you?"

Mason said yes, of course. Ben slid the stack of papers into an old briefcase and snapped the lid closed. He started out the door but turned back and grabbed the red editing pencil off his desk. "For good luck," he said, smiling, as he slipped it behind his ear.

***

Tony stared at the blank screen of his computer. He didn't have writer's block. He'd never been cursed with that affliction. He was, however, struggling with the fact he couldn't write a word about what had happened to him in Italy and New York. It was a remarkable story, and being forced to keep it to himself was driving him crazy.

As Ben walked by, carrying a hot cup of coffee from the break room, he asked, "You doing okay?"

"Yeah. Well, mostly." He looked up at his boss. "I had a great interview with Saxman Bells this morning. It'll make a nice feature. I even got an audio clip to include with our online version."

Ben nodded his approval and said, "Maybe it's time to have a couple of beers at the Iron Range and debrief a little. Tonight?"

"Yeah, thanks. I'd like that."

It was Monday afternoon, and Tony and Doug had only been back in Orney for a week. It felt great to be home, but Tony was still unsettled. The adrenaline drain, the devastation over losing another woman he cared for deeply, and the lack of sleep had combined to render him a physical and mental wreck.

On the previous Tuesday, he had called Powell at *The New York Times* to turn down the job offer. Powell had been cordial but had clearly communicated he thought Tony was making a big mistake. As Tony gazed out the big windows at the front of the Crier building, he wondered if Powell was right. Tony noticed the sun had disappeared. It was beginning to rain. *Perfect.* He took a deep breath, sat up straight, and began to type just as Rich Davis came through the door.

"Hey, Tony! Welcome home!" the DCI agent called from across the room, brushing droplets of water from the shoulders of his suit.

Tony waved.

Instead of coming to Tony's desk, Davis headed for Ben's office, motioning to Tony to come join him. After Tony walked over and passed through the door, Davis pushed it closed behind him.

Ben looked up at the two men. "Hey, Rich. Welcome. Whose meeting is it this time?"

"It's mine," Davis said. "Well, actually, it's Lieutenant Coppestad's at the NYPD."

Ben's eyebrows went up, and Tony immediately tensed.

Davis pretended not to notice and handed Ben a slip of paper. "Here's a Zoom link to pull up on your computer. Our friends in blue back in New York have some information they'd like to share with you."

Ben opened the program and punched in the number. Almost immediately, a picture of a meeting room appeared on the screen. Tony came around Ben's desk to watch, with Davis right beside him.

Seated at a conference table in New York were Coppestad and four others—three men and a woman.

When Coppestad spoke, the picture immediately changed to feature his image.

"Agent Davis, good morning. Mr. Harrington, nice to see you again."

Tony was surprised. Coppestad almost sounded like he meant it.

The lieutenant continued. "I assume the third person in the office is Ben Smalley, yes? Nice to meet you, Mr. Smalley. Your reputation precedes you. My name is Lieutenant Keith Coppestad. Perhaps Tony has told you I'm one of the team leaders in the Major Cases Squad of the NYPD."

"Thanks," Ben said, "I know Tony met with you, but that's about it." He shot Tony a sidelong glance. "What can we do for you all?"

Before Coppestad spoke again, the man next to him leaned over, touched his arm, and spoke into his ear.

"Ah, yes," Coppestad said. "I've been reminded to make sure

you're the only ones in the room, and that no one else is connected to this call. I don't mean to go all Spookville on you, but we have to be sure we know who's hearing this."

"No worries," Ben said. "It's just the three of us. So...?"

"Well, we decided you and Tony should have this story first, since Tony led us to it. We're holding a press conference tomorrow morning at 9 a.m. Eastern. If I have your word you won't publish until tomorrow morning, I'll share some important information with you now."

Ben looked to Tony, hoping he knew enough about what was happening to have an opinion about the embargo. Tony didn't hesitate. "Yes. Say yes."

"Okay, Lieutenant, you have our word. Fire away."

Coppestad told them that on Friday, his task force had gone to the apartment of Roberto Costello in Manhattan with a search warrant. They had obtained the warrant based, in part, on information Tony had shared with them while in New York. Once they began looking into Costello's background, their suspicions grew. For example, how did a man with no apparent job live like a millionaire? They also knew he was related to the Montagna crime family, so they kept digging. They got lucky and found one woman who was willing to acknowledge that Costello had abused her. That was enough for a judge to approve the warrant.

They had found the apartment empty. Not just empty, but wiped completely clean. "Someone was very determined to make sure nothing was found in that apartment. We couldn't even find a stray hair in a drainpipe."

"Wow," Davis said from behind Tony. "That takes a real effort."

"Yeah, no kidding," Coppestad said. "Word on the street is that Costello heard we were looking at him as a suspect in a string of murders here, so he skipped town."

"And?" Ben asked, knowing the NYPD hadn't set up a teleconference just to tell him that they hadn't found anything.

Coppestad drew a breath and said, "And the woman told us Costello has a storage unit he rents in Brooklyn. Apparently, he stopped there the night she was in the car with him. He had put something in her drink, causing her to pass out. He must have thought she was still unconscious, and she never told him any differently. Turns out that was smart. She might not be alive today if he had known she'd seen the storage facility."

"Really?" Davis expressed his surprise.

"We got another warrant on Saturday, found the storage unit, and discovered everything."

"Everything?" It was Ben this time.

"Yes. Like many serial killers, Costello kept souvenirs from his victims. We're not revealing exactly what those were, but I can tell you we found clear evidence tying him to the murders of nineteen young women in five different states."

"Nineteen!" The number hit Tony like a shock wave.

"Yes. It's as horrific a situation as I've ever seen. But to you all, and to Tony especially, I have to say thanks. Because of him, nineteen families now know what happened to their daughters, sisters, cousins. Tony has given these families a precious gift—closure."

Everyone was looking at Tony as he leaned back against the wall behind Ben's desk, not knowing what to think or say.

Coppestad spoke again, "And Mr. Smalley, I want you to know, to my great embarrassment, we didn't make it easy for him. Tony showed real courage and no small amount of bull-headedness in bringing Costello to our attention and forcing us to look at him."

"No surprise there," Ben said. "Anything else?"

"Well, we'll send an encrypted email to you with the victims' names, cities from which they disappeared, and dates of their disappearances. Again, that's all we're releasing for now."

Ben said, "We appreciate it. It was kind of you to think of us out here. If you catch the bastard, I wouldn't mind another call."

"I will. Now we know who he is, we can get his picture out to everyone. I'm sure we'll get him, but even if we don't, we should be able to put him out of business. He won't dare show his face in public."

Expressions of appreciation were shared again, from all quarters, and the group ended the teleconference. Tony and Davis found their way back to the chairs in front of Ben's desk. As they settled in, Ben turned to Tony and said, "You found a serial killer. You went to a funeral and ended up chasing a serial killer. Good grief."

Tony didn't say anything, and Ben continued, "So this is the guy who also killed your cousin? I'm surprised you didn't mention it to Coppestad."

"Oh, I did, when I first went to see him in New York. I think he didn't bring it up because he doesn't need one more murder, especially one that occurred in a foreign country, complicating his case."

Davis nodded. "Makes sense."

"And besides," Tony said, "I'm not sure anymore that Costello killed Noemi."

The two men's jaws dropped. Tony would have enjoyed the effect if the facts hadn't been weighing on him so heavily. Of course, he couldn't tell them the whole story. He simply said that when he and Costello had fought, Costello had told him that he hadn't killed Noemi. Tony wasn't inclined to believe him until Costello referenced "doing the right thing" by not stepping up and telling him what had really happened.

"You're buying his story?" Ben asked, not as an accusation, but with genuine curiosity.

Tony shook his head and admitted, "I don't know what to believe. Considering what an evil bastard Costello was…is, it's easy to believe he killed my cousin. On the other hand, the way he expressed his denial, I don't know anymore. It just sounded like the truth. I'm torn. Sadly, I'll probably never know."

Ben nodded and said, "You may be right, but try not to let it fester. And," Ben's face brightened, "you can take your mind off it by helping me write a great article for tomorrow's paper."

Tony smiled. "Roger that."

Town Crier

Crier reporter's tip leads New York police to serial killer

Police say 19 murders of young women likely solved

Ben Smalley, Editor

New York, NY – A tip from Tony Harrington, a reporter for the *Orney Town Crier*, has helped New York police solve 19 cases of young women and girls killed in, or missing from, locations in five different states, NYPD Lt. Keith Coppestad told the *Town Crier* in an exclusive interview on Monday.

Information supplied by Harrington caused the NYPD Major Cases Squad to obtain a warrant to search an apartment and storage unit leased by a Roberto "Robbie" Costello of Manhattan, New York.

In the storage unit, located on the west side of Brooklyn, NY, police found evidence Costello was involved in the disappearances and likely murders of 19 young women and girls, some as young as 15 years of age. The searches were conducted this past Friday and Saturday.

Coppestad said Costello's apartment had been emptied and "wiped clean," indicating he has fled to avoid capture. A warrant has been issued for his arrest, and his picture has been distributed to news media organizations and law enforcement agencies all over the country. Coppestad expressed confidence that Costello will be found and prosecuted for his alleged crimes.

Coppestad said police in various jurisdictions had recovered about ten of the young women's bodies previously, in cases where the killer had left them in places where they could be found. As a result of the information discovered Saturday, police have recovered another six bodies, Coppestad said. "Sadly, it appears all of the missing women and girls were killed," he said.

Harrington said he reported Costello to the Major Cases Squad of the NYPD after observing him with a young woman on the night the girl was killed.

"I didn't really do anything, except what any good citizen would do," Harrington said. "I happened to be in the right place at the right time. When I suspected I had observed something important, I told the police about it. The NYPD gets all the credit for following through and bringing closure to the families affected by these tragedies."

Coppestad said a task force formed to find the serial killer has been expanded temporarily to include officers from the other jurisdictions involved in the...

***

Tony was playing the upright piano in the back room at the Iron Range when Doug and Ben walked in together. They were chatting like old friends, smiling and enjoying an occasional laugh. It made Tony wonder what was up. He finished his jazzed-up version of Todd

Rundgren's "Hello, It's Me," closed the cover over the piano keys, and carried his Diet Dr. Pepper over to his friends' table.

"You two are looking chummy tonight. What's going on? Did Ben finally hire an obit writer for the *Crier*?"

Doug laughed, looked at Ben, who laughed, too, and said, "In a word, yes!"

Tony plopped down in a third seat and said, "What?"

Ben said, "I'm sorry I didn't tell you sooner, Tony. I meant to. But the leadership at the radio station spilled the beans to their employees a full two days before the date we had agreed we would make it public."

Tony was baffled. "What are you talking about?"

Ben said, "I bought the radio station. KKAR. I signed the papers Friday."

"What? Really?"

"Yes, really. As you know, I've been struggling to make the *Crier* work financially. Hell, print media all over the world is struggling. Then I had this idea: if I could combine the radio and print enterprises, we could save a ton of money. One newsroom, one website, one advertising sales staff, one accounting department...It goes on and on."

It made complete sense to Tony, and he acknowledged so with a smile and a nod. Then he said, "What about the government? Won't the FCC or the FTC or one of those wagons full of bureaucrats want to prevent this? I thought they didn't like it when media consolidated."

Ben pursed his lips, then said, "Historically that's been true, but look at the mega-mergers of media companies that have occurred. I'm hoping this will be a small enough deal the powers that be won't give us a second glance. Hell, I'm more than hoping. I'm moving forward with the assumption no one will squawk. If someone does, we'll just have to deal with it."

"Any other downside we...I mean you, will have to consider?"

"Saying 'we' is just fine by me," Ben said. "I need you guys fully on the team. And in answer to your question, yes. Combining the two businesses means some people will lose their jobs. I hate to see that in a town like Orney, or anywhere, but it means we can keep the best people from each organization and really make this operation something special." He was revving up again, sounding like a kid who's been told the Avengers are real and they want him to join up. "And think about it from the merchants' point of view. We can offer our advertisers more comprehensive packages for less money. Most importantly, if this works, I can keep both the newspaper and the radio station in business."

Tony looked at his boss. He had to ask, "Was it really that bad? Were we at risk of closing?"

Ben ran his hand through his hair "I dunno. Maybe not closed down completely, but we were this close"—he held up his thumb and index finger, spaced a quarter-inch apart—"to having to cut staff and start functioning more like a small-town weekly paper rather than a legitimate daily."

"And if that had happened, you'd be gone, right?" Tony didn't know why he was pushing his boss. He feared his pissy mood was interfering in what should be a celebration, but he couldn't help himself.

Fortunately, Ben didn't seem to mind. He said, "Frankly, gentlemen, yes. I love Orney. I really do. But I can't see myself settling for a second-rate product. If I couldn't afford to hire and keep great people like the two of you, then I'd have to go somewhere else where I could."

Doug was practically dancing in his seat. He held up his beer. "Here's to the new Ben Smalley enterprise, and the reporting team of Harrington and Tenney." They clinked bottles and drank. "I would have insisted on Tenney and Harrington, but I'm feeling generous tonight."

They laughed, the slight dig jostling Tony out of his mood, but only a little.

***

At 2 a.m., Tony was still wide awake. He couldn't stop thinking about it all: Costello's crimes, witnessing the murder, his own close call with death, everything he owed his friend Doug, his affection and devotion to Ben, and the rescue—please, God, let this work—of the *Crier*. He also thought about Angelica. Even getting used to thinking of her with that name was difficult. *How many times did I whisper 'Erica' as we were making love? Was she laughing at me the whole time? Was she really no better than a prostitute, using her body to keep her position in the family and the benefits that come from that?* He almost couldn't bear to contemplate the answers to those questions.

And of course he thought of Noemi. He was still devastated by the knowledge he would never again sit with her in the warm Italian sun, laughing about his latest misuse of the language or admiring her as she danced. *What had happened that day? Costello was there. She died. Was it really an accident? No, that's not what Costello had said. He'd said he had done a good deed by not telling people what had really happened. If he wasn't the one who had killed her, and it wasn't an accident, then what was the real answer? What the hell happened that day? And how could a dying man be so... God, I don't know what to call it. And why the bizarre comment at the end? He told me to go fly...*

Wait. Tony sat up. *Oh, my God.*

Chapter 32

Amalfi, Italy

It was mid-morning the following Friday. The sun was shining on the front steps of the Hotel Santa Caterina. Tony marveled at the perfect weather. He knew the sun didn't always shine. If it never rained, the mountains wouldn't look so green, and the flowers wouldn't be so beautiful. However, in all his trips here, he had rarely seen dark skies and rain. *Do magical elves come out in the middle of the night and spray their elixir on everything? I wouldn't be surprised.*

It hadn't been easy to convince Ben to let him return to Italy so quickly. The *Crier* really did need its senior reporter, especially in light of the attention the article about the New York murders was getting and the announcement about the acquisition of the radio station. Tony also suspected Ben was worried he was off on another attempt to find Noemi's killer. Tony had finally convinced him this was not the case. He had simply left some family business unfinished in Amalfi, and it needed his attention right away.

Tony smiled broadly when he saw Montay waiting for him in front of the taxi at the edge of the sidewalk.

"Welcome back, my friend. I heard you came in last night. I was hoping to drive you today. Where to? Enzo's? The Don's? The inside of Mount Etna?"

Tony laughed. "No, Montay. No active volcanos today. In fact, we face no dangers today, except from overeating and sunburn."

"Wonderful! To Enzo's then."

"Yes, and you'll join me at the table for breakfast. Then I have an important task to do."

After stuffing themselves appropriately with omelets, pastries, fresh fruit, and juice, Tony and Montay waddled back to the taxi.

"Okay, boss. Where now? I know a nice coffee shop with bagels and cheeses—much wonderful."

"You're joking."

"Yes, joking. So?"

"Take me to the school. It's nearly lunch time, and I want to say hello to Amedeo."

Twenty minutes later, Tony returned to the cab waiting outside the school and told Montay, "Amedeo didn't show up for school today. They called his home, and he's not there, either. We need to find him."

"Perhaps the Cathedral? He often goes there to practice the piano."

Tony was glad to hear it. "Let's try it."

But once again, they struck out. The piano was silent, and no one they asked had seen Amedeo all morning.

Tony leaned back in the passenger seat of the cab. He was riding in the front now. "Think," he said aloud.

Montay hummed quietly while he awaited instructions.

Suddenly Tony sat upright. "Shit!"

"An idea? Apparently a bad idea?"

"The seawall. Get me down the mountain to the seawall as fast as you can. To the spot where Noemi died."

Montay didn't reply. He simply put the cab in gear and stomped on the gas.

Minutes later, the cab screeched to a halt and Tony jumped out, telling Montay to stay inside. His fears were realized. Amedeo was standing atop the wall, facing the sun, his eyes closed.

Tony approached him slowly and quietly.

Without opening his eyes, Amedeo said, "Stop there."

Tony stopped. Amedeo was just a couple of meters away. So close, but still too far to risk lunging at him.

Amedeo said, "Walking to school this morning, I heard you were back."

Jeez, how fast does news travel in this town? "Good morning, my friend. It's good to see you too. Your English is still excellent."

"Yes. Very good. Thanks to my friend Noemi." Amedeo opened his eyes as tears leaked onto his cheeks. He looked down over the far side of the wall, watching and hearing the waves crash into the rocks.

"Amedeo, look at me."

The child turned toward the voice.

Tony said, "I know what happened. I know everything. And it's going to be okay."

"Of course you know. That is why you come back. All will not be okay. All is terrible. I did not want you to know. I did not want Signora Moretti to know. Now they will take me away." He looked back down into the surf.

"Take you away? No, no. No, Amedeo. I came back to tell you it's okay. It was not your fault."

The child screamed back at him. "It was my fault. She was a...

a beautiful dancer. A perfect dancer. I came, and she fell."

"Amedeo, listen to me. It was the kite, wasn't it? You wanted to show her the kite."

"Yes..." He began to cry. "I came here to see her. To show her. The wind pulled it from my hand. She tried to grab it. She fell, and now she's dead! It was me"

"No, Amedeo. You cannot be blamed for the wind. You cannot be blamed for her mistake. It was an accident. A terrible, horrible tragedy. Now it's over, and we have to live our lives."

"I don't want to live. I want to die. I can be with her if I die, yes?"

"Amedeo, do you remember her funeral?" Tony was desperately trying to think of something to bring him down off the wall before he jumped or before the wind claimed another innocent victim.

"Yes, I do. You played for her."

"That's right. But do you remember all the people who were there? Remember how the whole town grieved at losing her?"

"Yes. She was loved."

"You are loved too, Amedeo."

"Not like her."

"Yes, like her. And I can prove it to you."

Amedeo looked puzzled, and Tony continued, "Do you think you weren't seen that day? You think no one knows what happened? You're wrong. Everyone knows what happened. The woman in the shop across the street saw you. She wouldn't tell me because she loves you and didn't want you to suffer for a silly accident. The other merchants further up the hill, they wouldn't tell me what happened. They told me to forget it. They urged me to go home because they love you." As he spoke, the truth of what he was saying dawned on Tony. "Even the polizia know what happened. The chief himself wouldn't tell me what he knew. He wanted to protect you. *You,* Amedeo. And finally, a very bad man who was after Noemi—who had followed her here from America—he was watching when it happened, and even *he* protected you. He kept your secret even though it cost him dearly."

"So what? How does that help?"

"Amedeo, all of these people protected you because they care about you. They want you to live a long and happy and successful life. They will be devastated if you die. If you take the easy road, the road that leads over the wall and into the rocks below, it will be a very selfish thing. Do you think Noemi would want you to be selfish?"

"No, she wouldn't... no."

"Do you think Noemi wants you to suffer because of her accident?"

"Well, no, I guess not."

"So come over here to me, and let's go honor Noemi's memory by having a gelato and listening to you play the piano."

The tiniest of smiles crept into the corners of his mouth. "Will you play first?"

"Absolutely." Tony smiled and held out his hand, and Amedeo jumped into his arms.

***

Tony's Aunt Martina was astonished to see Tony standing with Amedeo at her door. "Tony! You back! Come in! Come in!" She turned in toward the kitchen. "Carlotta! Tony is back!"

Tony's mother stepped into the hall from the kitchen, saw Tony, and rushed to him with her arms outstretched. After what seemed like years of hugs and kisses from both, Tony finally had the opportunity to say, "Aunt Martina. Amedeo has something important to tell you. Can we visit with you alone for a minute?"

The two sisters looked at each other, shrugged, and laughed. "Of course, Tony. Anything for my two favorite men."

When they were seated in a small parlor, Aunt Martina looked to Tony, but he turned to Amedeo and said, "Go ahead. It will be fine. I promise."

Amedeo hesitated, started to say he was sorry, stopped, and started again. "It's about Noemi," he said, tears welling in his eyes. "I was there when she fell. I know what happened. It was my fault."

Martina looked up at Tony sharply. Fire was burning in her cheeks even as her eyes looked confused and questioning.

Tony shook his head quickly and vigorously, and Martina settled back.

"Amedeo. Tell her the whole story."

He did. When he had finished, Martina sat quietly for a long moment, and then said, "Amedeo, come here."

The boy inched slowly off his seat, frightened of what was coming. However, Martina pulled him close, wrapped her arms around him, and spoke into the hair on top his head, "You are a very brave boy, coming here and telling me the truth. You cannot know how good it is for me to know what happened. I have been awake night after night, wondering how could this happen? Thank you, Amedeo. Thank you."

"But I…"

"Hush," Martina said. "It is over now. I can sleep. Noemi can dance with the angels, and Tony can go find a nice Italian girl to marry and make babies for his momma. And you, Amedeo, you can become a great pianist and bring much honor to our village. Will you do that? For me and for Noemi?"

"I will try," he said, wiping tears from his face.

Tony said, "Oh, we can't forget. Amedeo has a gift for you."

The boy smiled and disappeared back into the foyer. He returned with a vase full of flowers he and Tony had picked up from a merchant in the village. "For you," he said proudly.

"Martina took the vase and turned quickly toward the kitchen, hiding her tears from the boy.

"I'll just put these in water and be right back. I have a gift for you too."

Amedeo looked to Tony as if to say, "How can that be?" Tony just shrugged and said nothing.

Soon Martina returned. "Follow me," she said, and led them to the foyer. She opened the armoire and removed the big, beautiful kite Tony had left with her after Amedeo had refused to take it.

This time, he reached out and grasped it firmly, his eyes alive with excitement.

"I kept this for you," Martina said. "Tony gave it to me, and now I give it to you. Every time you launch it into the sky, you will think of Noemi, yes?"

"Yes. I will never forget her. I will never forget any of you. Thank you."

With promises from Tony that they would play the piano together again before he left town, Amedeo was out the door with his kite in tow.

As soon as the door closed, Aunt Martina wrapped her arms around Tony, buried her face in his chest, and cried like a baby.

Chapter 33

Orney, Iowa

Suddenly, it was fall. It had been an eventful summer, long and hot and filled with important news. A tornado had struck a neighboring town. National politicians had begun showing up, building support for their presidential bids in the following winter's Iowa caucuses. The legislature had struggled to reach agreement on a budget, dragging the annual session into July—the longest session in the state's history. And naturally, the merger of the *Crier* and KKAR had resulted in many challenges and opportunities as everyone got used to working in new teams and in new ways.

It was Sunday morning, and Tony was sitting at his desk at home, reading the *Sunday New York Times* online. He preferred reading newsprint, but getting the *Times* online was faster and killed a lot fewer trees.

He stopped short when he saw the headline: "Longtime head of Montagna crime family dies." Tony read the article with obvious interest and learned that Stuffy Montagna apparently had died in his sleep of natural causes. The article went on to describe Montagna's longtime career as a criminal and later as the founder of one of the most powerful crime syndicates in New York. Ironically, the bigger he'd become in the criminal world, the less trouble he'd faced with authorities. He had not been arrested in more than twenty years and had not served jail time in more than forty.

Tony had to admit to being relieved the old man was gone. Now, his sword of Damocles was a little less pointed and aimed a little less directly at his head.

***

The following Thursday, Tony was at his desk, finishing a story about the local college comptroller who'd been caught embezzling, when the delivery woman from UPS stopped at his desk with a package. It was addressed to him and marked "Personal."

Tony signed for it, shook it once for no reason he could articulate, and ripped open the seal. Out of the box and onto his desk, wrapped tightly in clear plastic bubble-wrap, fell a gun. Tony recognized it immediately. It was the gun Mickey had used to kill Costello. The gun that had *his* fingerprints on it.

Tony quickly shoved it back into the box and glanced around to ensure no one had seen it. Double-checking the box, he spotted a simple piece of generic stationery, folded and taped inside the flap. He pulled it off and unfolded it. The note, written in a florid, refined script, simply said, *"You're welcome. Love, Erica."*

Afterword

The Third Side of Murder, I can say honestly, was the most fun to write of the first three Tony Harrington novels. It was, of course, enjoyable to get Tony out of the Midwest and into more exotic settings, such as Italy and New York City. I've been fortunate to travel to both places, and I love them both, so bringing them to you was a genuine pleasure. I hope I did them justice.

It was also interesting to explore the world of organized crime which, fortunately, Iowans rarely encounter. I have no insider knowledge of that world, but I did spend a lot of time researching it. I tried to include enough facts to be realistic without using any real names or sharing anything that will cause one of those enforcers to pay me a visit.

Lastly, I enjoyed creating another love interest for Tony who was different from those in the previous novels. I tried to make her equally compelling but clearly conflicted in multiple ways.

Sadly, the economic challenges of rural Iowa and other parts of America, as described in the book, are very real. As noted, small towns have struggled for most of fifty years. Unfortunately, the larger communities in rural states—communities of 10,000 to 100,000—are now feeling the same drain. The march of technology and chemistry continues, and the number of people needed to work on farms gets smaller and smaller.

I should mention, however, that some cities in Iowa are thriving. As families leave rural communities, they're moving to larger cities and finding work in banking, insurance, technology, manufacturing, and other enterprises. If you're not from Iowa, you may not realize Des Moines is one of the largest centers in the world for banking and insurance, or that central Iowa has become a major hub for the high-tech industry, with large campuses hosting Facebook, Microsoft, Apple, and others, or that some of the highest quality manufacturing occurs here, from companies such as Pella Windows, Vermeer, John Deere, and Sukup Manufacturing.

Yes, I'm proud to be from Iowa, and despite all its challenges, I am optimistic about its future. This is primarily because the good people you read about in these novels—those who care about their neighbors and strive to do what's best for their families and their communities—are the most realistic aspect of my stories. Those people live in Iowa. They are why, when we travel to New York or Italy or anywhere else in the world, just like Tony, we are always happy to come home.

Acknowledgements

As always, I need to thank members of my family for their unwavering support of my work. My children and siblings often are the first readers of a draft novel, and they always provide excellent insights and suggestions. Two of my sons, Luke and Alex, have been particularly helpful recently, covering my routine tasks at home so I can spend more time writing.

I want to thank you, the readers and purchasers of my books. Supporting authors and booksellers is critically important to keeping this aspect of our culture alive. I'm amazed every day that I am able to be a part of this world, and I appreciate you for making it happen. My appreciation also goes to the crew at Bookpress Publishing. I couldn't ask for a better partner in getting my stories from manuscripts to finished products in readers' hands.

To repeat an acknowledgement I've made before, I suggest we all thank the men and women who strive every day to keep daily and weekly newspapers, and other forms of news media, alive and available to everyone. The economic and operational challenges of running a high-quality and viable news organization are enormous, and we're fortunate to have people in our communities who are dedicated to the effort.

Thomas Jefferson said democracy cannot exist without a free press. He was right. As a result, we owe our friends in the media a tremendous debt. I hope my tales of Tony Harrington and his friends and co-workers in the world of small-town newspapers pay proper homage to the journalists doing this work in the real world.

Lastly, it is important to note that this is a work of fiction. Take to heart the standard disclaimer language: "Names, characters, businesses, places, events, locales, and incidents are either products of my imagination or used in a fictitious manner. Any resemblance to actual persons, living or dead, is purely coincidental."

Enjoy Joseph LeValley's other Mysteries/Thrillers
featuring journalist Tony Harrington

Burying the Lede and *Cry from an Unknown Grave*

Critics and Readers Love Them!

- **Publishers Weekly:** "Fans of reporter sleuths...will be pleased."
- **U.S. Review of Books:** "Don't miss it!" — RECOMMENDED
- **Midwest Book Reviews:** "Nearly impossible to put down."
- **Online Book Club:** "Heartily recommend."
- **Danielle Feinberg, Pixar Studios:** "A gripping, page turner!"
- **BookLife Prize (9 of 10):** *"Filled with suspense"*

Get Your Copy Today!

Joseph LeValley's books are available from your local bookstore, Amazon, Barnes & Noble, or the author directly at **www.josephlevalley.com**.

Check the website for more information about books and public appearances, to preview chapters of upcoming books, and much more!

Coming Soon! Tony Harrington's next adventure!
Performing Murder